FIRST TIME IN PAPERBACK!

"There is never a dull moment in this history cum western crafted by a master story teller."
—*Ohioana Quarterly*

THE PROPOSITION

Liam was in the bunk house when Patrick arrived after dark on Friday. Patrick was stunned by his brother's face. His pale skin seemed to hang loosely around his sunken eyeballs. Liam looked diseased although he protested his fitness for ranch work.

"But you look like hell."

"I haven't been sleeping. I'm damned glad you're here. There's something I want to show you after the others bed down."

"What?"

"I can't say. But you'll see it outside before morning."

Liam spent the entire night standing close to the window of the hired hands' cabin. Whatever Liam had expected never came. But he waited all night anyway. After two days on horseback, Patrick had to sleep and he left his brother alone at the window.

Saturday, Alexander McSween and half a dozen Regulators sat around at the large table. That Governor Axtell had revoked their commission as lawmen did not trouble anyone. Patrick struggled to keep his eyes open when the lawyer stood up to address the assembly.

"Boys, Sherriff Brady and the governor have tried to make all of us into outlaws. Right here and now, I am making a pledge to you. I'm offering five hundred dollars to the man who kills William Brady."

THE SONS OF GRADY ROURKE

DOUGLAS SAVAGE

LEISURE BOOKS NEW YORK CITY

A LEISURE BOOK®

December 1996

Published by special arrangement with M. Evans and Company.

Dorchester Publishing Co., Inc.
276 Fifth Avenue
New York, NY 10001

For further information, contact: M. Evans and Company; 216 E. 49th Street; New York, NY 10017

The name ''Leisure Books'' and the stylized ''L'' with design are trademarks of Dorchester Publishing Co., Inc.

Printed in the United States of America.

In the memory of Joseph and Rachel Savage, to whom America was the goldeneh medina.

A man can commit murder here with impunity.
—John Tunstall, 16 November 1876
Lincoln, New Mexico

What they didn't burn, they stole.
—Susan McSween
Lincoln, New Mexico

THE SONS OF GRADY ROURKE

Chapter One

THE DEAD MAN'S JOURNEY—*JOURNADA DEL MUERTE*—THE
locals called it: the blistering ocean of sand and sage
between the Rio Grande River to the west and the Sacramento mountain range to the east. The bones of men and
horses had bleached in the mile-high desert for three hundred years. Spanish conquistadors were the first white men
to explore this furnace of southeast New Mexico Territory
and the first to perish. Even in the heart-stopping cold of
January with its blinding snows, the lifeless land was still
the *Journada del Muerte*.

In the thin air, the two riders coming down the mountain
were sharply etched against the hard, blue sky. Steam blowing out of the ice-encrusted nostrils of their mounts and the
two pack horses surrounded the horsemen in a white veil of
horse breath. Descending down the eastern face of the
Sacramento Mountains, the four horses walked slowly and
painfully on cracked hooves. What little moisture the high
desert had sucked out of the air in the fall had frozen solid in
the sandy ground. The icy earth offered only a steep path
paved with shards of glass. Blood seeped around well-worn
iron horseshoes. Behind the traveling band, the White
Mountain ridge crept slowly toward the setting sun as the
trail pointed down and to the east; toward the headwaters of
the Rio Bonito.

Thick fur coats made the two riders look like mounted

bears. Their little caravan followed the southern side of the river where the water had stopped flowing from west to east three months earlier. With ice crunching under his animal's feet, the lead rider looked north, over his left shoulder toward Capitan Mountain. It formed the snow-capped northern side of the steep valley that the Rio Bonito split down the middle. Three frozen rivers cut parallel scars through the arid land: the Rio Bonito to the north on the riders' left, Eagle Creek to the south, and the Rio Ruidoso still further south. All of the frozen streams joined the Rio Hondo over the eastern horizon.

When the riders looked at the sky, they saw that the white sun would stay high long enough for them to make Fort Stanton, ten miles into the valley. Both riders knew the trail since boyhood. Words were not wasted in country where opening a man's mouth would make his cracked lips bleed like his horses' soles. Beyond the fort lay the clapboard settlement of Lincoln. By January 1878, the bleak one-road town had been at war with itself for a year.

"THOUGHT THEM BOYS was dead." The cold traveled through the younger man's teeth until his forehead throbbed. He secured the tent flap behind him.

The clerk at the sutler's tent did not stay outside long. He braved the evening cold only until he was satisfied that the sound of horses was not warning of a thirsty squad of the 9th United States Colored Cavalry.

"Don't matter," the older man said. He had known better than to go into the gray cold. If the riders were Buffalo Soldiers, they would find their way to a barrel of corn whiskey on their own. The sutler's tent was the one place at Fort Stanton where the all-black cavalry troopers were equal to their white officers. "You sure it's the Rourke brothers?"

"Damned sure," the clerk said as he rubbed his hands furiously over the pot-bellied stove at the center of the large tent. A stove pipe climbed toward the top seam of the canvas shelter. "I knew the older one before the war."

"Oh. Which brothers was they?"

"Sean, the oldest. Think the other one with him must be Patrick, the middle brother. Liam was just a kid when I last seen them over ten years ago. Heard he was riding with the Seventh. Maybe he got himself killed with the rest of them at Bighorn. Likely as not."

"Likely as not. Come help me with the firewood."

The clerk took an armload of dried pine and shoved it into the stove. Resin crackled and hissed. He paused when he heard horses whinny from the wind stinging their watery eyes.

"Guess they come home to claim the old man's land." The old sutler took off his gloves when the last log went into the large stove. "Such as it is." A stream of tobacco juice landed and sizzled in the fire.

In the darkness under a brilliant moon, Fort Stanton was an indistinct change in the icescape. It was not a walled structure, but merely a collection of snow-covered log buildings erected in the valley halfway between the Sacramento Mountains and Lincoln. The buildings stood along the perimeter of a parade ground. From a distance, the thirty-three-year-old fort looked as though a hillside worth of trees had simply collapsed, rolled down Capitan Mountain, and stopped in a dirty pile of timber beside the frozen Rio Bonito. Confederates had occupied the place briefly during the war. Apaches finally drove the Rebels out. Paths through the knee-deep snow carved a lacework pattern between the buildings, huts, and corrals for the post's horses. Thin horses huddled against the nighttime cold under rough-hewn lean-tos built within the pens. Steam rose from fresh manure that hit the snow hard and round from poor forage.

Sean and Patrick Rourke tied their weary animals to a hitching post outside the fort's administrative hut. A black private in blue greatcoat escorted the brothers into Captain

George Purington's office. The white officer came around his desk to extend his right hand. His cigar remained clutched between his teeth.

"I'm Captain Purington, brevet lieutenant colonel of this post. You boys look like you could use a drink."

"Thank you, Colonel." Sean spoke for the two brothers. "That would be welcome."

The two civilians sat down opposite the small desk. The sentry went back to the frigid darkness as the commanding officer poured three glasses before returning to his seat behind the desk. The newcomers removed their heavy mittens and opened their fur coats. With chapped red hands, each brushed melting snow from his wild beard. The fort's commander handed the men glasses and kept one for himself.

"The hair of the dog, boys," the soldier smiled, lifting his glass.

A lantern on the officer's desk cast cozy yellow light on the riders' weathered faces. The lamp light made only faint shadows on the young face of Patrick Rourke, not older than twenty-five. But on Sean's face, only seven years older, the flickering light crashed against creased and bluish flesh to the right of Sean's nose. A jagged fissure was gouged from the bridge of his nose. Between his beard and his hairline, the right half of his face was badly mangled. Beneath his eye, the skin lacked the wintery red of his left cheek. The world had not been kind to the young man.

Sean felt the officer's eyes quickly studying his burned face. Brevet Colonel Purington's eyes narrowed for a moment. Without meaning to, Sean's right hand touched his poorly healed wound.

"Shiloh. I was sixteen. Wore the gray."

Purington nodded. He frowned, remembering worse wounds.

"I wore blue in the east under old 'Useless' S. Grant. Saw the elephant in the clouds above Chattanooga. Already seems like a lifetime ago; like it was someone else and not really me."

"Yes," Sean sighed. His right hand went down to his tattered knee. His left hand lifted his glass again.

"So you're old Grady Rourke's boys?"

"Yes, sir." Patrick spoke for his brother whose face was still remembering. "We've been on the trail for a month. Snow laid us up on the train six weeks ago. Not even the Southern Pacific could break through in the west."

The soldier played with his cigar.

"Understand Grady was in the Army? Mexico, wasn't it?"

"Yes." Patrick spoke warmly. "He was decorated at Sierra Gordo in '47. He was discharged in '50. He was real proud of his years in uniform."

"I understand that. Too bad: his accident and all." The officer seemed saddened. "No details that I can really give you boys. Stoved up by his horse is all I really know. My condolences."

"Thanks. Guess we need a place to sleep. Stable would be fine, Colonel."

"Nonsense. You're sons of a military man. I can put you up with my non-commissioned officers. Sorry you'll have to bunk with darkies. But they're damned good soldiers. The Ninth is a good bunch."

"That would be fine, sir. The way we smell, they may take more offense at Patrick and me."

The officer stood in a cloud of cigar smoke.

"Then you'll be going on to Lincoln tomorrow?"

"Yes, sir. First light—weather permitting, of course."

"We'll put some hot food into you first. I'll have the orderly hay your animals tonight, too." He flicked his ash onto the earthen floor. "Ain't one of Grady's boys in the service now?"

"Yes," Patrick said proudly. "Liam's mustering out soon from Colonel Miles' command up north."

"The Nez Perce campaign?"

"Yes, sir. Gone after them runaway Indians making for Canada. We left California before he could wire us."

"I can tell you that they rounded up every last one of them. Chief Joseph himself surrendered in October. The other chief—Looking Glass—was killed. Sad business."

The two brothers shuffled toward the door. Their long fur coats nearly touched the dirt floor. They carried their battered, wide-brimmed hats.

"Thank you, Colonel. Liam must be on his way then."

"Till tomorrow, boys. Good night." Captain Purington opened the door to darkness and a biting wind. Powdery snow blew in and dusted his beard.

"Private, escort these men to the sergeants' hut. They'll bed down there tonight. And have someone tend to their animals."

"Yes, sir. Follow me, please."

Grady Rourke's sons pushed their hats down low over their ears and bowed their faces into their collars to avoid the wind. Without looking up, each brother instinctively found his horse's forehead and rubbed his animal's nose as they passed. The trooper blinked new snow from his eyes as they walked toward one of the camp's small cabins. Yellow lamp light cast inviting warmth from dirty windows fogged by the breath of two soldiers who watched the men approach out of the darkness.

"Colonel's orders," the young trooper said as the night wind and swirls of powdery snow blew the three men into the warm cabin. Half a dozen black men stepped back from the freezing air. Two of the troopers still wore their blue flannel blouses. The others were already in their long woollies.

"Take a load off, sir," the man closest to the door said as he smiled toward Patrick. "Hang your coats there by the fire to dry."

"Thank you, Sergeant," Sean said for the brothers. "We don't mean to be in the way."

The trooper pointed toward pegs in the log walls near a stone hearth that blazed with pine timbers. Patrick suspended both coats on the pegs. Melting water quickly formed a mud puddle on the dirt floor.

"Carry on, Private," the sergeant nodded. The young trooper sighed and marched grimly into the night. The wind stopped whistling when the door closed heavily.

"I'm Sean Rourke. This here is my little brother. I used to soldier."

The sergeant squinted at the older brother's wrecked face. He recognized a soldier's face and he knew that extending his hand was premature civility. So he only nodded and pointed toward a small table.

"The coffee is hot, sir, and you're both welcome to bunk down tonight. The biscuits are hard. But they're warm and will fill you till morning."

The two brothers sat down and sighed at the sudden comfort. The congenial sergeant stepped toward the fire and retrieved a small sack from the mantel. When he laid it on the table between the brothers, he could smell the whiskey.

"Help yourself to our tobacco. Save yours for the trail."

The brothers thanked the big man in unison.

"We have four empty bunks, so you can take your pick."

"Thank you," Sean said wearily. He felt his scarred cheek warming from the fire and sensed how hard his southern accent fell on the sergeant's ears. The older brother looked up and extended his right hand toward the soldier. The trooper touched the veteran's hand carefully, as if it were a fragile thing of value.

"We're much obliged, Sergeant."

The soldier nodded and released Sean Rourke's firm handshake. Then he pulled his government issue suspenders off his wide, blue shoulders. The braces dangled against his sides.

"Then we'll turn in, Mr. Rourke. We've had a long day out in that there cold."

"If you don't mind, Sergeant, my brother and I'll just sit by the fire for a little while until we thaw." Sean's torn face and graying beard opened into an honest smile.

"Very well, sir. Light up, if you want. We can sleep through hail and high water, that's for damned sure." The noncommissioned officer glanced sideways with a narrow grin. His head and kindly face gestured toward a clay jug wedged into a corner where the thick logs came together.

"There's some medicine in the jug if you need to help your circulation."

Grady Rourke's sons smiled and nodded gratefully.

The other troopers had said nothing. With a chorus of "night, then" one at a time, each of the still dressed cavalrymen stripped down to his long woollies. The men climbed into their bunks and pulled heavy gray blankets up to their chins. The sergeant who had been talking laid an armload of new logs into the hearth before he bedded down last.

The quarters were warm and comfortable. Within five minutes, six soldiers were sleeping soundly. Patrick stood up, leaned toward the corner, and fetched the jug and two tin cups. He poured a dose of sour mash whiskey into each cup on the coarse table. When he sat down again, Sean nodded without a word. After lifting the cup to his cracked lips, he sighed deeply.

The fire crackled and sent embers looping upward into the stone chimney.

The two brothers sipped their whiskey for half an hour in silence. The wind moaned against the frosted windows almost as loudly as the severe snoring that rumbled from the soldiers.

Sean squinted toward the windows on either side of the doorway opposite the hearth. He watched the bright fire reflecting on the glass. Ice crusted around the edges of the panes and refracted the flames like cold prisms of crystal. As the cabin's warmth and the bitter medicine worked together, the one-time Confederate looked hard at the windows. The firelight dancing in the windows looked familiar and the night wind groaned like wolves at the door. Closing his eyes, Sean still saw the flames inside his exhausted head and the wind made the pitiful sound he had heard rising from a score of dismal battlefields fifteen years earlier. The howling grew until it sounded like a thousand men lying in their own blood and baying for water like wild, wounded animals.

Patrick sipped and watched the lines around his brother's closed eyes. The creases seemed to deepen as Sean's trail-numb mind drifted across the years of pain and defeat.

"Sean?"

The older brother opened his eyes slowly and turned his face toward his brother. In the fireplace light, the right half of Sean's face looked to Patrick like an ancient and gnarled oak tree—the kind in which mystical oriental kings buried their children in the tales of far away, which Patrick could vaguely remember in his mother's own voice.

"Are you all right?"

Sean turned back toward the iced windows. He laid his hand across the top of his tin cup as if to say that he was finished drinking.

"Well enough."

ONE OF THE sergeants had stoked the fire back to life by the time their guests rubbed their eyes and climbed out of their blankets. Someone put a hot tin cup into Sean's hand before his eyes were open.

"Thanks."

"Ain't nothin', sir. You'll need some heat in you just to make it to the mess tent."

The travelers were surprised to see that the sky was still the hard blue-black of morning twilight in the mile-high morning. Although the wind had stopped howling from the western mountains, the pre-dawn air remained painfully cold. The civilians buried their faces in the collars of their ankle-length coats that dragged on new, powdery snow. Half a dozen cavalrymen in blue greatcoats escorted their guests to breakfast. Low in the east, the sky over Lincoln, New Mexico, was just turning pink. When Patrick looked up, he could still see a few bright stars shining. The moon had set and the stars did not twinkle in the thin, brittle air.

In the mess tent reserved for noncommissioned officers, the atmosphere was wonderful with the hearty scent of sour-dough biscuits fried in bacon fat, strong coffee, and tobacco smoke. To Sean Rourke, the large tent smelled better than any woman he could remember. Breakfast comforted the brothers to their bones.

By the time the brothers pushed themselves outside, the stars were gone and the sky was clear and blue. The blinding snow in the valley was too bright for either brother to make out where the plain ended and the western mountains began. The snow cap on Capitan Mountain to the north was too painfully bright to look at.

The two travelers were surprised to find their mounts and pack horses already tacked and ready for the day's ride to Lincoln. Two troopers held the reins and halters.

"Thank you," Sean said to one of the soldiers.

"The smithy reset the hind shoes of the bay, sir." The private glanced at the brown animal that had snow glistening on his whiskers. "Said one was coming loose. So he done them both to set the angles right."

Sean reached into his fur coat's deep pocket.

"Will you give your smithy a gold piece for us?"

"No need, sir. Besides, he won't take it from you. The old man said you was a soldier once."

"Then tell your man that we said thanks."

"I'll do that, sir."

The tall youth handed the leathers to the two brothers. Sean and Patrick mounted slowly with their heavy coats holding them back. The orderly stepped back and looked up at Sean's ruined face. Gathering his reins, Sean straightened in the saddle and snapped off a brisk salute with parade ground precision.

Both orderlies took one step back, squared their heels, and returned the military courtesy with equal dignity. Sean nodded and led his brother east across the ocean of unspoiled snow.

THE ROURKE BROTHERS slowly followed the frozen Rio Bonito eastward for ten miles. After half a day, the frozen river turned south.

"La Placita should be a mile beyond the bend." Sean's words came with a cloud of steam. He was not yet accustomed to calling the town by its new name, Lincoln.

"I suppose," Patrick stammered with lips too cold to work.

Sean reined his horse northward, away from the Rio Bonito. Directly ahead, Capitan Peak glistened brilliantly high in the southern sky. Leaving the river trail, the men guided their horses between waist-high gray boulders. The sun gave the icy rocks the glitter of diamonds. Rounding a slight rise a mile from the river, they stopped side by side. Beneath them in the midday sunshine was a run-down ranch house and crumbling outbuildings. Without a word, they spurred their mounts forward at an easy walk.

The four horses had to pick their feet up as they made their way over downed fence rails, which lay in heaps where a fence line had once stood. The riders drew rein and stopped five hundred yards from the ranch house. They glanced at each other and then back at the Rourke family ranch. At least a hundred head of cattle pawed the snow in search of grass. Some of the steers walked casually upon the weathered front porch.

"Pa's?" Patrick said as his lips cracked from a single word.

"No. Look at them ears. Seen it before down Pecos way in Texas." Sean pointed to a thin steer fifty yards distant and not the least fazed by the horsemen.

Squinting into the sun, Patrick could see that each steer had the same ear defect or wound: Each animal's right ear was cut lengthwise to its base. Where the ear met the head, the lower half of the ear's underside flapped behind the eye. Every animal grazing had the same mutilation.

"A brand?" Patrick held his hand over his mouth when he spoke to ease the pain of the cold wind against his gums.

"John Chisum's brand. He calls it the 'jingle-bob.' Didn't know he had cattle this far north. But we ain't been home in six years. Guess things change."

"Maybe Pa bought them?" Patrick sounded hopeful.

"Ain't likely." Without more, Sean spurred his horse through the cattle, which shuffled out of the way of the two riders and their pack horses. The droopy-eared steers seemed unafraid of mounted men as if they had experienced them often. When the brothers reached the house, they dismounted and led their four horses into a clapboard barn. It was too cold to leave their horses outside for long. Unsaddling their mounts and untacking the draft horses required ten minutes. The hungry horses nosed around for forage and found only moldy hay. But they snorted with relief to be sheltered from the biting wind.

Walking to the house, Sean used his hat to swat the rump of a steer that had claimed the front porch as his own. Before stepping off the porch, the animal left a hard and steaming cow pie behind, aimed with precision at the spot where Sean took his next step. With a curse, the older brother wiped his boot on the wooden railing before he opened the unlocked front door.

Inside, ragged furniture was covered with six inches of clean snow. One of the front windows was completely gone. Patrick went back out into the sunny afternoon. Sean went directly to the single large fireplace where he found unburned logs piled neatly against the stone. He knelt, removed his gloves, and worked to kindle a fire. His hands were stiff and his fingernails were blue from cold. By the time the fire was catching, Patrick entered with a hammer in his hand. He quickly pulled faded curtains across the broken window and nailed the cloth to the window frame to keep the winter outside.

"Pa had a tool box," Patrick said with three rusty nails in his mouth.

A thin veil of white smoke rolled through the large room until the hearth began drafting into the chimney. With the door closed and the broken window covered, the house slowly warmed.

The Rourke brothers idled in the center of the room. They seemed uncomfortable, as if they were trespassing and expected to hear footsteps on the front porch. But the only noise was from the nearby cattle and the crackling hearth.

Sean peeled off his heavy coat and draped it over a high-backed, leather chair—a father's chair. The coat blew a small cloud of snow onto the snow drift in the middle of the floor. Water was already seeping from the drift and running between the floorboards. Patrick wiped snow from a second chair before he laid his coat down. The brothers stood side by side with their palms opened toward the blazing hearth.

"Smaller than I remember it," Sean said into the fireplace.

"Me, too. Guess we growed over the years."

Sean shrugged. As he warmed to the fire, he moved around the room, but came back to the hearth every few minutes to open his hands above the flames. Patrick kicked snow away with his boots and made tracks across the floor.

The ceiling was not flat. It was gabled down the center of the room and housed a single loft above a wooden ladder. From below, several travel trunks were visible, aligned neatly like small wooden coffins awaiting their final resting place in the frozen earth.

A single doorway opened along the long wall. Bright sunlight shone upon rusty hinges on the half-open door. Inside, a small bedroom contained a single bed, which stood high off the dusty floor. At the narrow end of the living room was a tiny kitchen with closed cupboards, a dry sink, and a large pump with a wooden handle. Walking closer, Patrick saw open tin cans with jagged tops pointing toward the rough hewn ceiling; it was as if the owner had started dinner but had not had time to finish preparing it. Looking down, Patrick saw that each can was still full of something frozen and unidentifiable. Whatever it once had been, it had half rotted during the fall before freezing in the high-country winter.

Stepping back into the harsh daylight of the living room, Patrick came closer to his brother's side. Sean frowned down at a waist-high bureau against a wall. On top, wooden picture frames sat in puddles of melted snow. The melt water ran brown with dust and grime. The frames will filled with browned portraits of dour faces—painfully rigid from holding their breath for the long exposures of the photographic processes common to the West.

"I remember that one," Patrick smiled at a portrait of three scruffy little boys.

"We don't look real happy," Sean said without emotion.

"Except for Liam."

The youngest child—no more than five years old—wore the smudged mouth of a boy who could not hold still while the plate was exposed.

"Liam always took Ma to heart," Patrick said warmly.

"'God sees smiles,'" Sean said softly as if reciting something important learned at school.

"You remember Ma saying that to us?" Patrick sounded surprised.

Sean's broken face smiled awkwardly. He seemed out of practice.

"I knowed her before you did, little brother."

Patrick gently touched his tall brother's shoulder and looked down quickly before his eyes showed wet.

"Pa." The smaller brother studied a stern face with hollow cheeks and a double row of brass buttons running down the puffed-out breast.

"I remember his uniform from Mexico. He was proud of it." Sean did not seem to notice that the frame held two portraits in the glass. The second showed a man in a Confederate uniform with corporals' stripes. The beardless face was untouched by the ravages of war.

"Pa must have put you in the frame with his picture."

"Or Ma did."

"Don't matter who, does it?" Patrick stopped short, wishing that he had not spoken quite so quickly.

"Don't matter at all," Sean said as he laid the double frame into the last of the snow melting on the little bureau. He turned when he heard cattle hooves on the front porch. "Think I'll go outside and make some fresh beef for dinner. Why don't you broom out the kitchen?"

"All right."

"Tomorrow, we'll ride to town to find Lawyer McSween what wrote us to come for probating Pa's will." Sean heaved his soggy coat over his shoulders. He paused to examine the cylinder of his Peacemaker revolver. He knew that its six chambers were loaded. But he checked anyway as he walked quietly into the blinding sunshine.

Inside, Patrick Rourke heard his brother's spurs jingling on the porch followed by the clatter of cattle feet. He knew that Sean would guide one of the steers toward the barn before putting it down. While he waited for the single report from a .45-30 cartridge, Patrick picked up his father's framed face and gently wiped snow melt from the knotty wood. He studied Grady Rourke's clear, pale eyes, which stared straight ahead. Patrick blinked as if his father's youthful eyes were watching him. Then he looked at his brother's face from sixteen years earlier. Sean's eyes were slightly pursed at the bridge of his nose. It was a teenage warrior's face that seemed grimly aware of its certain future.

Patrick did not startle when a single pistol shot cracked outside. From inside the barn, the thin mountain air muffled the round into a faraway pop like dry kindling under foot. He set the double frame back where it belonged.

"We come home, Pa."

Chapter Two

THE ROURKE BROTHERS RODE INTO LINCOLN FROM THE WEST.
Their steak dinner and their steak breakfast did not keep
them warm during the short ride to town. Scarves of coarse
wool held their sweat-stained hats down over their ears.
Riding with their heads down against the wind, the Rourkes
had to squint their eyes within the shadows cast by the hats'
wide felt brims. An all-night feast of clean hay and rolled
oats found in the barn put the light back into the black eyes
of each rider's horse. Oats burn slowly inside a horse, and
each animal carried his feet high as their warm bellies and
thick winter coats kept the mounts comfortable under the
bright midmorning sun. The men felt the confidence of their
heavy Colt Peacemakers rubbing against their hips beneath
their fur trail dusters. The sun glinted off the riders' spurs.

Riding slowly eastward, the brothers followed Lincoln's
only dirt road. The hamlet was nothing more than a single
row of wind-burned and sun-bleached adobe structures on
each side of the street, 5750 feet above sea level. Behind the
single-story buildings on their left, the frozen Rio Bonito
river bed ran east and west, parallel with the street. Its near
bank was hardly twenty yards from the rear of the ragged
buildings on the north side of the road.

They passed the town's only two-story building on their
right. Men already bustled in and out of the prosperous
mercantile. The sign said J. J. DOLAN AND COMPANY. Ten

yards further into town stood a single-story adobe building on their left, opposite the Dolan store. To the right of the building, a large corral was empty of livestock.

"Let's try the store, Patrick."

Without comment, the younger brother steered his mount toward Dolan's hitching rail. They dismounted and went inside.

Half a dozen men stopped chattering when the brothers entered. The travelers' beards, trail coats bulging at the right hip, and their general disrepair called the patrons' attention to the strangers. The brothers unwrapped the scarves covering their heads and removed their hats. They walked on stiff legs toward a ratty bar along one wall.

"A little early in the day for hard liquor, boys," a friendly man said behind the bar. His pot belly was stained with tobacco juice. "Coffee's strong and hot, if you have a mind."

"Coffee would be just fine," Sean said. His left hand reached across his chin to pull the right fur collar of his coat high up on his disfigured face.

"Here you go," the barkeep smiled. If he noticed Sean's face, he did not even blink.

"Thanks."

"You boys passing through?"

"No, sir. We live here. Leastwise our folks done for years."

"Oh?"

"We're Rourkes. I'm Sean and this here is my little brother, Patrick."

The barkeep squinted in the bright sunlight streaming harshly through wavy windows. He studied Sean closely.

"I'll be damned. Old Grady's boys come home? Yes, I can see it now. Around your eyes. Just come in?"

"Yesterday. Ain't had time for a bath or shave yet."

"Guess not. Sorry to hear about your pa. He had friends here in Lincoln."

"Yes," Sean nodded, lifting a heavy coffee cup to his

beard. "Lincoln. When did it get a new name?"

"Back in '69, I suppose. When we finally got a Post Office. Old-timers like me still call it La Placita del Rio Bonito." Though blond and blue-eyed, the barkeep's Spanish accent was perfect from a lifetime in New Mexico Territory, where native Mexicans and Mescalaro Apaches still outnumbered the *Anglos.*

"We're looking for a lawyer, Alexander McSween. Know where we can find him?"

"Jail more 'n likely," someone behind the brothers piped up.

The brothers turned toward the man behind them: another *Anglo,* middle-aged, with a frightened, hungry look in his eyes.

"Jail?"

"Yes. McSween's under arrest for stealing from old Fritz's estate. Got took to Mesilla to tell it to the judge down there."

"Emil Fritz," another man joined in. "Used to be one of the owners of Dolan and Company. Consumption killed him when he went home to Germany a while back. Old McSween had his dirty little hand in the cookie jar." A gathering of townsmen laughed together around the brothers, who were suddenly uncomfortable with so many strangers blowing tobacco breath down their necks.

"McSween has papers for us," Sean said firmly, hoping to bring the conversation to a quick resolution.

"See the Wortley 'cross the street?" The barkeep pointed out the front window toward Lincoln's only boarding house and hotel. The brothers squinted toward the snow-covered street and nodded. "Well, ride past it, and past the Mills' house. The fenced-in building on the left will be McSween's house. No one's home now." The cluster of men chuckled. "His law office is next door in Tunstall's store." The man said Tunstall as if the word had a bad taste.

The brothers laid their empty cups down on the bar.

"Thanks for the coffee. What do we owe you?"

The barkeep smiled with strained courtesy.

"Nothing this morning, boys. It's on old Grady. Ask for Shield. He's McSween's partner."

"Shield," Patrick repeated.

"McSween's wife is Mrs. Shield's sister," one of the nameless men offered.

"Thanks, again," Sean said as he walked an anxious step ahead of Patrick into the sunshine. They mounted, crossed the street toward the Wortley Hotel, and continued slowly past an apparently deserted adobe structure surrounded by a fence. The place looked like a small fortress. Within minutes, they reached the second large building on the river side of the street. Its front porch ended at the street. The entire rear of the building was a corral, where a lone horse stood quietly, fetlock-deep in new snow. The brothers tied their animals to two of the beams that held up the porch roof. They entered the single-story building. A young, thin-faced boy with pale blue eyes stood behind a counter.

"Is this the Tunstall store?"

"Yes, mister. Can I help you?"

"We're looking for a Mister Shield. Supposed to be a lawyer."

"He's in the back. I'll fetch him. Who shall I tell him?"

"We're Rourkes."

The young man nodded as if his early morning customers were expected.

"What about you?" Patrick said toward the clerk's thin back.

The boy stopped, turned and grinned. "William Bonney." He waited with a look of cheerful anticipation on his clean-shaven face. For a moment, he studied each brother's blue-gray eyes.

"Mr. Shield, please," Sean said impatiently.

When the clerk continued on his way, he looked disappointed and continued to watch the brothers over his shoulder until he disappeared into an open room. He quickly returned with a tall, well-dressed man behind him.

"I'm David P. Shield. May I be of service?"

The boy returned to his post behind the counter.

Sean and Patrick removed their hats.

"I'm Sean Rourke. And my brother, Patrick."

"Grady's sons?"

"Yes, sir. Come to see Mr. McSween. His letter three months ago is what brung us home."

"Yes. Of course. We were sorry to hear about old Grady. Won't you come back, please?"

The dapper, middle-aged gentleman with a handlebar mustache led the brothers through the rear of the Tunstall store. He stopped at a small cubicle and gestured for his guests to enter first. The brothers took seats close to the adobe wall and their host settled into a wicker chair on castors close to a rolltop desk.

"I'm Alex McSween's partner and a lawyer. We all felt bad about Grady's accident. Didn't find his body for a week. His friends buried him behind the house, beside your Ma and their babies." The lawyer nodded gravely. "Your father's will is in our files and I am authorized to share it with you in my partner's absence." He paused to collect his thoughts. "I have to report that Alex was called away on legal business to Mesilla. I don't expect him back for several weeks."

"We heard he was in some kind of trouble." Sean was already out of patience and it was not yet ten o'clock.

"So he is," Mr. Shield nodded with discomfort in his calm voice. "Trumped up charges of abusing an estate in his care. Dolan's people and the House are behind it."

"Oh. Who's Mr. Tunstall what owns this store?"

"I can tell, Sean, that you don't dance around the issues. I like that in a man." The lawyer reached into a desk drawer and pulled out a wooden box. "Cigars, gentlemen?"

Sean reached into the open box held open in front of him. Patrick waved it past. The lawyer took a cigar and returned the box to his drawer. He struck a match on the bottom of his boot and offered the fire to Sean.

"No need, sir." Sean bit off two inches of cigar and began slowly chewing it. Shield smiled and brought the flame up to his own cigar.

"As I was saying, how long has it been since you boys were home in Lincoln?"

"Five, maybe six years," Sean said with his lips barely opening. Shield handed his guest a brass spittoon. Sean nodded and used it.

"That's long enough to be out of touch with Lincoln affairs and all of the players. Do you want to get to your father's papers first, or get reacquainted with local politics?"

The brothers glanced at each other. In the brief silence, Shield took a drag on his cigar and spoke first.

"You planning to stay here? Maybe work your father's ranch?"

"I suppose," Sean said before spitting again.

"Then perhaps a little local history would do you both good." Shield spoke to Sean whom he now knew did the talking for Grady Rourke's heirs. The lawyer leaned forward toward the older brother. He looked for an instant at Sean's scarred face and then forced his eyes to study his cigar that he rolled in his fingers, clean as a woman's hands.

"You asked about Mr. Tunstall. John Tunstall is the business partner of Mr. McSween. They own this store. The other mercantile in town is Dolan and Company, known here as the House." Shield's lips curled slightly. "Dolan and his kind think they own the town. Except for Alex and me, they probably do. They own the law, for sure."

"Who's the law?"

"Sheriff Brady. William Brady. To be fair, I have to say that there was a time when Brady's heart was in the right place. But not any more. When Jimmy Dolan hums a tune, Brady starts dancing."

The brothers looked sideways at each other. Sean spit

into the brass cuspidor.

"John and Alex formed this general store in the spring of '77. Tunstall is the controling partner and Alex is buying into it. They bought this place from Lawrence Murphy who was the founder of Dolan's store before he sold the House to Dolan. Murphy started the House at Fort Stanton, but had to move off the fort in '73. Your Pa ever mention Murphy?"

"No. Never mentioned Tunstall neither."

"Tunstall's not from the territory. He's from England, near London. Alex met him up in Santa Fe two years ago. John was running his daddy's business in Victoria, British Columbia, before Alex talked him into going into business here."

"Why would they set up a mercantile across from Dolan's if Dolan owns the town?"

"Alex knew that the House was financially shaky. Thought Tunstall could take them on."

"How would McSween know that?" Sean spit and wiped his chin with the back of his hand.

"Alex was the attorney for the House for three years. He knew the books."

"Is that legal?" Patrick looked closely at the lawyer with the well scrubbed hands.

"This is Lincoln, boys."

"How'd that sit with the House?" Patrick's eyes narrowed as the town's political situation took root in his mind.

David Shield smiled easily and pointed over his shoulder with his thumb. The brothers noticed for the first time that the shutters on the windows were made from plates of half-inch-thick steel. And the windows were set into massive adobe walls. The Tunstall Store and the McSween–Shield law office was a fortress. Patrick nodded.

"I see. What about Pa's papers?"

"Right here, Sean." The lawyer opened a drawer and pulled out a large paper envelope tied with a string. He pulled the string, untied a neat little bow, and opened the packet. Two folded documents fell onto the desktop. "Alex saw to your father's affairs all clean and legal-like. I can assure you of that."

Sean thought of Alexander McSween using his confidential knowledge of J. J. Dolan and Company to compete against him.

"We come home yesterday to cattle running over Pa's ranch. Looks like the Chisum jingle-bob mark. How's that?"

Shield leaned back and his wicker chair creaked. He dragged on his cigar.

"You boys have been away a long time. It's Chisum cattle, all right. John Chisum bought a spread south of here. Guess Texas got too small for him." Shield chuckled to himself. "Chisum started ranching in the territory back in '68, I guess. He ran his herd on a two hundred mile spread in Pecos Valley. Built his South Spring River Ranch where the Rio Hondo meets the Pecos, sixty miles from Lincoln. Chisum sold out—lock, stock, and barrel—to Hunter and Evans out of St. Louis about three years ago. But they kept Chisum on to round up the cattle and manage things. He's probably running forty thousand head by now. Your daddy leased Chisum grazing rights to his pasture land." Shield laid his white hand atop the empty envelope that had "Grady Rourke" written across the flap. "Alex and I have kept the rents in Tunstall's bank until you boys could get home. We have all the records for you, too." Shield nodded with sudden gravity. "Records to the penny."

"Tunstall's bank?"

"Yes, Patrick. The only one in town." The lawyer's smile was the face of a man who held all of the aces. "Here's the lease for the cattle."

Patrick picked up the document and leafed through its three pages. When he handed it to Sean, the older brother merely glanced at it.

"Where's Tunstall now?" Sean asked as he handed the document to Shield.

"Home. Ranch a few miles out of town. He was laid up all summer with the small pox. He's still getting his strength back." Shield looked up at a large, colorful calendar that hung from a nail in the adobe wall. Monday, January 21st, 1878, was circled in ink. The lawyer nodded toward the wall. "He'll be back here in three days, Monday."

Sean made another deposit into the spittoon.

"Could we get to the will, sir?"

"Indeed. I should wait for Justice of the Peace Wilson to disclose this instrument to you, but we can dispense with the formalities, if you have no objetions."

"We rode hard for three hundred and fifty miles, Mr. Shield. Just give us the high points and we can do the legal business when Liam gets here."

"Your brother. Yes. Alex wrote to him, too, through the War Department. That letter did not come back, so he must have received it."

Shield stood up and walked to the doorway. He leaned out toward the spacious store area.

"Billy? Come on back for a minute, will you?"

"I ain't got no one to cover the counter," a voice called from beyond the little office.

"Won't take long, Billy."

The boy with the cheerful face stepped into the office. His thick hair curled over his ears. His smile was filled with protruding, front teeth. Only his merry eyes showed any trace of intelligence to the sitting brothers.

"This is William Bonney. He clerks for Tunstall."

The brothers nodded and fidgeted with their hats in their laps. Bonney studied Sean's wounded face until the older brother blinked. Then the youth leaned against the door frame. His hands were clasped behind him.

"You witness this, Billy." Shield took his seat and adjusted steel-framed spectacles on the end of his sharp nose. He opened the document very carefully and studied it

silently for an instant to allow the drama to rise until the
Rourke brothers leaned forward.

"'I, Grady Rourke, an adult white man of sound mind
and disposition, do declare this instrument to be my Last
Will and Testament dated this 19th day of August 1874. I
have three living children, Sean, Patrick, and Liam Rourke.
My wife, Shannon O'Casey Rourke, has predeceased me. I
hereby devise and bequeath all of my property, real and
personal. . .'"

Shield looked over the tops of his spectacles directly
toward Sean. Then he looked back to the document.

"'. . . real and personal, to my sons Patrick and Liam. I
specifically disinherit my oldest son, Sean, who left home
last year and is fully emancipated and able to make something of himself on his own.'"

Sean's mouth dropped open revealing a half-dissolved
piece of cigar and browned teeth. Billy inched away from
the wall and stood with his hands at his sides. Patrick looked
at his brother as the lawyer continued to drone.

"'I nominate Alexander McSween, Esquire, to serve as
my executor without bond . . .' *et cetera, et cetera.* The rest
is pretty much legal boiler plate. And it's duly witnessed
here at the end by Lawrence Murphy and George Peppin—
he's Deputy Sheriff now. That's it, boys."

Sean sagged in his seat. He looked stricken to the heart.
The last time he had felt such a sickening churning of his
stomach was the sixth day of April, 1862. His regiment of
Confederates had stumbled into a stand of trees at Shiloh
Church near the Tennessee River. They were met by two
divisions of General Grant's Yankees. By the end of the day,
both bleeding armies would call the woods The Hornet's
Nest. After two ferocious days, one hundred thousand men
did battle there and twenty-four thousand fell. Sean's face
now twitched the way it had twitched at Shiloh—moments
before a red-hot fragment of iron peeled back his face, down
to teeth and bone.

Without a single word, Sean's hands dropped hard upon the arms of his wooden chair. He pushed himself out of the seat before Shield or Patrick could rise. Billy had to step sideways so Sean would not have to walk over him as he stomped, spurs jingling, through Tunstall's store. The front door slammed before Patrick had moved.

"I'm sorry, Patrick." Shield stood beside his cluttered desk. "I have no idea why your father made his disposition cutting Sean out of his estate. According to Alex, Grady never gave a reason. He seemed sane and in possession of his faculties when he wrote this. Nothing more was required. We certainly didn't influence your father, one way or the other."

Patrick stopped at the doorway where Billy Bonney stood, slightly wide-eyed.

"Mr. McSween didn't have to put ideas in Pa's head. He always done what he wanted to. We'll come back to finish this." Patrick walked quickly past Billy toward the door. The younger brother pulled his hat low over his eyes as the Tunstall Store door opened into piercing sunshine exploding against the snow-white street. Sean was already across the road.

"Whiskey!"

The barkeep was wiping yesterday's glasses when Sean Rourke threw open the front door closed tightly against the high-country January. Men and women stopped toying with the dry goods stacked floor to ceiling at J. J. Dolan and Company. They cleared a quick path for the tall man's long strides to the bar.

"Whiskey!" Sean said again as his open palm slammed down on the bar. The unburned left side of his face grimaced at the pain in his hand, which seemed to surprise him.

"There's womenfolk shopping here, Mr. Rourke." The barkeep still sounded pleasant, but with a trace of tightness in his voice. He swallowed his next word when Sean pushed his furry greatcoat back away from the Peacemaker hand-

iron on his right hip. The saloon keeper held his breath until
Sean reached deeply into his pocket in front of his iron. He
retrieved a five dollar gold coin that spun atop the bar.

"Keep 'em coming until that there half-eagle is drunk up.
It's late enough for me."

When the few men in the House started to back toward
the open door, the barkeep put a bottle next to one of his
clean glasses in front of Sean.

"I don't take to hard talk or spittin' when there's women
in here to shop, young fellow."

Sean's voice softened, but the live side of his face was
flushed and angry.

"It's your store. Them rules is fine."

Sean picked up the bottle and glass with one hand,
turned, and walked to a little table. He passed in front of a
round woman and her small child who clutched her dress,
which carried white snow and brown manure along the long
hem. The woman gasped when sunlight from the window
shone full on the dead side of Sean's face. The wounded
man turned away and sat down with his back to the woman
and the front door. He did not turn around when Patrick
entered with a light step. Patrick's spurs rang softly with the
clean, clear tone of Mexican silver.

The younger brother followed the barkeep's glance
toward Sean's hunched back.

"May I sit down?"

Sean did not look up. He spoke into his glass, already
emptied for the second time.

"It's my table, Patrick. You get the ranch."

Patrick sighed so loudly that the woman with the child
turned around from the pile of calico. He pulled out the
chair opposite Sean and sat down. Both men still wore their
filthy hats.

"It's not my fault, Sean. You know that."

"Yes." Sean did not look up. "Son of a bitch. I never done
him wrong. Pa had no cause for cutting me out like that. I

worked them fields till my hands bled just like you. And Liam weren't even in long trousers yet." He spoke only to the bottle. "I only went to California cause there weren't dirt enough to feed us all after the war. I sent money home, too, after Ma passed." Sean looked up from under his wide-brimmed hat. Patrick could see that the corners of his brother's eyes were wet. "Did Pa tell you that I sent money home?"

Patrick wanted to nod, but mumbled "No" before he could stop himself.

"Old man got the last laugh after all." Sean lowered his face. "Said he would." He filled the shot glass again and passed it to Patrick. Amber liquid dripped down the side when it stopped against Patrick's gloved hand. Sean lifted the half-empty bottle. "To Pa," he said, sucking at the bottle. Patrick did not lift the glass.

Before Patrick could speak, Sean swallowed a fiery gulp and pushed the bottle toward his brother.

"You can finish it. I'll take a room across the street. Pick up my things maybe tomorrow."

Sean stood up unsteadily. The cheap whiskey was already working. He shuffled to the bar.

"Do I have another one coming for my money?"

"If you want it, Mr. Rourke."

Sean opened his ungloved palm and held it out until the barkeep laid another full bottle in it. Sean nodded.

With the bottle in his right hand, he walked slowly to the door. He waved with the other hand toward Patrick. The younger brother watched the brilliant halo of sunshine swallow Sean when he slammed the door behind him. Sean's long coat cut a man-wide path through fresh snow between the House and the Wortley Hotel across the street.

Chapter Three

A MAN CAN GO INSANE LIVING ALONE. AFTER FOUR DAYS IN
the haunting silence of his father's empty house, Patrick
brooded about how long it might take, precisely. By Tuesday, January 22nd, the night wind whining across the roof
sounded like a woman crying. Patrick as a grown man of
twenty-five years lay awake in his bedroll on his father's
bed. The night wind reminded him of a four-year-old
boy's wide-eyed memory of the sounds his mother had
made when Liam was born at first light. He knew that a
sane man living alone should be dreaming about another
kind of woman.

At Sean's side on the long ride across desert and mountains toward Lincoln, Patrick could ride a hundred miles
without exchanging a single word. But that was a different
kind of silence. It was not at all like the loneliness of an
empty ranch house creaking with memories and ghosts.

Monday had marked only the third day of the brothers'
separation. But it was the third day after nearly three months
of riding together. Patrick worried about his sanity when he
caught himself standing on the front porch and looking over
the backs of John Chisum's cattle toward the mountains. He
was watching for his brother Liam riding down the Sacramento Mountains, past the Sierra Blanca's extinct volcano.
When he had realized that he must look like his mother
scanning the blue horizon for her three sons, Patrick

laughed out loud with only steers to hear him. That worried him even more and he resolved to make his peace with Sean the next day.

No new snow had fallen since Friday, so the drifts were brown along the single street splitting Lincoln down the center. Warm droppings from horses melted the snow down to the frozen sand. Manure and wads of tobacco chew turned the road into a cold slurry of noxious vapors that lingered on the painfully cold air.

Patrick opened the wooden gate to the large corral adjacent to the east side of the Wortley Hotel. The square paddock was larger than the L-shaped, single-story boarding house. He uncinched his saddle and heaved it atop the fence. His tall horse snorted with relief and trotted into the center of the corral to rub noses and reacquaint himself with Sean's animal who walked over to his companion of the long trail. Each horse welcomed the other with a long musty breath into the other's flared nostrils. They faced each other nose to nose, nodded, and took one step forward until their faces could touch the other's back where their manes ended. In a cloud of steam in the morning chill, the animals began to merrily nibble each other's withers with equine good cheer.

Patrick smiled and turned his back on the paddock. Without a front porch to clean the snow and muck from his boots, he left muddy footprints on the faded carpet in the lobby of the Wortley Hotel. He had to stand still for a moment until his eyes adjusted to the subdued light after the blinding sunshine of his ride into town.

Dirty hat in hand, he surveyed the small front parlor and the clerk's desk close to the far wall. The clerk's cleanly starched white shirt made his Spanish face appear even darker. His black eyes were bright and pleasant.

"*Buenos dias, señor,*" the short man smiled, "do you wish a room?"

"No. Thank you." Patrick walked closer, conscious of the

trail he was making on the floor. "I'm looking for Sean Rourke. I'm his brother."

"*Sí,* you are the new owner of your papa's ranch, no?"

Patrick looked down at his gloved hands locked to the brim of his faded hat.

"Is Sean here?"

"He is in the back; that way." The clerk gestured toward an alcove beside the end of the desk.

"Thank you," Patrick said softly. His spurs jingled too loudly for his cold ears as he walked into the shadow of the archway. He entered a tiny cantina with a few bare wooden tables across the hardwood floor. The floor boards were wide and coarse and they creaked as Patrick made his way toward the only occupied table where a round shouldered man sat alone with a bottle.

Sean looked up. His eyes were as red as the right side of his chewed-up face. Squinting a scowl of recognition, he lowered his face toward an empty plate on the table. All but traces of red sauce had been erased by pieces of dark bread, which had gone down like saw dust.

"May I sit?"

Sean shrugged and his brother pulled out the second chair. He laid his hat on the table. Sean picked it up and dropped it to the floor. The younger brother leaned sideways in his chair, retrieved the hat, and tucked it into his lap.

"We need to talk, Sean."

"Ain't you got a ranch to run?"

"You know I ain't no rancher and I ain't no cattleman. I can't do it alone."

"Your Pa done it alone."

"I ain't Pa."

Sean only exhaled into an upturned shot glass.

"You can get your own bottle, if you want. This one's mine."

"No, thanks. It's a little early for me."

"Not me. I started three hours ago." Sean chuckled for the

first time since Attorney Shield's office four days earlier.

"What have you been doing for the last few days?" Patrick asked gently.

Sean lifted his empty glass toward his brother as if toasting him. Then he refilled the glass but left it sitting in a little alcohol puddle on the rough table.

"I've been home." Patrick spoke cheerfully, as he answered a question that had not been asked. "Mucking out the barn, mainly. Even the horse chips is froze by morning. I can't manage it alone."

"Hire somebody. From what I hear, there ain't no shortage of able bodies in Lincoln."

"You've learned more about the town?"

Sean could not resist being drawn into the conversation. The two eldest Rourke brothers had always been close. Not even the war could come between them. Only Grady Rourke was able to do that and he had done it from the grave. But the older brother liked talking about things he knew about.

"The House owns the Wortley Hotel, too. That Tunstall fellow and McSween set themselves against the House. The townsfolk chose sides. Half and half, sounds like. And both sides got guns." For the first time, Sean focused his bloodshot eyes squarely on his little brother. "Damned town is a garrison. That's why Shield's office looked like a fort."

Sean broke the moment of civility by looking past Patrick. The younger brother followed his brother's gaze over his shoulder.

Twenty feet away, a young woman was picking dirty breakfast plates from a corner table. Patrick studied her. For some reason, he had not noticed her when he had entered the hotel's small dining area. She was middle height, perhaps half-a-head shorter than the tall brothers. Her long hair was black but her bare arms were pale skinned. When she turned around, her eyes met Patrick's. The brother squinted at her sky-blue eyes. She blinked when Patrick blinked and she turned to continue cleaning the cantina's tables.

Patrick turned back toward Sean who closely watched his brother's reaction.

"She ain't Mexican, leastwise not full-blooded," Sean said into his glass. He spoke very softly, causing Patrick to lean toward him. "Her Ma was white as the snow outside; her Pa was a local."

"I didn't even see her when I come in."

"She's like that. Like a piece of the furniture. Keeps to herself and don't say nothing. Name's Melissa. Melissa Bryant."

"Nothing wrong with a good woman who keeps her mind to herself." Patrick almost whispered, leaning halfway across the table. In the back of his mind, he felt relieved that an attractive woman close to his own age still caught his eye. Perhaps his mind was not yet lost.

"She don't say nothing. Ever." Sean was looking past his brother's shoulder again toward where Melissa Bryant was bending over a wooden pail of soapy water. The bloodshot eyes focused on her bottom. The brother took a deep breath, through his nose.

"Never?" Patrick asked without turning around again.

"Manuel—the Mex at the desk out front—says she got done by a bunch of Mescaleros and Navajos back in '70. In May, it was. Near Fort Stanton. Half a dozen done her." Sean was whispering and his sweating face and glistening, red eyes looked serious. "Left her with a little girl. They live near here in a place the House give them."

Patrick nodded. The story depressed him further. It reminded him of the hard country in which he had grown up and to which a letter from a stranger had brought him back.

The young woman walked quickly past the brothers into the shadows of the narrow hallway leading out of the room. Patrick concentrated on her as she went by. In the warm, firelit room, she wore light clothing in which to work. Her long skirt and short sleeves fit closely. The younger brother was surprised that the firm, pale body underneath was not like the few women leading children he had noticed in town. The other women in heavy winter clothing would have required leather stitches to keep their calico from exploding. Perhaps laboring as a house maid at the Wortley Hotel kept Melissa trim. Patrick wondered.

"What do you mean 'she don't talk?' "

"Manuel says she ain't spoke a word since the Apache raid eight years back." Sean shook his shaggy head. "They must have done her something awful." He looked up toward the arch where the woman had disappeared.

"About this ranch business, Sean. We can't let Pa's will come between us like this. It ain't right."

"It's what Pa wanted." The malice was gone from Sean's voice. He stated only the bare facts. For the first time, Patrick noticed that his brother had a wad of chaw stuffed into the side of his face that had been destroyed. The bulge gave the illusion that the missing meat had returned to balance his face.

"Why can't I deed you half of the land? We can go back to the lawyer right now and fix it. Put an end to this."

"No. You can't speak for Liam. He's your partner now, not me."

"What if Liam don't come?"

"Gotta wait. McSween's letter to us said that he wrote to Liam, too. If our little brother ain't dead and scalped up north somewheres, then he'll come when he can." Sean took another swig. "Till then, I ain't coming between you and Liam like Pa done between you and me."

Patrick put a hand on each side of the narrow table, lowered his head, and sighed deeply.

"All right. Until Liam gets here. What will you do until then?"

"I got a room here. I can work. And I still got my share of the California coin. I won't starve." Sean smiled weakly, but that was enough for Patrick to see the first glimmer of his real brother in nearly a week.

"You'll be all right?"

"Sure. You go on now."

Patrick knew Sean well enough not to press the fragile peace.

"I'll go on over to the House and get some supplies for the ranch."

The younger brother pushed back from the table and stood up.

"No. You can't go there."

"Why not?"

"Chisum's cattle." Sean toyed with his empty glass, moving it in little circles through the liquor wetting the table. "The House don't take kindly to Chisum. He's in with Tunstall and McSween. You better get your stores at Tunstall's for a while."

"That don't make no sense." Patrick said as he brushed his long hair from his brow.

Sean looked up. Brown tobacco ooze trickled from the corner of his mouth when he spoke firmly, "This is Lincoln."

"All right. I don't need no trouble. You take care of yourself, Sean."

"Sure."

When the sitting man lowered his unshaved chin to his filthy shirt collar, Patrick put on his hat and walked out of the dining room. Sean listened to his brother's spurs loud on the hardwood floor. The drunken brother looked over toward the empty table where the woman had been working. He stared blankly ahead, as if she were still there, bending over, inside his alcohol-saturated mind.

Outside, the midmorning sun was blinding in the southeast sky. Patrick had to pull his floppy brimmed hat lower to shield his eyes. His rested horse came quickly to the side of the corral where his master waited. Sean's horse stood patiently close to Patrick's mount as the saddle was cinched tight. Patrick led his animal by the reins through the wooden gate. When he mounted, the other horse whinnied as his companion carried Patrick up the left side of the street.

Patrick tied his horse to the porch rail at Tunstall's, a hundred yards east of the Wortley. He stood in the cold sunshine to loosen the saddle's girth leathers.

"Might as well put him in the paddock."

Patrick was startled by the perfect, Oxford English at his shoulder. He turned around.

"I'm John Tunstall. We haven't met."

"Patrick Rourke."

"Grady's son?"

"Yes."

"Too bad about your father. Have you been to Mr. McSween?"

"We met with Mr. Shield last week. My brother and me."

"Of course. Alex should be back in a week or two."

Patrick was taken by the easy cheer of the Englishman. They walked his horse to the side of the store and the corral gate. An old, brown horse dragged his hooves in the snow when he ambled over toward the two men. Tunstall reached out to rub the animal's nose. The horse seemed startled by the hand on his face.

"He's quite blind," Tunstall smiled. "I call him Colonel. Bought him from the cavalry to save him from the butcher. Don't ride him much. Never in this cold. He's rather a pet these days."

Love for an old horse is a sure sign of a gentleman, and Patrick was won over quickly. After lifting his weathered saddle to the corral's fence post, he turned his horse out to make Colonel's acquaintance. The blind horse laid his ears flat back. Patrick's mount read the message and walked to a far corner.

"They'll figure it out," the shopkeeper smiled. "Come on in."

Patrick followed the Englishman into the store.

Tunstall took off his long duster, shook off a few flakes of

wet snow, and hung it on a wall peg. With his hat off, Tunstall looked younger than his twenty-five years.
Clean-shaven with bushy auburn hair, his hands were as
softly pink as the lawyer's. Patrick quickly sized up the
friendly merchant as someone who never broke a sweat
doing poor-man's work under a hot sun.

Patrick took off his fur coat in the cozy store. A blazing
hearth added to the sense of comfort and cheer. Several
round women navigated through bolts of cloth and piles of
tinware. As his eyes adjusted to the inside, Patrick noticed
Bill Bonney manning the clerk's counter. The boy's pale
eyes watched the women and ignored the few men who
were taking the measure of ax handles and leather horse
tack.

"You must have met Mr. Bonney already."

"Yes."

The young men nodded at each other.

David Shield walked out of his cranny office.

"Mr. Rourke? Nice to see you again. Have you decided to
have me admit your father's will to probate?"

"Don't think so, sir. My brother and I want to wait for
Liam coming down from Canada."

"That will be fine, Mr. Rourke. There's no rush really."

"Thank you." Patrick turned to Billy Bonney. "I need
some stores for the ranch: flour, sugar, maybe some sourdough starter if you have any this time of year, and a bottle
of whiskey, please. Oh, and do you sell glass?"

"Glass?"

"The front window is broke."

"Have to order it. Do you have the dimensions?"

Patrick pulled a crumpled piece of paper from his pocket
and handed it to the boy behind the counter. Billy squinted
his pale, narrow eyes and nodded.

"Take about three weeks, unless the pass on the stage
road thaws early. And we have starter, but this time of year
it's potato. That all right?"

"That'll be fine."

"Good." Billy began to search the spacious store for the supplies.

"Mr. Bonney? Small doses of everything, please. I only brought my riding horse."

"All right. And call me Billy. Everyone else does."

John Henry Tunstall ushered Patrick toward a table at the saloon end of the store. There were four tables; two were empty. The proprietor and the customer sat down.

"A drink, Patrick?"

"Just coffee, thanks."

"Two coffees, Billy."

"Thanks, Mr. Tunstall."

"Call me, John. I heard your brother took a room across the way."

"Yes. He's a little upset about Pa's will—giving everything to Liam and me. Can't hardly blame him."

"Perhaps not. But the Wortley is part of the House, you know." Tunstall saw Patrick nod. "They're a rough lot, Dolan and his kind. Is Chisum still running part of his herd on your ranch?"

"Yes."

Billy Bonney set two china cups of black coffee on the table. Tunstall thanked him like a proper English gentleman.

"Then you had better keep an eye on the cattle. The House makes part of its living rustling."

"Cattle thieves?"

"Yes. For years. And not just any cattle—Chisum cattle is their speciality."

"But the House is a bunch of clerks and one deaf and dumb girl."

Tunstall spoke over his steaming coffee cup close to his face.

"You met Miss Bryant?"

"Yes. I visited Sean before I came over here."

Tunstall nodded and sipped.

"She isn't deaf, just mute. Tragic story. Such a pretty girl, too. And her daughter is just precious. But the House isn't clerks. Jimmy Dolan runs with the Boys. You heard of them?"

"No. Only been back four or five days."

"The Boys are what these colonists call the Jesse Evans Gang: ruthless thieves and bushwhackers. The Boys do Dolan's dirty work: rustling and ambushing decent people."

"How do you know? About the rustling, I mean?"

"You saw Chisum's jingle-bob ear brand on the steers?"

Patrick nodded.

"Not long ago, my people raided one of the gang's cronies at a ranch south of town. Found a hole in the ground full of cow ears. Cutting the ears off is the only way to get rid of that brand. They're rustlers, all right."

"Anyone arrested?"

Tunstall laughed out loud. "Who do you think hand-picked Sheriff Brady for this town?"

The Englishman couldn't stop chuckling. The picture of Lincoln looked grimmer to Patrick than he had imagined.

"But how come my Pa's ranch ain't been rustled dry? Pa's been gone for months."

"I'm afraid your father ran with the Boys and Dolan. Not much and not often. But Grady was one of them all the same. They don't bushwhack their own, I suppose."

Patrick sat back against his chair. He looked stunned.

"I'm sorry, Patrick. I didn't mean to imply that your father was a cattle thief. Only that he bought at the House and welcomed the Boys to his home. Everyone in Lincoln has taken sides. Your father simply chose Dolan. He got everything and everyone that goes with it."

Tunstall stopped abruptly in mid-thought. He lowered his cup, put his hands palms-down atop the table, and closed his eyes. Patrick waited for a moment.

"Are you all right, John?"

The Englishman opened his eyes slowly, as if after a half-minute nap.

"Excuse me? Yes, yes, quite all right. I just get tired. I spent four or five weeks down with small pox last summer. Came down with it at Las Vegas. I should have spent more time recovering. But I had business back here in Lincoln. In the middle of October, I rode back on horseback—forty miles a day for three days. That was three months ago and my bones still ache from that ride. But I'm doing much better now."

"Good. You were speaking about Jesse Evans and rustling."

"Yes, the captain—that's what the locals call Jesse. The Boys even stole some livestock of mine."

Patrick watched his host intently.

"Back in September. Middle of the month. Stole my horses from my ranch down on the Rio Felix. Everyone knew the gang did it. So even Sheriff Brady had to go after them. Sent Dick Brewer, his deputy. Arrested the captain and three of the Boys down at Seven Rivers and threw them in jail up here in Lincoln. The sheriff of Doña Ana County refused to issue the arrest warrants so Justice Wilson—Justice of the Peace John Wilson—in Lincoln issued the warrants."

Billy Bonney stepped out of the shadows with a large pot of hot coffee. Without asking, he refilled the two china cups and stepped back.

"Tell Patrick how you got the captain out of jail."

Bonney looked almost giddy over the story's climax.

"Nonsense, Billy. Go help those ladies with that flour barrel."

"Yes, Mr. Tunstall."

"As I was saying, the captain and his gunmen were locked up. Toward the end of last November, the whole damned gang—twenty-five riders—broke them out of jail. I got a little of the credit just because I sent Evans a few bottles of whiskey while he was in jail. Folks thought I hid a saw in a fruit cake! But his men broke him out, not me."

Patrick concealed a faint smile behind his beard.

"Did you ever get your horses back?"

"Yes. Jesse promised me that he would return them when he was released. He was and he did. But I didn't have anything to do with his breakout."

"Of course not."

"Well, as I was saying: If your brother stays at the Wortley, he will either run with the Boys or get himself run over by them. He can't stay long over there without choosing sides. Everyone in Lincoln has chosen sides."

"Yes. You said that."

"It's true. And that's the end of it."

Billy came back without the coffee pot.

"Your supplies are ready. Packed small for behind your saddle. Four dollars, please."

"How much for the coffee?"

"On the house," Tunstall answered for Billy. "It was nice talking with you, Patrick. I hope things work out with your brother." The Englishman excused himself, stood up, and walked into Shield's back office.

Patrick reached into his pocket and laid four silver dollars on the table. Billy picked them up and went to the counter. Patrick followed him and picked up a canvas sack heavy with his purchases. The sack was only two-thirds full so it would dangle from the saddle's cantle.

Outside, the sun was well up and seemed to stop dead in the purple sky to the south. It was noon and Patrick regretted having already burned up half of the day. He walked to the paddock on the side of the store and waited for his horse to come over. Tunstall's blind horse followed the swishing tail. Saddling quickly, Patrick heaved the sack across the back of his saddle. The saddle was a cattleman's saddle designed for roping and cutting John Chisum's cattle: long toward the rear and secured by two belly cinches.

Patrick rode at an easy walk toward the west. The sun

was shoulder high to his left. He pulled his fur collar up high on his neck to keep the cold breeze out of his thick flannel shirt.

He glanced right as he walked his mount past the Wortley. Patrick did not see Sean. But Melissa Bryant stood ankle-keep in old and dirty snow just outside the door. Still in her short sleeves, she wrapped her arms across her full chest to keep warm. The brilliant sun was in her eyes, squinted nearly closed. Her long black hair shined against the drab adobe wall behind her.

Patrick looked down and kept going. When his eyes half hidden by his wide hat met the woman's blue eyes, he nodded and touched his floppy brim with his gloved hand.

The woman blinked and turned quickly, closing the door behind her.

Chapter Four

By Monday, January 28th, 1878, Patrick Rourke had stayed away from Lincoln for six days. During that time, he continued to work at making the ranch house livable. It seemed to him that he cleaned out enough cobwebs to knit a sweater. Mucking out the barn felt like working in a mine. The frozen piles of manure were like shoveling rocks. With the fences down, the cattle with mutilated ears strolled the brown and yellow snow up to the front door as if they were the real tenants of Grady Rourke's home. When mornings came cold and bright under a purple sky, dozens of them huddled to stay warm on the front porch. Patrick wondered if the weight of their thin bodies had shattered the front window—through which the night wind still blew hard against the faded curtain nailed across the sill and sash.

By Monday, six days had passed since the woman who had no voice had walked behind Patrick's chair in the cantina. He had felt or had imagined that he felt the coarse linen of her skirt just touch the back of his neck. She did not walk through his dreams until the third night.

Because of the woman, Patrick thought over hot coffee in a tin cup, because of the woman the cattle dozed this morning on his front porch. Since his third morning in his father's bed, each day he awoke from dreaming of Melissa Bryant. Instead of stepping out of his warm bedroll onto the ice-cold hardwood floor the instant his eyes opened, he lay there

52

with his hands folded under his head and thought of Melissa. Each morning, he wasted an hour trying to conjure every detail of his dream in his mind. Inhaling sleepily, he would imagine that he had her scent on his beard, instead of the stench of the night's cow droppings steaming on the front porch and seeping through the billowing curtain.

The morning hours spent remembering her were hours that would have been better spent on mending fences and patching the roof. But instead of stoking the fire in the hearth and baking a sourdough biscuit to go with his morning coffee, Patrick sat thinking about shining black hair, white shoulders, and sparkling blue eyes. In the moment when he had ridden past her and she had looked up and turned away, Patrick had seen eyes full of sunlight and a distant blind terror that haunted her memory. Each morning, as he lay there remembering the fleeting glance of pain in the corners of those violet eyes, he tried not to imagine that skin and that face screaming under a dozen brown bodies taking her, one at a time. For eight years, she had not used that voice again.

The only way to shake the last vision was to climb out of his blankets and let the deathlike cold of the floor snap his mind back to the business at hand. So Patrick had rubbed his eyes and grimaced when his stocking feet touched the floor. He built a fire and now sipped hot coffee at the small table in his dead mother's kitchen.

Rummaging through the old house, Patrick had found a loose board in the floor of his parents' bedroom. Investigating further, he saw that the timber was not nailed to the framing underneath. When he lifted the plank to inspect for rot or termites, he discovered a rusted, metal box no larger than a loaf of bread. Inside were gold and silver coins, just under one hundred fifty dollars. Within the treasure was a yellowed citation naming Master Sergeant Grady Sean Rourke a brave soldier at the battle of Chapultepec, Mexico, September 12, 1847. The citation was signed by Brevet Lt. Colonel Robert E. Lee and countersigned by Winfield Scott, General of the

Army. The long-hand signature at the very bottom belonged to James K. Polk, President of the United States.

Patrick had counted the coins into neat piles on the kitchen table, kept twenty-five dollars, and put everything else back into its place under the bedroom floor. The little box and a few hundred dollars under Grady's name at Tunstall's bank were all of Grady's life savings. The money, the rundown ranch, and a Presidential citation were all Grady Rourke had in the world—that, and three sons should Liam still be alive.

By the sixth day, Patrick knew that he could not repair and manage the ranch alone and that Grady's hidden money would not last long. To keep the ranch, he would need either a brother or a hired hand. That would require renting the pasture to Chisum's herd—up to the front porch, if necessary. And since Grady's estate could not be released until Liam returned or was declared dead by the Army, Patrick knew that he needed a job.

So on this cold and bright Monday, Patrick saddled his horse and rode again into Lincoln.

"Run out of sourdough already?" Billy Bonney asked cheerfully from behind the counter.

"No. I would like to see Mr. Shield, please."

"He's gone for at least a week."

"Gone?"

"Yep. Went down to Mesilla to see about getting Mr. McSween loose."

"What about Mr. Tunstall?"

"He's in the back. You can go on in, I suppose."

"Thanks."

John Tunstall stood up when Patrick knocked on the door frame of the open door.

"Good morning, Patrick. Have a seat."

"Thanks." Patrick sat down and set his hat on his lap. He opened his fur trailcoat wide in the room warmed by the fireplace.

"Is Billy getting more supplies for you?"

"No. I come in to ask for work. Seems I can't get at Pa's account in your bank till our other brother musters out of the cavalry. I can't get by just on the ranch. I don't even know what the cattle rents are."

"Chisum's herd?"

"Yes. I suppose I could go down to his place. Maybe he needs another hand?"

The Englishman put his paperwork aside to give his guest his full attention.

"John Chisum's ranch is South Spring River, fifty-five miles east of here where the Rio Hondo meets the Pecos River. It's a long haul if you're also running your father's spread alone. The cattle are probably putting twenty-five dollars a month into your father's account here at the bank. I'm pleased to tell you that the Lincoln County Bank is the only one in town. There are only two other banks in the whole territory. I'm an owner, but I'm carried on the charter as just the cashier. John Chisum is president and Mr. McSween is vice president."

"Chisum's in the banking business, too?"

"Yes, indeed. It's the three of us against the House and their whore sheriff. John probably runs eighty-thousand head now. He might pay you to join his operation here in Lincoln. Can you handle that sidearm?" Tunstall nodded toward Patrick's Peacemaker high on his right hip.

"My piece? I'm passable with it. But I was thinking of cow punching for Chisum, not using my Colt."

"You don't seem to understand yet." There was no trace of impatience in Tunstall's voice. "John Chisum has taken up with McSween and me. That puts him on our side of the fence. Dolan's gang is on the other side."

"Over cattle, too?" Patrick had never seen anything like this, not even in the far western gold fields where men killed each other over a scrap of bread.

"Especially cattle. Dolan's henchmen—the Jesse Evans

Gang—have made a fine living stealing Chisum cattle and selling it back to the Indian Agency for the Apache reservation. They hide the cattle down around Seven Rivers. Remember: That bunch wasn't above stealing my horses from my ranch down on the Rio Felix. And make no mistake," Tunstall leaned forward, resting his elbow on the lawyer's rolltop desk, "Jimmy Dolan is at the bottom of that cesspool. He owns the House, and the Boys rustle and murder for him."

"Murder? I thought Dolan was just another shopkeeper."

"Murder, Patrick. Just last year, he shot and killed Geraldo Jaramillo. Sheriff said it was self defense. But he shot him three times. Dolan is a killer and a rustler. He just lets Jesse Evans do his dirty work so Dolan can keep his hands clean. That's why Chisum could use one more gun here in Lincoln."

Patrick looked down toward his hat balanced on his right knee. He toyed with its faded crown. He had not come home to become a gunman.

"My brother's still at the Wortley, you know."

"Yes. And I've seen him—not in here, of course, but on the street—with some of Jesse's men. Sean is in rough company, I'm afraid."

"And if I hire on with Chisum?"

"Then you and Sean might very well end up on opposite sides of the street."

Patrick nodded.

"Then I can't do it. I can't take no job with Chisum."

Tunstall leaned back and folded his hands in his lap. His brow pursed with a moment's deep thought. He seemed genuinely concerned.

"Well, Patrick, even if you could hasten the probate process of your father's estate, Mr. Shield has gone to Mesilla for a week, maybe longer. Perhaps Liam will be here by the time Mr. Shield and Alex get home. I'm just thinking: Chisum has his men based out of South Spring River. No one really works this end of his spread. You're living on your father's ranch anyway. Why not hire on just to watch the Chisum cattle grazing on Rourke land? I can just about guarantee he'll pay two dollars a week for that. The Evans men shouldn't bother you much—especially with Sean living at the Wortley in House territory. Besides, I could probably arrange an increase in the grazing rents if you need it."

"What authority do I have over the grazing rights?"

"You seem to be running the spread. Sean has elected not to participate. Even though Chisum's lease was with Grady, you have certain rights as one of the heirs to the estate. After all, the lease will descend to you and Liam once the will is probated. I think Mr. Shield or Alex could get some kind of temporary order giving you power of attorney when the judge visits here on his circuit ."

"Would I have authority to cancel the lease altogether, if I wanted to?"

"I suppose. But you need the money."

"Yes. That's true."

"Then you'll continue the cattle grazing, for the time being?"

"Yes. I don't have much choice."

"Fine. I'll tell John when I see him. Now, about your hiring on to protect the cattle on Rourke land?"

"Do you speak for Mr. Chisum?"

"No one speaks for John Chisum except John Chisum. But we're partners. I can hire you until he disapproves. His money is good until then. And I'm quite certain he'll approve. One more gun is one gun not in Dolan's service."

Patrick looked down again. He studied his spurs where he crossed his legs.

"All right. Till Liam is accounted for and we can settle up Pa's business."

Tunstall patted his blackclad knees before he stood.

"Splendid. I'll have Billy put you on the payroll at once. Do you need an advance?"

"No, thanks. I still have some coin. I'll be on my way, Mr. Tunstall."

"John. Please. I'm John. Chisum is Mister." He extended his hand, which Patrick took. "And I hope that you can talk some sense into Sean before it's too late."

"Yes. I'll try. I'll look forward to meeting Mr. Chisum."

"Good. I'll send word to you if I have need to ride over to South Spring."

Patrick nodded, fixed his hat low over his eyes, and walked out of the office. Billy Bonney looked up and nodded cheerfully.

The Rourke brother's pace was brisk when he walked down the frozen street toward the Wortley. He left his horse in Tunstall's paddock where the animal rubbed noses with blind Colonel. Patrick's spurs made no sound on the packed snow that crunched underfoot. For a town where there were two clearly drawn sides and everyone was on one or the other, the townspeople were friendly. They nodded and touched the brims of their hats when Patrick passed them. *Anglos* in black suits or ranching clothing and Mexicans uniformly dressed like Indians or cow punchers were equally civil to the new man in town.

The crowd inside the adobe hotel surprised Patrick. The boarding house was full of hungry-looking men in shabby trail dusters and baggy pants. The dark-faced clerk at the desk nodded.

"He's in the cantina."

"Thanks."

Hat in hand, Patrick found Sean sitting at a large table where all seven chairs were filled. There were three bottles between them but Sean was the only one without a glass at his place.

"Patrick? Come to visit your ex-brother?"

"Sean."

When Sean stood up, Patrick noticed that his brother's eyes were not bloodshot and his breath did not smell like kerosine. He could smell strong tobacco instead. Sean pulled a chair from a nearby table and wedged it in close to his. He gestured toward the empty seat. Patrick remained standing and eyed the strangers at the table: young men in their mid-twenties with unkempt hair, scruffy beards, and heavy gunbelts. One of the men looked older, in his thirties. He alone wore a business suit and a clean, white shirt.

"This here is my little brother Patrick."

The strangers nodded.

"This is Jesse Evans," Sean said as if he had known all of his life the man smiling without pretense.

"Mr. Evans."

"They call me Captain. It's an honorary." Jesse Evans chuckled. When he stood up for a moment until the brothers got seated, Patrick was surprised that the cattle rustler was rather stocky and short, maybe 150 pounds on a 5-foot, 6-inch frame. His gray eyes were not killers' eyes. Greasy, blond hair fell over his forehead. "Come to join the Boys? Sean has decided to ride with us."

Patrick looked sideways toward his clear-eyed brother. Sean blinked and looked down at the table.

"Don't think so, Captain. I'm running our father's ranch until the lawyers get back and our other brother gets here. Then we'll settle up and get things back to normal." Patrick kept looking at Sean who did not look up. He sat on Sean's good side and could not see his shattered face.

"You had business with the Englishman." Evans did not ask a question.

Patrick wondered who had watched him.

"Yes. Banking."

"Oh. The Englishman and McSween think they can put the House under. What do you think?"

"I think it's none of my business, really." Patrick was not about to be drawn further into the village's civil war.

"That's my brother," Sean said quickly. "Keeping his nose to his own affairs."

"Admirable quality," Jesse Evans nodded. "Understand Chisum is grazing on your daddy's land?"

"Seems so."

"Chisum paying you rent?"

"Not directly. It goes into our father's account at the bank. For a while yet."

"Tunstall's bank, you mean. Tunstall and Chisum."

"There ain't no other bank in town," Patrick shrugged. "There weren't no choice."

"Guess not. If Tunstall and the lawyers had their way, we'd all owe our souls to their bank." The older man in the clean shirt beside Jesse Evans spoke. "I'm Jimmy Dolan."

Patrick looked Dolan in the eye. He wanted to see the rest of the story when it came at him. Dolan spoke without an Irish accent.

"The Englishman and McSween are swindlers and thieves. The ranchers here abouts have to trade their government script for real money at their bank. Tunstall gives them two-thirds of the face value. The exchange rate is thievery, pure and simple. And townsfolk who farm or want to buy land have to get credit at Tunstall and Chisum's private little bank. When they can't make the payments, the bank gets their land. They're breaking the ranchers' backs. You best not have nothing to do with them people."

Dolan was visibly angry. His words hissed out through clenched teeth. Patrick listened politely.

"And that there Britisher is buying up land what ain't legal for someone what ain't a real citizen."

"How's that?" Patrick leaned slightly toward Dolan.

"Your daddy and most of the folks around here bought their spreads by the new Desert Lands Act. Passed about a year ago. Folks can lay temporary claim to a whole section of U.S. Government land for twenty-five cents an acre if they promise to work it and irrigate it for three years. After that, they can buy clear title for another dollar per acre. But it's only open to real Americans, not

Englishmen. Tunstall had local people buy up over three-thousand eight-hundred acres in their names and then sell it to him. It's thievery and it ain't even American thievery! You keep clear of them Protestants. The House is Irish: Murphy started it and I bought him out. I come to this country back in '48 when I was a boy. The potato famine in '45 is what sent the lot of us over. Joined Mr. Lincoln's army when I was only fifteen. Served till '69. At least we're citizens now. Not like the Englishman and his Protestants. You hear me?"

"Yes," Patrick nodded. He glanced sideways toward Sean. "But it's too late. I'm thinking of going to work for Chisum. I ain't got help for Pa's ranch and I ain't got money to keep it going much longer. If Chisum wants to rent grazing rights, I got to sell it to him." When Sean looked away, Patrick turned back toward James Dolan. "I ain't got a choice. Leastwise not till Liam comes home ."

The owner of the House and the Wortley Hotel—who hired the likes of Jesse Evans to rustle Chisum cattle—shook his head as if truly disappointed.

"That ain't much of a choice, Patrick."

"Everyone keeps telling me that you can't live in Lincoln without you make a choice of sides. It don't make any sense to me. But I suppose I done what I had to do. I choose Tunstall and Chisum. I ain't going to lose Pa's ranch."

"All the same," Evans said, "you ain't chose right. Not like Sean here. He'll be riding with us and the House."

Patrick looked at Sean until the older Rourke brother had to turn his head to face Patrick squarely.

"I can come over here if you'll come back to the ranch, Sean."

"No. I'm part of the House now. And the House don't take to Chisum cattle or to their bank."

Before Patrick could respond, a sturdy middle-aged man entered the cantina. He was tall, in his late forties, and had black hair and a black mustache that curled down past the corners of his mouth. He wore a silver star on his shirt. Jesse Evans the bandit smiled broadly and waved. The lawman nodded and walked toward the table. Two of Evans' men moved their chairs sideways to make a chair-size space between them. The new man pushed a seat between them and sat down. He immediately looked at Patrick.

"You're Grady's other boy?"

"Yes. Patrick."

"I'm Sheriff Bill Brady. You're the one who ain't never soldiered?"

"Yes," Patrick stammered and looked down at his dirty hat atop the rough table. "Sean here and our brother Liam was soldiers. And our Pa. But I ain't been."

"That's all right, son. I didn't mean no disrespect. I wore the blue, like Jimmy here, in the war. I know Sean wore the gray. But it don't matter out here. I was a major in the New Mexico Volunteer Cavalry. Fought more Navajo and Apaches than Rebs during the war anyway."

Patrick nodded. He wished for a drink so he would have something to fidget with instead of his hat.

"You staying at Grady's place?"

"Yes. I'm running the ranch now."

"Alone?"

"I ain't got no help."

Sheriff Brady looked at Sean, then back toward Patrick.

"Guess not." The County Cavan–born sheriff spoke with a thick Irish accent. "Well, Lincoln's a good town. Hard, but good. When we get rid of McSween and the Englishman, it will be even better. Good place to raise children."

"Brady ought to know," Jesse Evans laughed. "He's got eight of them and another in the oven."

"That ain't no way to talk about my wife, Jesse," Brady said without malice.

"Well, it's true, ain't it?"

"It's true."

"The sheriff is a politician, too," Jesse offered to break

the momentary tension. "First Lincoln delegate to the Terri-torial House of Representatives back in '71."

"That was a long time ago," Brady smiled to reassure his outlaw friend. "Been sheriff here since '76." He looked over at Patrick. "When you get settled, you come on over to my place at Walnut Grove, four miles east of town. My wife, Bonifacia, will show you some home cooking like only a Mex woman can make."

"That would be welcome, Sheriff."

William Brady nodded and stood. He touched the brim of his hat, smiled warmly at Dolan, and walked over to the bar where he joined a few men drinking and laughing.

Turning back toward the company at hand, Patrick saw Melissa Bryant enter carrying a wooden tray. She set some plates in front of two dusty men sitting two tables away. From their side of the round table, both Rourke brothers watched the woman lean over the table.

"That's Melissa," Jesse Evans said softly. "She don't talk no more."

"I know," Patrick said without thinking. He watched Melissa standing on the far side of the other table. She faced Sean and Patrick without looking at them or seeing them. When she leaned forward, Patrick saw the weight of her breasts pull her low-cut blouse away from her collar bones. Her long black hair fell forward and covered half of her ele-gant face. Patrick exhaled so slowly that Jesse Evans turned full around to see what held the younger Rourke's absolute attention. The leader of the Boys smiled and turned back toward the brothers.

"You'd need cavalry spurs to ride that, boy," Evans said in a whisper. "You'd be bucked off for sure." The rustler's two friends chuckled without turning around. They knew from Patrick's face where his squinting eyes were focused.

"I suppose so," Patrick smiled. He looked at his brother who wasn't smiling. "But I have fences to mend and a leaky roof to tar first."

"Then you best get an early start to it," Sean said coldly.

Patrick regarded his older brother carefully.

"Yes. You ain't coming then?"

"Not today, Patrick. I'm having supper with my friends." Jesse Evans nodded.

"All right. I'll see you." Patrick pushed back from the crowded table.

"Whenever you come back to town."

Patrick stood, looked down at his brother, and walked out of the cantina. When he left, he did not glance over at Melissa as he screwed his hat down low over his forehead.

Walking back up the street toward his horse in Tunstall's corral, Patrick was overcome with a strange anger that simmered to a full boil by the time he threw his worn saddle over his horse's back. He hated feeling like the little brother. But Sean made him feel that way by catching him looking at the mute woman. He thumped down into his saddle so hard that his horse swayed slightly for the step it required to engage its hind legs. Riding slowly west, Patrick was too angry to notice Sheriff Brady watching him from the shadows of the front porch of the House.

An icy wind blowing down from Capitan Peak above Patrick's right side cooled his anger quickly. Walking his long-haired horse across the frozen Rio Bonito, his brain was too cold to think about anything other than getting home before his fingers snapped off against the leather reins.

When he knelt in his fur coat at Grady Rourke's hearth, Patrick's hands were so numb that he broke the first two matches when he struck them on the stone. He cursed the logs until they caught with a cold, yellow flame. By the time the fire had thawed his hands, Melissa Bryant had been in his brother's room for an hour.

Chapter Five

SEAN ROURKE DID NOT SPEAK HIS BROTHER'S NAME FOR A week. Friday morning, February 1st, Sean stood clean and sober in Sheriff Brady's office.

The single-story abode courthouse stood on the south side of the dirt street. In the bright morning sunshine, the thin air had warmed enough to turn the frozen street into slushy mud. It was comfortable enough to walk from the Wortley, across the street, and on up to the sheriff's office just past the Tunstall store. Walking past Tunstall's, Sean glanced left. He did not see Patrick's horse in the paddock, so he fixed his eyes on the street as he continued eastward.

Inside the courthouse, Sean could look across the street to the ancient stone tower that early settlers had built as a watchtower against Indian raids. The locals called it the *torréon*. Looking through a side window facing further up the street to the east, Sean could see early-morning customers staggering out of Ike Stockton's saloon adjacent to the Montaño store.

"Thanks for coming, Sean."

"Sheriff."

William Brady was cheerful in the cozy comfort radiating from a large, pot-bellied stove. He put a cup of coffee in front of Sean and splashed some whiskey into both tin cups. The lawman picked up his cup and wrapped his fingers around it as if to warm them.

"Any word from your brother?"

"Patrick? No. Ain't heard from Liam neither."

"Jimmy Dolan says you need some work?"

"Yes. Two weeks of boarding at the Wortley and Manuel's cantina have just about cleaned me out."

"I see. Well, I can use another deputy if you want."

"Law? I don't know."

"There ain't any profit from riding with the Boys. Fun maybe, but not much profit. You were a soldier and I need another man good with a shooting iron."

"You already have more guns than you got criminals, Sheriff."

William Brady smiled and nodded toward his steaming tin cup.

"Maybe. But word is that McSween will be coming home any day from Mesilla. He and Tunstall have quite a bunch of Mexicans riding with them. Thought your gun might even us up some."

"What about Patrick?" The brother looked squarely at the sheriff. The sun low in the east came through the window and cast horrible shadows on the burned side of Sean's face. The sheriff looked into his coffee cup.

"As far as I know, your brother ain't been to town since Monday. One of Jesse's men said that he was busy putting up his fence line. It ain't like I expect a war or anything. Maybe just a little trouble when McSween comes home. Probably nothing. You need the money and I need another gun. It ain't much more complicated than that."

Sean laid his coffee cup atop the desk between the men.

"What kind of trouble? McSween's nothing but a lawyer. He pushes paper."

"But he's got friends. What's worse, he's got a little army of cow punchers what protect Chisum's herd."

"From the way Jesse talks," Sean smiled tightly, "that seems like a reasonable precaution."

Sheriff Brady nodded. "I suppose. McSween and Tunstall

extort half of Lincoln county at their bank and Jimmy Dolan's House robs the ranchers by selling them goods at exorbitant prices and taking in the farmers' produce at outrageously low prices in exchange. Everyone has to choose their poison here." Brady nudged his cup aside, folded his hands on the desk, and leaned forward to lock eyes with Sean Rourke. "But Dolan ain't killed anybody; at least not over Chisum stock or money. McSween's gang don't seem so polite. Not after how Jimmy done him with old Fritz."

The force of Brady's narrow-eyed glare pushed Sean against the back of his chair.

"Everyone talks about this Fritz business, but no one will give it to me straight."

"Yes. You be entitled to that much, Sean." The sheriff stood up and moved toward the east window. His coffee and whiskey breath steamed the glass where he studied Stockton's saloon bathed in glorious high-country sunshine. "You know that Lawrence Murphy started the House. Emil Fritz was Murphy's partner until Fritz went back to Europe to die about four years ago. When some back-East insurance company refused to pay on Emil's life insurance, Murphy hired McSween to collect for the estate.

"Last summer, McSween wrung seven thousand dollars or so out of them. Then he stashed it in a bank in St. Louis, I think. Jimmy tried to get at the money to settle some old House debt of Emil's. When McSween stopped him, Dolan had Emil's sister swear out a complaint that McSween embezzled that money from the estate and hid it." Brady turned from the window and smiled. "Emil's sister don't even speak English."

Sean looked at Brady with the sun full on his mangled cheek.

"How come you know so much about all this legal business?"

"Because, Sean, I was appointed executor of old Emil's estate back in '76. I resigned as administrator to run for sheriff. That's when the House hired McSween to go after the insurance company."

"And that's why McSween is down in Mesilla now?"

"Yes. Dolan had a warrant issued for McSween's arrest. McSween, his wife, and Chisum were riding to Las Vegas, New Mexico. Deputy Sheriff Adolph Barrier—an honest man, for out here—arrested the lot of them on the stage road two days after Christmas. He released Sue and Chisum, but dragged McSween down to Mesilla to be arraigned in court. It's been five weeks now. They ought to be coming back up here any day. I expect the lawyer won't take too easily to a drumhead hearing."

The ex-Confederate knew about drumhead courts martial well enough. Sean nodded.

"I ain't seen Mrs. McSween since I come to town. Is she here?"

"No. She went on east. To St. Louis, maybe. She and McSween come to Lincoln in the spring of '75. Married about two years before that. She wanted to come out here for her asthma. Her cough got better and her husband got himself arrested." Brady chuckled to the frosted window. "Funny, in a way. McSween was born on Prince Edward Island. I suppose that makes him and Tunstall both British. But McSween speaks American."

Sheriff Brady returned to his seat behind the desk.

"I could use one more gun, if you want the work. I won't bother you unless I need you. You won't have to wear no tin star. The town will pay you two dollars a week just to be something of an auxiliary deputy—for emergencies and such."

Sean nodded and smiled behind his beard.

"Emergencies and such? Least you're honest about it, Sheriff. Does the town council have to approve of putting me on the payroll?"

"Jimmy Dolan approves."

Sean nodded. "All right, Sheriff. It's better than the

county poorhouse till we can close my father's estate."

Each man stood up. Sean put on his faded, floppy hat.

"You could move back into Grady's ranch with Patrick and forget the whole thing."

"No. I can't. I accept Mr. Dolan's offer. I'll thank him when I see him."

The lawman pulled two silver dollars from his vest pocket and laid the coins into Sean's gloved palm.

"I already done that for you, Deputy."

Walking back toward the Wortley, the midday sun hung in the violet sky over Sean's left shoulder. Most of Lincoln had taken root over the years on the north side of the single street, on the narrow strip of dirt-poor land between the road and the Rio Bonito. The hotel, the McSweens' fenced-in compound, Tunstall's store, the old *torréon* with its surrounding fence, and a few tiny homes all stood on the frozen strip of land. Sean walked on the undeveloped side of Main Street where only the Cisneros spread broke the snow-covered monotony between the courthouse and Dolan's mercantile. He had to pull his fur collar up around his face against a chilling, dry wind that blew across the Rio Bonito's ice.

The good side of Sean's face was red from cold and his nose protruding from his beard was moist by the time he stood at the far end of the half-mile long town. The Wortley was at his back as he looked up at the House.

Sean tried to smile, but his face was too cold. He kicked snow and slush from his boots before he walked inside the House—his new boss.

J. J. Dolan and Company owned forty acres around the large building. Sean removed his hat after closing the door behind him. Townspeople milled about the first floor piled high with bolts of cloth, barrels of flour and sugar, and shelves of canned goods brought by wagon down from Albuquerque or west from Texas. A pink-faced boy walked out from behind a counter.

"Can I help you find something?"

"I'm Sean Rourke. Looking for Mr. Dolan."

"He's in the lodge room."

"What?"

"Upstairs, Mr. Rourke. Is he expecting you?"

"I don't know. Sheriff Brady just hired me as a deputy."

The little clerk's rosy face opened broadly.

"Well, why didn't you say so. Go on up, Deputy."

Sean looked around and moved the brim of his hat through his gloved fingers until the battered hat made a complete revolution. The clerk waited patiently while Sean surveyed the entire establishment for steps. He saw no stairs.

"How?"

"You must be that new man whose pa writ him out?"

Sean's eyes narrowed. Only half of his cold face was able to squint. The clerk tried not to eye the half that was purple and rigid.

"You gotta go up from out back. That way." The clerk pointed toward a closed, back door.

"Thank you," Sean said. His voice had become as cold as his hands and feet. He walked quickly outside and turned left. A wooden ladder was airborne and coming down toward the snowy ground. It thumped on the hard earth and leaned against a second-floor, open window. Sean raised his right hand to shield his eyes when he looked up. Even though the sun was directly behind him where he stood within a fenced paddock, the sky was so bright that it hurt.

"Come on up, Sean." The voice was Jesse Evans'.

Sean put his hat back on and climbed the ladder. He crouched down to get through the window which was quickly closed behind him when he stepped onto the wooden floor. He straightened and looked around while his eyes adapted to the dim light.

"Understand congratulations are in order . . . Deputy."

Evans smiled warmly. "Welcome to the lodge room. You know Mr. Dolan here, and John Riley and Billy Mathews."

Sean shook hands with Dolan, and then his two partners. John Riley spoke with another Irish accent, but Jacob "Billy" Mathews did not.

"Deputy," Dolan nodded as if he need not bother to ask if the job were offered and accepted. "This is where the bachelor partners of the House live. We only eat over at the mess in the Wortley."

Sean looked around at the rather tidy room which was wide open throughout the second story like a hay loft. Bunks against the walls were also neat as a barracks.

"Can't allow clutter when we all live together up here."

"But there ain't no stairs?" was all Sean could mumble.

"Safer that way. In Lincoln, anyway," Billy Mathews said cheerfully. "Heard you went with the Confederacy?"

"Yes."

"Me, too. I was born in Tennessee. Been a miner too, before Lincoln."

The Battle of Shiloh was in western Tennessee. Sean's mind was momentarily flooded with horrors. He turned toward Dolan.

"Just wanted to say thanks for the work, Mr. Dolan."

"Glad to have you aboard, Sean. You'll earn your three dollars a week."

Sean thought of the two silver dollars new to his pocket.

"Thanks. Sheriff Brady said he don't expect trouble."

"Neither do we," Jesse Evans answered before Dolan could. The cattle rustler gently laid his hand on his heavy gunbelt and sidearm. Sean nodded thoughtfully.

"The sheriff said that McSween should be coming back soon." Sean focused on Dolan's completely clean-shaven face. John H. Riley stood at Dolan's side. Riley's face wore only a closely trimmed mustache on a triangular face with broad forehead and short hair. Dolan had the round, clean face of a schoolteacher rather than a merchant and occasional shootist. Riley looked more like a cavalry sergeant trying on civilian, bankers' clothes. Sean tried not to look at Riley's protruding ears and Riley tried not to study Sean's scarred face.

"McSween will be home soon enough," Jimmy Dolan said without worry in his clear voice. "I wouldn't worry about one Protestant lawyer."

"Sheriff says he rides with some rough people."

"The captain here is rougher," Dolan smiled with a glance sideways toward Jesse Evans who nodded with pleasure. "Don't give it another thought. If you don't mind going back the way you come up, we'll all go over to the mess for a bite." Dolan took a gold watch out of his vest. "It's already one o'clock. Manuel should have his fire going by now, boys."

A murmur of voices filled the bachelor quarters as half a dozen men pulled coats from wall pegs. Billy Mathews heaved the window open and gestured toward Sean.

"Watch your step going out. It takes a while to get used to it."

"Thanks."

Crossing the street in single file, Dolan paused for an instant to allow Sean to take his place behind Jesse Evans who led the way to the Wortley. Dolan fell into step behind Sean. Marching silently under a perfect sky, their long coats swayed across the ankle-deep snow, cutting a wide path from the House to the hotel. With eyes lowered against fierce sunlight, they looked like armed monks bound for vespers.

Just at the hotel side of the street, four small boys as dirty as the melting snow ran headlong into the House men. Waist-high to Jimmy Dolan, they skidded to a stop, panting hard in the cold, thin air. They had charged out of the hotel's corral where a dozen horses had ignored the boys' snowball fight with frozen clods of manure. When the leading boy bounced off Jesse Evans, Dolan recognized the bunch of them as scruffy sons of loyal House patrons. They returned the cheerful Irishman's smile.

The boys laughed in merry chorus until, one by one, they saw Sean Rourke who looked up from under his wide-brimmed hat. Sean grieved in the same instant that each boy gasped wide-eyed at the new deputy's destroyed face. He silently lowered his face into the lonesome shadow of his hat.

"Run along, boys," Dolan said gently. They did, looking over their shoulders as they trotted into the street.

When the men entered the hotel with Sean between Evans and Dolan, everyone inside immediately understood the newcomer's place in the field troops of the House. The Mexican behind the front desk wiped his hands on his apron as he approached the group hanging their trail dusters along the wall. Jesse Evans stood close to Sean.

"*Buenos dias, Capitan* Evans." The dark-faced man smiled at Sean, "Deputy." Then he ushered them into the cantina. Melissa Bryant stood beside a large round table. She waited for the company to take their seats before she moved without a word to stand between Sean and Jimmy Dolan. Lincoln's newest lawman looked up into her blue eyes. In the shadows of a corner, a child stood in faded calico. With large black eyes in an Apache face, the little girl watched her mother whose arm gently touched Sean Rourke's shoulder.

PATRICK ROURKE LAUGHED out loud when he caught himself speaking calmly to the nearest, droopy-eyed steer. That he would unconsciously take the counsel of beef amused and frightened the rancher. In the six months since Grady Rourke's death, the Chisum cattle had pushed over most of the post and rail fence that had stood in the rocky ground like a square parapet surrounding the little house on all sides. The fence once kept the cattle at least twenty-five yards from the house.

The fence could not withstand tons of shuffling hooves
and months of winter wind howling down from Capitan
Mountain to the north and the Sacramento Mountains to the
west. Patrick wondered how long the fence had guarded the
homestead and he wondered where the rails had once been
trees. Lincoln was dotted with knotty little trees. But only
the distant mountain ranges had stands of old wood, and
even that was sparse under the summer's ferocious sun and
winter's withering cold.

Patrick remembered the old fence as having always been
there, gnarled and enduring. Its shadows were part of his
boyhood memories when he and his brothers played at hunting and tracking his mother's barnyard hens. That his father
must have hauled the timber down the mountain had never
crossed his mind until his last solitary week of trying to
repair half a year's neglect and abuse.

Where the posts had been snapped clean through at
ground level, the frozen earth would not suffer ten strong
men to dig another hole for a fresh beam. So he could only
put back the horizontal rails between vertical posts that had
survived the grazing herd. As sections of fence took shape,
open segments between broken posts became funnels that
seemed to attract the cattle into the gap. The breaks in the
fence forced even more cattle to scratch their scrawny sides
against the square, coarsely-hewn pillars holding up the
front porch.

The lone rancher cursed the animals out loud and they
only shook their uniformly torn, jingle-bobbed ears to mock
him.

The steers' feet made so much noise crunching on the
frozen ground that Patrick did not hear the lone rider come
slowly up the lane that branched off the road to Lincoln. If
the rider had heard the rancher conversing with his cattle,
Billy Bonney did not say and Patrick did not ask.

"Patrick." Billy climbed down from his horse. The
mount's mousey brown ears were laid flat back in the

uneasy company of hundreds of milling steers. "Mr. Tunstall wanted me to look in on you." The rider stood beside his horse who twitched against the taught reins in Billy's gloved hand.

"Glad for the company, Billy. Better put your horse in the barn so these damned cattle don't spook him. You'll have a long, cold walk home."

Billy nodded and walked toward the dilapidated barn. Inside, he untacked his animal and let him drop his face into a pile of still green hay. Three other horses nickered from inside their stalls. Bright sunlight streamed in through narrow fissures in the weathered siding and glowed brightly on a few nail heads on each stall door. Billy knew that these nails must be new. Patrick had been working hard during the week since his visit to town. Before leaving his saddle on the cold dirt floor, he retrieved a small sack, which had dangled behind his seat. Then he walked back into the sun, which hurt his pale eyes after his few minutes inside the barn.

"I brung you some coffee and sourdough. It's from Mr. Tunstall." Billy spoke in normal voice and the thin air barely carried his words across the 20 yards to Patrick.

"Huh?"

"I said Mr. Tunstall sent some supplies with me."

"Oh. Thanks. Come on in and I'll put on a pot."

Billy Bonney was shivering by the time they reached the front porch. A warm horse under him had kept him comfortable for the easy ride from town. Patrick did not wear a coat and his shirt was damp with sweat from wrestling steers and timber. Perspiration leeched through the crown of his hat.

"You can hang it there," Patrick said as his guest peeled off his trail coat which dripped condensation onto the floor under the wall peg. He adjusted the walnut-handled Peacemaker high on his baggy trousers. Two logs quickly flamed when laid atop red embers simmering in the main room's hearth. Billy held out his red palms toward the fire.

"That's better."

Patrick opened the gift sack in the narrow kitchen. He smiled at a small bag of coffee beans. He threw a handful into a small, square mill, which he hand-cranked for half a minute. The aroma made him close his eyes and inhale deeply. He opened the stopcock on a water barrel and filled a tin pot. The fresh ground coffee floated on the icy water.

"This won't take long," Patrick said as he set the pot close to the blazing fire. "That was nice of Mr. Tunstall."

"Weren't nothing. Wanted me to make sure you was comfortable out here all alone."

"Getting by," Patrick nodded with fatigue in his voice. He pulled his father's rocking chair closer to the fire. Billy pushed a straight chair closer and sat down. He pointed his muddy boots toward the warming coffee pot.

Patrick studied Billy's face, which he had never really observed close up. Without his hat, Billy looked even younger. He was clean-shaven. Patrick noticed for the first time that Billy's two, upper front teeth protruded and gave him the look of a cheerful, gray-eyed squirrel. Even with a heavy six-shooter strapped to his narrow hips, Billy was as nonthreatening as a nineteen-year-old boy could be. It would have been hard for Patrick not to like him. It helped that Patrick was no more than six years older than Tunstall's clerk.

"Have you seen my brother?" Patrick tried not to sound very curious.

"Not hardly. I don't go to the House or the Wortley. Wouldn't be welcome. I seen him maybe twice on the street is all. Once he was with the dumb girl what works for the House."

Patrick's face was poker blank.

"Melissa?"

"Yeah. She's hung like a Holstein."

"I ain't much noticed." With the toe of his boot, Patrick nudged the coffee pot closer to the fire. The smell of fresh coffee was beginning to drift deliciously into the spacious room.

Billy inhaled slowly and collected a teenager's thoughts.

"I always thought Manuel or even Jimmy Dolan was doing her."

Patrick shrugged and watched the fire.

"You'd think them boys would get all the mares they wanted at the Indian Agency." Billy smiled. "I hear them Apaches put out for blankets."

Patrick looked Billy in the eye.

"But I don't know that for sure," the boy said earnestly.

The rancher nodded.

"Your brother got hisself a new job."

"Doing what?"

"Deputy. Sheriff Brady hired him. Dolan, really."

"Deputy? Sean?"

"According to Brady. Sheriff sticks his head into Mr. Tunstall's store maybe once a week. 'Keeping the peace,' he calls it. But he's just nosing around for Dolan and Riley. But it's still a free country, mainly. So we don't bother him."

"Why would the sheriff need another deputy?"

"Probably knows that McSween is on his way home. That makes Dolan nervous."

Billy smiled toward the coffee pot where steam began to rock the tin lid. Firelight shining in the boy's eyes illuminated a face clearly content with being on the right side of the street.

"Guess my brother needs the money to live on."

"Seems so."

Patrick glanced toward the bureau with its browned glass portraits of his father and Sean, each in his generation's army uniform.

"Ain't like Sean to sell his gun."

"But that's what he done. And took up with the dumb girl, too. All in the same week." Billy sounded impressed.

"Is he riding with Jesse Evans?"

"The captain he rides for the House and the sheriff he rides for the House."

Patrick leaned forward, half out of his chair. He picked up a kindling stick from a pile near the hearth. He used the stick to push the coffee pot away from the fire.

"Mr. Tunstall sent you out here to tell me about Sean?"

"Wanted to make sure you was still going to let Chisum's stock graze your land if your brother's took up with the folks what rustles Chisum cattle."

Patrick sat back into the rocking chair.

"My brother needs the money and so do I."

"Good." Billy looked over at Patrick and he grinned innocently. "Only difference seems to be that your brother talks to the dumb girl and you talk to cows."

The rancher brother's bearded face hardened.

"Is she a whore?"

Billy became thoughtful for a moment.

"Not strictly."

Patrick's face softened, strangely relieved by Billy's careful answer.

"Sean ain't been with a woman he ain't rented since Shiloh, that I know of. Sixteen years."

Billy shrugged and sniffed the coffee. "Her mouth is broke and his face is broke." The clerk smiled, full of the power of his own reasoning.

Chapter Six

THE GUNFIGHTER TWIRLED HIS SIX-SHOOTER IN HIS RIGHT hand. He watched it intently with squinting eyes as if the blue iron were some kind of ballet. Two revolutions forward; two revolutions backward. Then a blue blur and the gentlest rubbing sound of warm metal against hard leather. The hand hovered motionless, poised just beyond the grip of the 1872 Remington, single-action Belt Revolver. The gunman had paid an extra ten dollars for the pearl grips which glowed the amber color of old ivory where the afternoon sun landed warmly. Like a bullfrog tongue taking a fly, the hand hardly twitched and 2 $\frac{1}{2}$ pounds of steel spun again first forward, then backward, then swished back into the oiled holster low on the killer's right hip.

"You ain't going to be happy till you shoot your balls off, Rob." Billy Bonney spoke cheerfully through his buck-toothed smile.

"It's not loaded, Billy," Robert Widenmann said with a slightly nasal, Michigan accent. The brilliant sunshine coming through the windows of the Tunstall store made the mid-westerner's white, starched sleeves glow. A dime, pocket novel of the Wild West protruded from the back of his baggy trousers and rode up the thick gunbelt's row of .44 caliber cartridges. The twenty-four-year-old immigrant from Ann Arbor to New Mexico Territory saw the winterscape of Lincoln County's high plains against far blue mountains through the eyes of a ten-year-old boy. John Tunstall had hired Widenmann to do clerking and handyman chores for the store a year earlier. The clerk practiced his quick draw in front of the mirror in his room.

"All the same, Rob, it still makes me nervous when you play with that thing."

Before the clerk gunman could respond, the boots thumping on the front porch sounded like a full squad of cavalry from Fort Stanton. In an instant, Billy realized that the heavy lock-step jingled with spur, heel chains.

"Sheriff Brady's boys," Billy said gravely. Rob Widenmann unbuckled his gunbelt and tossed it under the counter with the speed trained into his shooting hand.

Four armed men and an icy wind entered the general store on Friday, February 8th.

"Where's Mr. Tunstall?" William Brady asked softly. His eyes quickly took the measure of the large room. At midday, there were no women shopping for fabric or flour. They were all home preparing noontime supper for their men and children.

"He's at the ranch," Billy answered with strained courtesy. The other clerk backed quietly into the shadows between two barrels of molasses.

"I got this here writ," the sheriff said. "It's a Writ of Attachment. We're here to seize by lawful process ten thousand dollars worth of goods to secure Alexander McSween's debt to the Emil Fritz estate."

Two deputies stood at Brady's left elbow and a third stood in front of the closed, front door. Their trail coats were pulled back to reveal their sidearms.

"This ain't McSween's store, Sheriff. It's Mr. Tunstall's." Billy kept his hands flat on the counter. "I ain't packing, Sheriff."

"Then you come around here, Billy. You too, Rob."

Widenmann took one little step out of the shadows when

Billy walked to the front of the counter. Brady studied both young men.

"Billy, we need to inventory the store. McSween was arraigned six days ago down in Mesilla for embezzling money from old Emil's estate. McSween is Tunstall's partner, so what's Tunstall's is McSween's until the judge says otherwise. Now you just give me the keys to the stock rooms."

Bonney looked at the deputies. Even with their eyes nearly hidden under the brims of their hats, he recognized them as employees of Jimmy Dolan.

"I ain't got the keys," Billy said firmly. "Besides, I ain't seen nothing in the weekly about Mr. McSween being before the judge."

"It won't be in the papers," the sheriff said calmly. "McSween was arraigned secretly in Judge Bristol's home."

"That legal?"

"It was for the judge. Now—the keys, Billy."

"Ain't on me, Sheriff. I'm telling you."

Rob Widenmann exhaled loudly as if he had overfilled his lungs when he was summoned from the protection of the syrup barrels.

William Brady took four steps away from his deputies and stood in front of the lanky man from Michigan. Brady held out his hand—palm up—without a word. When Widenmann held the keys above the sheriff's gloved hand, they jingled as Widenmann's hand shook.

"This is your house, Rob!" Billy said coldly. His blue-gray eyes narrowed on his boyish face. Tunstall allowed Rob to board in the back in exchange for his odd jobs.

Slowly, Widenmann put the keys back into his pocket.

"I'm sorry, Sheriff. I can't give you no keys till Mr. Tunstall comes up from his ranch. I'm real sorry." The voice was pleading although neither the sheriff nor his grim deputies had made a single threatening gesture.

"Me, too, Rob. You're interfering with the execution of

lawful process." Brady's voice was gentle. Sweat ran off Widenmann's nose. "I'll have to take you in till Tunstall comes into town. I'm sorry."

The sudden prisoner swallowed hard. He shuffled without a word toward his coat which hung on the wall.

"William Henry," Brady said toward Billy Bonney, "you go fetch Tunstall. Tell him I have a writ to seize McSween's half of this partnership. My two deputies will guard the store and keep it closed down until he comes back to town."

"But, Sheriff, we do a hefty business on Saturdays. We can't close tomorrow."

Brady stepped over to the teenager and blew his whiskey breath into the boy's face.

"You can ride down to Rio Felix, or you can keep Rob company in a nice, cozy cell until Tunstall comes up in his own good time. You decide, Billy."

Bonney's thin lips opened around his crooked front teeth.

"I'll fetch Mr. Tunstall. I'll head out just as quick as I can get some supplies and a pack animal. It's thirty miles in this here cold."

Brady nodded and sighed alcohol vapors into Billy's eyes.

"Good boy."

NIGHT WIND FILLED the curtains nailed to Patrick Rourke's front window. Only the crackling fire in the hearth broke the terrible Sunday silence that clanged through Patrick's mind like an off-key tune. At least the house smelled warmly of pine resin popping in the logs in the fireplace. The repaired fence around the house kept the cattle far enough away that their tons of green manure froze before the stench could reach the shattered window. Patrick had weaved ropes between sections of broken fence where surviving posts were too far apart for their rails to connect.

From outside, the wonderful scent of the fire was the only

sign of life within. The two oil lamps in the main room cast no light through the curtains across the window. A brilliant half moon in a hard, clear sky illuminated the dirty snow. Under bright stars and the moon, hundreds of Chisum cattle stood in tight clusters to insulate themselves from the night-time cold. When the beef moved slowly, they looked like the shadow of Capitan Mountain moving across the snow as if the mountain were stealing away in the dark. A quarter mile down the lane, Dick Brewer thought that the black shapes looked like a ghost herd of buffalo slipping silently away from the arrows of long-dead Apaches.

"Yo there, in the house!"

Patrick was startled by the shout outside. He looked up from the little table in the single large room. He had been concentrating hard on sewing buttons to his salty shirts. His hands were so stiff and sore from field work that he could hardly steer his mother's old needle. He looked over his shoulder toward the billowing curtains and the closed door. Silently, he cursed the voices which he imagined hearing even in his sleep.

"In the house!" the voice shouted again.

For an instant, Patrick felt relieved. Then he forced his tight right hand around the walnut grip of his Peacemaker revolver. He stood, looked quickly at the weapon's cylinder, and then eased over to the wall. He stood with his back pressed flat against the wood between the door and the open window. Patrick leaned toward the curtain.

"Come on up slow," the voice inside the house called into the night.

"I'm coming up dismounted. It's Dick Brewer, Mr. Rourke."

"Tunstall's man?"

"Yes, sir. Billy said he told you about me."

Dick Brewer was Tunstall's ranch foreman.

"You come up."

When Patrick heard boots on the front porch, he opened

the door a crack with his left hand. He kept the Peacemaker raised behind the door. In the red light of the blazing hearth, Patrick saw a snowman in trail duster. Ice crystals were white around the stranger's mouth and hung like tiny icicles from his eyebrows.

"Let me lay my gunbelt down."

The visitor dropped his belt to the porch floor. It landed at an unnatural angle where it rested on a fist-size brick of steer manure. With the door open wide to the bitter wind, Patrick could see that the cowboy-style saddle had no rifle in its scabbard.

"I'm Dick Brewer."

Patrick studied the red face of a young man in his early twenties. The rancher lowered his handiron that had caught Brewer's gaze. He watched Patrick ear down the hammer, which had been cocked.

"Best put your animal in the barn so he don't freeze."

"Thank you, Mr. Rourke." Brewer slowly picked up his gunbelt far from the single holster and handed it through the doorway. "So it don't freeze neither, please."

Patrick took the weapon, closed the door, and returned to his chair by the fire. He laid the belted holster atop his ladies' work of buttons and thread. The sidearm was an aged Remington, '58 Old Army revolver refitted for cartridges from its Civil War original, cap and ball vintage. It was a poor man's piece, Patrick thought. He was somewhat comforted by the notion.

Brewer knocked on the door, although Patrick heard his spurs on the porch first.

"It's open," the rancher called from his rocking chair by the fire. "Come in and thaw. Hang your coat by mine there."

"Thanks." The cold man pushed his long coat against a wall peg.

Dick Brewer walked on unsure legs, wobbly from a long ride. Wearing his stirrups cavalry long, at least his knees had not frozen in flexed position. He walked toward the fire, turned toward Patrick, and then backed up so close to the hearth that Patrick waited to see smoke rise from the standing man's trousers. Brewer opened his palms wide and held them behind his back.

"Take a seat, Dick."

"Don't think I can just yet, Mr. Rourke."

"Please, I'm Patrick."

"Thanks. Billy called you Mr. Rourke. But he's like that sometimes."

"You want some coffee? It's hot down there behind you. I'll get a cup."

"Not yet. Don't think I can bend my fingers around it just yet."

When his guest smiled, Patrick saw a strong, youthful face, clean-shaven except for a small, frost-covered goatee affair. His hair was thick and curly with ringlets around his forehead where his tall hat had made a deep depression above his clear, gray eyes. He was tall and not heavy, but built solid and wide through the shoulders like a man who works hard labor for his wages.

"Guess my legs'll sit now." Brewer hobbled toward the straight-backed chair opposite Patrick's rocker.

Patrick stood and found a clean tin cup in the kitchen. He knelt to fill the cup, which he set on the table between them, and refilled his own cup. He sank back into his father's chair.

"Thanks. I'm Mr. Tunstall's foreman down on the Felix. He sent me to ask for your help."

"Help? My plate's pretty full just getting the fences back up here."

"I know. Sorry about your Pa. We all liked him. Sheriff Brady shut down the store yesterday. Billy rode down yesterday evening. Rode all Friday afternoon and all night. I started before daylight this morning. The other clerk—the dude, Widenmann—he got himself arrested by Brady for not handing over the keys. Two deputies are living in the store now to keep people from buying there. They come to take half of everything. Said it were to do with Mr. McSween 'bezzling from the Fritz family. The old man died in Germany last year, I guess."

Patrick put down his cup and looked down at his ragged shirts that had more button holes than buttons.

"Deputies? Was my brother Sean among them?"

"Don't know. Billy didn't say. Does he ride with Brady or the Boys?"

"Evans' gang? I suppose he does now."

"Oh. Them Boys take what they please from Chisum's herds. Took Mr. McSween's ponies last November, too." Brewer shrugged toward the breezy curtains that let in the distant rumblings of the cold cattle with their jingle-bobbed, Chisum ears.

"What does Mr. Tunstall expect from me?"

"He wants you to come down to Rio Felix with me tomorrow. He's expecting trouble from Brady. Tunstall ain't gone back to Lincoln yet. He wants some guns to ride with him when he does."

Patrick looked into the fire.

"I didn't come home to get into no gun fights, Dick. I'm a rancher now. Trying, anyway."

"Mr. Tunstall don't really expect no gunplay if Brady comes. He just wants us to stand up with him if Brady's men try to take Tunstall horses for this McSween business. He says that Mr. McSween is buying into the store a little at a time, but he don't own any interest in Rio Felix or Tunstall's horses. He just wants us to stand up with him if Brady comes down or to ride with him back into town."

"But there could be shooting."

"I don't think so. Brady ain't no killer like the captain or Jimmy Dolan. I have to say that Brady just tries to walk the line between Dolan and our side. He ain't a bad man. Not like Dolan and Evans, anyway. Brady's got a house full of babies. He ain't likely to go spoiling for a killing fight. We just want it to be even, that's all. The Rio Felix spread can be a two-day ride from here in the winter."

Dick Brewer became more animated as the blood returned to his cold face. He was earnest and courteous. Like the amiable Billy Bonney and the wide-eyed Rob Widenmann now in jail, Tunstall seemed to attract decent young men trying to make an honest living in a clapboard town.

Patrick raised his tin cup to extend the momentary silence so he could think. He had a ranch to run single-handed and the Englishman was inviting him to take sides in a little war in which Patrick had neither an interest nor a stake—except for the cattle grazing on old weeds under new snow that paid him just enough to hang on to his father's land. The cattle belonged to John Chisum and Tunstall's bank was supported by Chisum's sterling name.

"All right, Dick. There's a cot up in the loft with some blankets. There's water and a wash basin in the kitchen." Patrick gestured toward the back cranny.

"That will be fine. I ain't been horizontal for two days."

Patrick nodded.

"And there's a jug of jack back there to warm you up, too."

Brewer licked his cracked lips.

"Then I'll say good night. I appreciate the hospitality."

Dick Brewer stood on legs still shaky. He shuffled toward the clay pot of whiskey and carried his tin cup.

Patrick laid his hands on the arms of his chair and began rocking slowly, like an old man. He looked above the hearth toward his holstered handiron that hung from a peg on the thick wooden mantle. The fire glowed red on his hard face.

"I SHOULD GO."

Melissa Bryant reached up and placed her hand gently upon Sean Rourke's shoulder. As if her thin fingers were a

great weight, he sat down slowly into the hard chair close to
a black, pot-bellied stove. She placed a warm cup of coffee
into his open palm.

"Maybe another few minutes."

She nodded, turned, and ascended a wooden ladder
toward a small loft illuminated by a single oil lamp damped
low. Sean could not stop watching the white calves of her
firm legs where her skirt ended as she climbed. She was
barefoot in the stove's heat that filled her small, one-room
home. The loft was little more than a ledge that obscured
one-third of the pitched, timber roof.

Upstairs, Melissa had to crouch deeply to keep her head
from banging into the roof's thick beams. Unlike the stur-
dier adobe structures erected throughout Lincoln, her home
was slapped together from old barn siding. It had been the
Wortley's storage bin until Jimmy Dolan offered her the
place rent-free so long as she worked the cantina. That freed
one more room at the hotel for Jesse Evans' men to triple
bunk for a dollar per week.

The Apache raid in May 1870 had left her an orphan and
pregnant. The town adopted the fifteen-year-old girl and gave
her food. Lawrence Murphy had contributed one of the
House's rooms at the Wortley. But Murphy was gone and to
Jimmy Dolan, business was business. To Melissa, the live-in
pantry was home. The House let her have odd pieces of fabric
too short to sell. She used it for curtains of happy colors.

If Melissa gave up her voice when the painted warriors—
boys mainly—took her innocence, she had carefully nursed
the infant along with her fury. The eight-year-old child
sleeping in the loft had never heard her mother sing her to
sleep.

Melissa stroked the sleeping girl's forehead and blew out
the lamp. When she came down the ladder backwards, Sean
forced his eyes to watch the rusted old stove. Holes in its
thin sides glowed like orange eyes from the burning logs
within.

"Is Abbey asleep?"

Melissa nodded.

Sean took to the dark-faced child quickly. The first time she peeked from behind her mother's skirt to look up at him, Sean instinctively flinched. He knew what his burned faced did to the eyes of small children. But Abigail Bryant only blinked and smiled with her large black eyes. She showed no fear as if a child's inborn revulsion at the hideous had all stayed behind in her mother's abused body at the moment of birth.

For two weeks, Sean walked Melissa and her daughter the short distance from the hotel to their hovel. It was an accident. They had walked ten steps behind him when he was going outside to see to his horse for the night. In the iron-cold darkness, Sean offered to walk them home before he realized that he had no idea if they had a home nor where it might be. Melissa had looked up into his weary eyes and nodded. Something in his eyes made her accept the invitation of a stranger who wore a black revolver and who had dirty fingernails. She saw a place called Shiloh, Tennessee, in his battle-dulled eyes, but she did not know it.

The woman sat in a chair close to Sean so the stove could warm her, too. A lamp on the little table made her fine, pale skin appear yellow. The flame made shadows move quickly across her cheeks when she blinked or sipped her coffee. Only twenty-three, there were webs of small lines around her eyes and at the corners of her mouth. Having a child by violence—and having no mother to help—had aged her face beyond what New Mexico sun and cold could do to it. Sean watched her face with its deeply blue eyes, full eyebrows and inviting mouth. He only looked away when her eyes met his.

They sat without words for a long time after their coffee cups were dry.

"Sheriff Brady came by the hotel this afternoon. Wants

me to ride with his deputies to Tunstall's place in the morning."

A sudden gust of wind whined past the shuttered windows. Melissa turned to look at him closely. He saw the worry around her eyes.

"We just have papers to serve on Tunstall. Shouldn't be no trouble. I'm his deputy now. I need the work."

Melissa looked away toward the stove. She folded her hands in her lap and lowered her face. In the gray shadows of the nighttime cabin, the man and woman sat side by side and two feet apart. They watched the stove together as if it were grand opera.

Sean waited another five minutes. Then he put a hand on each of his knees. He still wore his trail coat, open in front.

"Well." He stood up and rubbed his hands together to warm them before opening the door to the night wind.

Melissa stood and handed him his hat.

"Thank you for the coffee, Melissa. We'll ride out tomorrow morning early. Should be back by Wednesday night late or early Thursday. I guess it's twenty-five miles to Rio Felix."

Melissa stepped to the door and opened it. The moon made the left side of her elegant face shine ghostly white. Sean blinked at the sudden beauty of it. He fumbled with his hat.

"Tell Abbey I said good night."

Melissa smiled tightly and Sean stepped into the snow. Putting his hat on for the walk back to the hotel, he felt stupid for having said such a thing.

WITH FIRST LIGHT, Sean led his rested horse from the Wortley's paddock to the hard dirt road. He was surprised to look up at Jesse Evans who smiled broadly from atop his mount. Three of the captain's Boys sat their horses close by. Sean looked up into each unclean face. Jesse's blond hair glowed in the first light of daybreak. William Brady was nowhere to be seen.

"We're the posse, Sean," Jacob "Billy" Mathews grinned. Jesse's Boys smiled too broadly. Only Billy wore a tin star on the outside breast of his fur, trail duster. Two of the men held the halter reins of pack horses loaded down for overnighting in the harsh country.

"Where's Sheriff Brady?"

"He ain't coming. No need, really. He's on his way to the jail to let young Rob Widenmann out before he pees hisself from fright." Deputy Mathews chuckled.

Sean gathered his reins, mounted, and adjusted his Colt Peacemaker. With his outlaw deputies, he rode south out of Lincoln.

Chapter Seven

MONDAY AFTER MIDNIGHT, SLEET EXPLODED FROM THE WINTER clouds atop the Sacramento Mountains to the west. Jagged ice pebbles pummeled the six riders and eight horses until they had to stop and pitch camp. Two of Jesse's men had bleeding faces from hail wounds by the time they pulled their blankets over their ice-crusted beards. They tied their scarves and bandannas around their horses' faces to prevent laceration of the equine eyeballs or, worse, a mass runaway of the terrified animals upon which their lives depended.

By midmorning Tuesday, February 12th, the posse's piss-and-vinegar bravado was frozen hard and yellow. Hiding their faces deep inside their raised collars, the riders walked their mounts and the pack horses slowly southward down the main wagon road. They dismounted to lead their animals by hand across treacherously lumpy ice that in two months would flow as the Rio Felix. Half a mile south of the river, the men stopped on the crest of a slight rise. They looked down with snow-blinded eyes to the large ranch carved out of the wilderness by John Tunstall, loyal subject of Queen Victoria.

"Nice horses," Deputy Billy Mathews nodded as his sore eyeballs focused on the paddock beside Tunstall's fine adobe house. " The sheriff will be pleased with us."

Jesse Evans' spurs jingled at his mount's sides and he pressed forward, leading the posse down the little hill. A white cloud of horse breath moved with the six men. With the enemy of the House in sight, Deputy Mathews did not mind the outlaw going first.

By the time the riders pulled rein in front of the ranch house, Tunstall stood on the front porch. He was unarmed. His ranch foreman, Dick Brewer, stood at his side and casually held a Winchester rifle pointed toward the manure-stained snow.

The front door opened and Billy Bonney came out. He carried an old Sharps repeating rifle cradled in the crook of his left arm. The boy smiled broadly around his squirrel, front teeth. Three more armed men came out of the house.

Six against six, Deputy Mathews thought. Been against worse, Jesse Evans figured silently.

"We come by order of Judge Bristol," Mathews said calmly. Even odds encouraged him. But he pondered if twelve fire-warmed hands were better than a dozen frozen ones. "We have a lawful writ to attach Alexander McSween's horses boarded down here on your ranch. They be security for McSween's bail bond for the Fritz estate case."

"These horses are mine," Tunstall said with a forced smile.

"You and McSween is partners. What's his is yours."

"You're on private property, Mr. Mathews," the Englishman said firmly.

"Ain't that right?" Billy Bonney said cheerfully.

Jesse Evans rode forward one horse length to come up beside Mathews.

"We have papers," Jesse said. His blue eyes quickly surveyed the men on the porch. They stood in the shade of the overhanging roof which put morning sun in a violet sky directly in the posse's faces. Damn, Jesse thought.

"Not today, boys. Sorry to send you back up that cold road empty-handed." Tunstall's Oxford accent never seemed to sound hostile.

Without another cordial word, Tunstall waved his gloved
hand. Slowly, five armed men came around the porch corner
from the corral on his right. Four men came single-file from
the paddock on his left. The last man around the corner was
Patrick Rourke.

Behind Jesse, Sean Rourke's numb face hardened. Its live
left cheek was an unhealthy white from the cold, and the
right side above his frosted beard was the sickening purple
of the poorly hanged. The two brothers glared at each other,
but Sean, blinded by the sun, could hardly see Patrick.

Looking up, the younger brother saw a man he hardly
recognized in the fierce sunlight and in the company of
grinning outlaws.

Looking down and lowering his face until his hat
shielded his burning eyes, Sean blinked at the kaleidoscope
of starbursts and flaming diamonds on the backs of his eye
balls, induced by snow blindness. Where Patrick's outline
stood shimmering in the shadows, Sean saw a six-year-old
boy raising his small hands to his bruised face to deflect the
hammer blows from Grady Rourke's farmer-sized fists. The
older brother blinked hard when he remembered those ham-
mers on his own thirteen-year-old face after he rushed
between his father and the boy.

Closing his eyes against the throbbing sunshine, Sean
Rourke jerked his reins and pulled his horse out of formation. With his back toward John Tunstall, he walked his
mount slowly up the road toward Lincoln, two bone-numb-
ing days away.

"You ain't seen the last of the law, Englishman," Jesse
Evans said for Deputy Mathews.

"That's right," the real lawman stammered toward fifteen
armed men.

One by one, the posse with lowered heads and icicled
beards turned northward to follow the swishing tail of
Sean's horse.

John Tunstall turned smiling to his army.

"Well executed, lads. They won't be back. With luck, they'll freeze between here and Lincoln."

Patrick swallowed hard and looked around Tunstall toward the snow-covered lane. His brother was invisible inside a soft blur of brown horseflesh and shimmering clouds of horse breath.

THE TEXAN EVEN looked like Texas. Tall, broad-shouldered, with a clean-shaven chin square as a barn door, John S. Chisum stood in the sunshine and twirled his black, waxed mustache to make certain that it had not frozen. Deep-set dark eyes squinted at the expanse of South Spring River Ranch that stretched over the horizon in all directions on the west side of the Pecos River frozen north and south. The house stood just south of where the Rio Hondo met the Pecos from the west. Deep crows' feet creased from Chisum's eyes to his slightly prominent ears. His short, thick hair and lined, wind-burned face had the look of a middle-aged cowboy, but his crisp black waistcoat gave the cattle baron the solid presence of a well-heeled banker.

Chisum stood beside Alexander McSween, Attorney at Law. McSween's round face with its drooping mustache was red from the cold wind. Thirty-five years old, he was slightly round and pink from a lifetime hunched over a desk.

"Then I'll be on my way, Mr. Chisum," the dark-faced Adolph Barrier said cordially. The Deputy Sheriff from San Miguel County, New Mexico Territory, had escorted McSween from his Las Vegas arrest down to Mesilla for the drumhead arraignment before Judge Bristol.

McSween put out his cold hand which the lawman shook warmly.

"Couldn't let you get hurt without a ruling from the judge," the lawman smiled.

"I'm grateful," McSween said earnestly. "I wouldn't have lasted long in Brady's jail."

"Maybe. Maybe not. All the same, you just make certain that I can find you if Judge Bristol wants to see you again. Or I'll be going to jail instead of you. I was ordered to take you to Lincoln, you know."

The lawyer's tired eyes were locked on the deputy's face. "You won't have to hunt me."

Deputy Barrier only harrumphed as he put his boot in the stirrup and heaved his heavily furclad body into the saddle. He adjusted the long duster to fall on the top of his boots.

"Good luck in Lincoln, Mr. McSween." Barrier touched the corner of his floppy hat. "Mr. Chisum." Tapping his spurs on his cold mount's sides, the animal moved out at a brisk trot to keep warm.

Chisum and McSween watched until the deputy disappeared over a small hill with the Rio Hondo on the backside. He had a long, lonesome ride northward.

"Good man, that one," Chisum said gravely.

"Could use his kind in Lincoln County," McSween nodded inside a cloud of steam.

"Not likely," the cattleman said dryly. "Let's go inside before we catch our death out here."

The two men entered the sprawling, single-story house. From here, Chisum had built his herd of eighty thousand cattle. After selling out to a beef syndicate, he and his brother Pitzer Chisum stayed on to manage the spread and its jingle-bobbed steers.

McSween and the cattleman took chairs near a massive fireplace.

"How long do you think Sue will stay east?"

"I told my wife to avoid Lincoln's troubles as long as she could stay with her family in St. Louis. I don't know when she'll lose patience with that and come back."

"She's a strong-willed woman," Chisum said.

"Have to be to put up with me."

John Chisum nodded thoughtfully.

"How's the rustling been in the six weeks I've been away?" McSween had spent a month in Mesilla.

"Same. Pitzer found a mass-grave of ears down at Beckwith's ranch a while back."

"Ears?"

"Yeah. It's the only way to hide my brand on stolen cattle. The ranchers down around Seven Rivers make a handsome living off my spread. Jesse Evans and his Boys do most of the field work, I'm told."

"What about the town?"

"Still even up, as best I can tell. Two new guns came to town while you were away: two of Grady's boys."

"Oh? Which two?"

"John says the older two, Sean and Patrick."

"They probably found my partner who has their father's will. Have they taken sides already?"

"I guess the older one—got his face shot up or burned in the war—has hired on with the House. John hired Patrick to watch my herd grazing on Grady's land. The boy moved into Grady's spread alone and needed the money till Grady's affairs are settled. I told John it was fine. At least we got one of them and the House got one. Better than Dolan getting both of them."

"There's a third brother," the lawyer remembered.

"Still north with the cavalry, last I heard."

"Well, David and I will have to wait for him before we can close Grady's estate. Maybe things will quiet down by then."

"I don't know, Alex."

"Something else?"

Chisum sat calmly and looked into the fire.

"John's man Brewer told me that Brady sent a small posse three days ago to Rio Felix to seize some horses to secure your bond or the like. Something about you and John being partners in the store. That damned Fritz estate business could get ugly."

The lawyer stood and paced in front of the hearth. The fire and his anger brought color to his soft face.

"Dolan really put the hot iron to me. Trumped up the whole thing. I never took a dollar from Emil's insurance policy. His sister who swore out the embezzlement complaint can't even speak English hardly. Dolan put her up to it. Had to. And Brady goes along with him."

"Sheriff Brady don't have much choice," Chisum shrugged. "Sometimes I think he really does mean well. But the House owns the town and Brady is stuck in the middle. I can't believe Brady would spend half his life in the Army just to come out here to become one of Dolan's Irish lackeys. It don't make sense to me."

McSween stopped pacing and turned to look down at his host who was keeping him out of William Brady's jail.

"If Brady can send a posse made up of Jesse Evans' gang out to steal my horses from John's ranch, Brady is in the House camp up to his ears. Governor Axtel should get off his pompous ass and come out here to clean up this outhouse of a town."

"I don't know about that, Alex. The Sante Fe crooks probably sleep with the House crooks and Axtel eats out of the Santa Fe gang's hand."

The lawyer sighed.

"You're right. I hate to drag you into all this."

The cattleman laughed.

"Alex, I was 'into all this' before you and Sue rode into town three years ago. The House has been rustling my cattle since before you ever heard of Lincoln. That's one of the reasons I sold out. Let someone else worry about my beef winding up at the Indian Agency through the back door." Chisum chuckled. "The House owns the town and Tunstall and I own the only bank there. It's still an even match. You're welcome to stay here as long as you like. It's safer for you. And I'm also being a little selfish: When Sue comes back, I'll get some of her cooking, too."

Alex McSween, fugitive, smiled and sat down. He was safe in the center of John Chisum's vast empire, well guarded by armed cowboys.

"Real food. That would be nice, John."

Chisum smiled broadly but did not look sideways at his guest.

"Yes. And you ain't had that other thing for two months neither."

The lawyer nodded without a word.

"MAMA WANTS TO know why you ain't going out with Mr. Evans?"

Abigail Bryant was given her mother's maiden name since Melissa had never had any other one. The little girl was proud of knowing her letters taught in Lincoln's only, one-room schoolhouse. She handed the long-hand note back to her mother. Melissa stood beside the small table that she had just wiped dry. Early morning sun splashed the cantina tabletop with a shiny, skewed square in the shape of a window.

"Just ain't," Sean Rourke said, looking up at Melissa instead of Abigail. He sat in front of an empty plate and half-empty coffee cup. Melissa pushed the rag into the belt securing her dirty skirt. She reached for a large clay pot. Sean placed the palm of his hand on the cup.

"No thanks. I've had enough."

Melissa pulled back from the pot. She sat down at Sean's table. Abigail stepped backwards until she felt her mother's knees. Then she eased back into Melissa's lap. The mother gently wrapped her arm around her daughter's narrow waist. The black-eyed child who looked like her Apache father rested her elbows on the table and her olive-skinned chin in her palms.

Sean had to smile at the child's friendly round face. Her eyes seemed to sparkle when Sean was near and he could feel her affection. Abigail never seemed to notice the wretched damage to the man's face. He could almost forget about it until he felt the narrow-eyed stare of some other cantina patron watching him from across the little room. Melissa's beautiful but weary face did not match Abigail's cheer. The silent woman shrugged as if to repeat her scribbled written question.

The part-time deputy looked down at his clean, breakfast plate.

"My brother rides with Tunstall now. There ain't nothing between us anymore. But if Jimmy Dolan wants the sheriff to make some kind of case downriver, I ain't about to draw down on my own kin. I done that in the war." Without looking up, Sean realized that he had not mentioned that grotesque time for over a week. He wished that it had been longer. He suddenly felt the dead side of his face become warm.

He caught himself waiting for Melissa to respond. When he looked up, she reached out and laid her calloused, washerwoman hand atop his. He nodded. Abigail scrunched up her shoulders and wrinkled her dark nose with a smile.

They looked up toward the sound of spurs jingling on the wooden floor. Jacob Mathews took long steps to Sean's table.

"Morning, Sean. Abbey; ma'am."

"Billy."

"Sheriff says that if you ain't going down to Tunstall's, it'll be all right with him. Sheriff says he'd be all alone in town otherwise. Says you be his chief deputy around Lincoln till the posse comes back in two or three days. Might be longer, driving them ponies twenty-five miles in the snow."

"All right, Billy. Sheriff Brady can count on me."

The hard look in Deputy Mathews' eyes said "If he could count on you, you'd be outside cinching up your saddle."

"Sheriff'll be pleased to hear that, Sean. I'll tell him 'fore we ride."

"Billy? Do you know if my brother is at Pa's?"

"Don't know." Jacob's face softened behind the sweat and stable grit sticking to his stubbled cheeks. "But Billy Bonney ain't opened Tunstall's store today and I seen Dick Brewer ride hellbent for leather out of town before first light two hours ago. And Tunstall hisself lit out before dark last night. Going down home, most likely."

"Thank you, Deputy Mathews."

The lawman saw the sudden pain on Sean's mangled face. He put his hat on his greasy head and glanced down at Melissa.

"Ma'am." He touched Abigail's nose with his index finger and she giggled. The child regarded all of Lincoln's men as her fathers. Jacob turned and walked quickly from the comfortable cantina.

Melissa read the hurt in Sean's eyes. These were not eyes that shrank from work or confrontation. Until this bright morning.

Sean looked past the woman toward the window sculpted in the two-foot thick adobe wall. White plaster covered the inside walls. He lost himself in the shaft of dazzling light raining in on a peaceful Sunday morning, February 17th.

THE HARD FREEZE along the Rio Felix had broken during Saturday night. Warm air churning up from the south arrived after dark, just as John Tunstall arrived from Lincoln. Sunday would be chilly but bearable. High wisps of cirrus clouds promised a week of clear sky and above-freezing weather.

William Bonney and Patrick Rourke were up early at Tunstall's ranch beside the still frozen river. They had been busy since sunrise dumping clumps of green hay throughout the two paddocks where Tunstall's horses grazed lazily beside the few animals belonging to Alex McSween who boarded sixty miles to the northeast at South Spring River.

Patrick had done the same thing for his horses in his father's barn two days earlier, just after Billy Bonney had ridden in at full gallup to beg him to ride again to the Rio Felix. Lincoln had been buzzing that Sheriff Brady was collecting a regiment of a posse for one more raid on McSween and Tunstall livestock. Challenge from another posse did not seem possible to the two young men under Sunday afternoon's perfect, purple sky. The air, the sky, even the livestock, were all too peaceful.

They were so confident of a tranquil Sabbath beside the river that they did not look down the narrow road all day— until they heard the sound of a horse pounding hard over the rock-hard ground. They had to shield their eyes with their gloved hands before they could make out Dick Brewer flying toward them. He had the reins in one hand and his other hand tightly gripped his horse's flowing mane.

Though above freezing, the mile-high air was still cold and thin enough that Brewer could not speak when he executed a flying dismount, allowing his winded horse to jog without him toward the corral. The rider stood ankle-deep in old snow. He hunched over with his hands braced upon his flexed knees. Dry heaves convulsed his chest as he gasped for air. His nonstop, twenty-five-mile gallop had only been broken by stretches of rough trotting to rest the horse.

The ranch foreman's lips were blue and his cheeks were bright red. His ears under his hat brim were menacingly pure white from incipient frostbite.

Billy Bonney put a hand on Brewer's twitching back and one on his chest to keep his from crumbling to the ground. Patrick steadied him with hands on both shoulders.

"Just breathe slow, Dick," Billy counseled. "You'll freeze your lungs for sure if you keep panting like some old boiler about to blow."

Brewer could only nod and wheeze hard. The commotion brought John Tunstall to the front doorway.

"Dick? You all right, old man?" Tunstall walked into the brilliant sunshine.

The young foreman looked up. Tears were streaming freely from his burning eyes. "They're coming right behind me, Mr. Tunstall." Brewer's voice was hoarse, not much beyond a winded whisper. "Brady's men! Near on fifty of them! Like an army. The Boys is with them, too."

"Evans?"

"The captain and the Boys and another three dozen. Coming for them horses what they says belong to Mr. McSween."

Tunstall touched Brewer's sagging shoulder and Patrick moved his hand out of the way.

"Now you just get hold of yourself, Dick," Tunstall smiled and spoke soothingly. "Sheriff Brady won't put up with any trouble."

Brewer straightened his back and took off his hat. His hair was soaking wet and began to steam in the cool air. He wiped his wet face with his furclad arm.

"Brady ain't leading them. Deputy Morton is in charge with Billy Mathews. Brady stayed behind."

"When did they leave?"

"Probably this morning," Brewer stammered. "Could be here after dark or at first light Monday."

Tunstall's face darkened. Brady ate at his enemy's table. But the Englishman still respected Brady for trying to walk the narrow line between the House and anarchy. Anything would be possible without Brady's influence so far from home.

"Very well, Dick. Thank you for coming down here. Now you go on inside by the fire." Tunstall glanced toward Billy. "Help him inside, please. Patrick? You better bring everyone inside, too."

Patrick nodded and headed for the large barn.

Tunstall stood alone outside. He looked toward the west where the large red sun was close to touching the snow-capped Sacramento Mountains. It would be full darkness in an hour. He turned and walked slowly into his home five thousand miles from his father's house in London.

By the time Dick Brewer was breathing normally over a cup of steaming coffee, Patrick led six cowhands into the spacious main room of the ranch house. They wore only light jackets over their heavy shirts and trousers covered with leather chaps. Their labor in and around the barn kept them warm.

"Boys, Deputy Morton is leading a posse down here to steal the horses." Tunstall spoke softly in his genteel, English accent that inspired Lincoln's *Anglos* and *Latinos* alike to listen attentively to his face and to chuckle behind his back. "Those horses are rightly mine and not Alex's. I don't believe that I can trust Morton with those animals. Men, I want five of you to ride with me to drive the bunch of them up to Lincoln. If we can get them into town before Morton gets his hands on them, at least Sheriff Brady will do right by me, I think." He paused and looked around the room. Some of his men were looking down at the shiny hardwood floor. Tunstall moved his gaze to the men whose eyes met his own.

William Bonney took a step forward; then Dick Brewer, whose legs were still stiff and sore. Only one other cowhand took his place beside Bonney. With a shrug, Patrick stepped up beside Brewer. No one else moved.

"Then this will do, boys. It'll be dark in an hour. We'll leave at dawn. Billy, let's take two pack horses with supplies. Don't know where we might have to camp. It'll be slow going with the stock. The rest of you can go on about your business around the ranch."

A chorus of subdued voices mumbling "Yes, Mister Tunstall" rose and faded quickly as the nongame hands hurried out into the evening twilight. Tunstall walked to Patrick.

"This isn't your fight, Patrick."

"I know. There shouldn't be any if we can leave before

Morton and Mathews get down here. Either way, I am on your payroll."

"Chisum's. Not mine."

"What's the difference?" Patrick looked Tunstall in the eye.

The Englishman thought about it and smiled broadly with a nod. There was no difference.

"Then let's get some food on the table for everyone and the five of us can turn in early. We have some hard driving come morning."

Without further discussion, Billy Bonney, Patrick, and one of the ranch hands headed for the large kitchen stocked to feed a dozen men all winter. John Tunstall threw his heavy coat over his shoulders before walking outside. He stood alone on the front porch for half an hour. He watched the orange sun drop behind the distant purple mountains to leave a blue-black sky behind. In the still blackness of the Sacramento Mountains silhouetted against crystal stars in a perfect sky, Tunstall thought of London's smokestacks driving black soot into a wet gray sky. He thought of the endless city's noise and clatter and violence. The chilly breeze washing his face had started in California and had remained clean for eight hundred miles. The Englishman smiled at his new country.

THE NOISY SPURS and boots on Tunstall's porch an hour before daylight belonged to Robert Widenmann who had ridden all night. A full moon illuminated his way. Fortified with black coffee, eggs, and grits at Tunstall's table, Widenmann stood in the middle of the main room. He played with his well-oiled Peacemaker, twirling it as he imagined Buffalo Bill would do it.

Armed men were posted at the bottom of the lane where it met the stage road north to Lincoln. The shivering sentries beside a roaring open fire heard only the wind as they strained to hear approaching horsemen.

By eight o'clock, the Englishman, Bonney, Brewer, Widenmann decked out like a Mexican bandito, Patrick, and one of Tunstall' s regular hands, drove eight horses up the stage road. The horses were all legally Tunstall's. He had carefully cut out his own animals and left McSween's few horses behind in the paddock where they never lifted their fuzzy muzzles from piles of rich hay. An hour along the road, the horsemen drove the livestock down an overgrown and little used trail that left the main road. The rugged trail went westward off the north-south wagon road. Hills and switch-backs would hide them from the posse on the main road.

Two dozen men rode slowly up the lane at ten o'clock. Jimmy Dolan rode with them. Lightly falling snow had already filled the hoof prints of Tunstall's escape.

The riders stopped at the front porch and were met by three cowhands who shook their shaggy heads when Dolan demanded Tunstall. The owner of the House was furious, but took comfort from seeing a few animals left behind in the paddock. Those would have to do.

Dolan ordered Deputy William Morton to take thirteen of the posse's twenty-four men back up the main road to find Tunstall and arrest him for evasion of a lawful writ of attachment. Dolan and Billy Mathews stayed behind with the rest to round up McSween's horses.

Morton turned his horse northward with a dozen men at his flanks including Jesse Evans, his Boys, and Sean Rourke.

The man with half a face had stayed behind in Lincoln for three hours yesterday morning. Melissa Bryant kept filling his coffee cup each time he said that he had enough. She kept watching him to make certain that he did not take horse. And Sean was content and untroubled. Then little Abigail turned her merry eyes toward him and said sweetly, "Mama and I are glad that you ain't got the fight in you no more."

Sean was in the saddle within fifteen minutes. He rode

hard for an hour to catch the posse. For a long day on the road and a cold night under his blanket beside the road, he had tried mightily not to think about Melissa standing in the sunshine and wiping her violet eyes with the filthy sleeve of her blouse.

The posse followed the main road for a dozen miles under an overcast sky. William Morton reined his mount to a stop and the others stopped. A narrow trail cut left, off the stage road. The trail northward looked fairly untrammeled. But the trail to the west was blemished with frozen brown clods of horse droppings on muddy snow.

"That way," Deputy Morton said through the ice clinging to his beard. Thirteen men followed "Buck" Morton into the thickets. For six hours, the tracks of horses freshened ahead of the posse. By four-thirty Monday afternoon, the horse droppings they followed were not yet frozen and patches of snow were yellow.

The armed men stopped. Morton spoke softly on clouds of steam.

"Take to them trees, boys."

The lawmen led the posse into a stand of trees beside the trail. Utter silence was broken only by the sound of their horses snorting as they put one hoof slowly in front of the other. They climbed a small hill that overlooked the trail below.

Buck Morton said nothing. He pointed down the tree covered slope at four men riding slowly ahead of maybe half a dozen unsaddled horses. They walked near the frozen Rio Ruidoso.

Morton stood slightly in his stirrups to survey the little caravan below. He smiled and pulled his Winchester, lever-action rifle from the scabbard on his saddle. With his knees locked and his backside out of the saddle, the deputy drew his bead on Tunstall's cold forehead. He looked over the rifle toward Jesse Evans.

The captain nodded.

Only ten miles from Lincoln, Morton squeezed the trigger. His horse jumped sideways at the report but did not unseat him.

Before John Tunstall could look up the hill to see what had exploded in the woods, what felt like a strong wind seemed to blow him backwards, out of his saddle.

Dick Brewer, Rob Widenmann, and the hired man instantly gathered their reins and bolted down the trail, leaving their little herd to scatter and Tunstall to bleed on the snow, alone.

Half a mile behind Tunstall, Bill Bonney and Patrick Rourke rode hard toward the sound of the shot. They skidded to a stop in the cover of the thickets beside the trail. They watched in silence and did nothing as Jesse Evans led the posse down the hillside toward Tunstall.

By the time the posse arrived, John Tunstall was dead.

Jesse Evans dismounted and kicked Tunstall's lifeless body. Warm blood oozed from the hole above the left eye. Evans smiled up at Buck Morton. Then he knelt on one knee and drew John Tunstall's revolver from the dead man's belt. He put one more round for good measure into the corpse's right shoulder with Tunstall's own handiron. Standing beside the body, Evans turned and put another round into the face of Tunstall's horse.

Evans held Tunstall's warm weapon shoulder high. He squinted one eye and took aim at a nearby tree. He fired, knelt again, and returned the piece to Tunstall's bloody hip.

"He fired three times at us, Deputy. The iron will prove it for sure."

Buck Morton gathered his reins.

"Round up them horses, men, and let's move on. We'll all be home by suppertime."

Ten men left Morton's side and collected Tunstall's horses.

Sean Rourke hardly moved, except to control his wide-eyed mount for each of the discharges of the weapons. With his mouth open, he drew rein to steady the animal. He had never seen a man gunned down in cold blood. The look he cast Morton and Evans was anguished disbelief. The once wounded soldier felt suddenly like Cain.

Morton understood.

"You ride with the House now, Rourke. Let's drive on."

"You ain't just going to leave him."

Sheriff Brady's man smiled.

"Wolves got to eat, too."

When the lawman spurred his horse into a loping canter, Sean remained fixed beside John Tunstall, dead, and the Englishman's patient horse, dead.

When Sean's nervous horse made a slow turn, the rider surveyed the surrounding woods. He saw no one and heard no one. Beside Billy, Patrick's wide eyes met his brother's grim face, but Sean saw only trees heavy with glistening snow.

Sean kicked his animal's sides and galloped up the trail toward the posse that had abandoned him. He left Tunstall lying face-up and wide-eyed. A gentle snow fell softly into the body's open mouth.

Chapter Eight

As Buck Morton had promised, his posse was home for supper, Monday evening, February 18th. John Tunstall's weary horses milled about the corral beside the Wortley Hotel. The possemen who had families took the comfort of their wive's hot food and the happy unwashed faces of their children.

Sean Rourke had no home. He sat alone in his darkened room at the hotel. He had led his tired horse on foot past Melissa's door. He knocked, assured the woman and her child that he was safe, gave no details, and pulled his mount by its bridle to the Wortley's paddock where the animal visited Tunstall's confiscated livestock.

With fresh snow on their shoulders, Billy Bonney, Rob Widenmann, and Patrick Rourke rode slowly into Lincoln at ten o'clock. Thick snow flakes absorbed the sounds of their horses and no one was on the single street to hear them when they turned their animals out in the paddock at Tunstall's store. Old blind Colonel shuffled over to the three new horses. Deep hollows above Colonel's lifeless eyes gave away his advanced age. He raised his muzzle and rubbed whiskers with the newcomers. He sniffed the night air for his master who had saved him from being sold as a side of beef at the Indian Agency store. Disappointed, Colonel stumbled to a solitary corner of the corral where he waited alone.

The deputies whom Sheriff Brady had assigned to seize

Tunstall's store had long since gone to their own homes and families. Only one guest at the Wortley saw the lantern light in Tunstall's window when Billy built a fire in the pot-bellied stove. Sean Rourke saw the light cool and yellow on the snow under the window in the adobe wall. Then he pulled the curtain across the hotel window and returned to his chair in the dark.

By the time the lawmen returned to Tunstall's store Tuesday morning, the place was empty. Billy and Patrick left before daybreak to return to the trail.

Townsfolk already buzzed with rumors of the Englishman's death on the road to Lincoln. He had fired on the posse, they said, and he got what was coming to him.

The rumors stopped briefly when a buckboard appeared on the dirt road leading to Fort Stanton. The wagon drew gasps when it stopped at Tunstall's store where three burly deputies stood guard.

Dr. Taylor Ealy, twenty-nine, helped his dazzlingly beautiful wife, Mary, out of the wagon. The woman held the hand of her two-and-a-half-year-old daughter. Their four-month-old baby nestled in her physician father's arms. Sheriff William Brady met the Ealys on the frozen street.

"Attorney McSween sent for us, Sheriff. I'm a doctor and a Presbyterian minister. We're here to start a church." The University of Pennsylvania graduate introduced his family to the law of Lincoln County.

"McSween and Tunstall ain't here, Dr. Ealy. McSween should be back any day now. I'm afraid that Mr. Tunstall done got himself shot out in the country. He was evading lawful process. Guess them Britishers don't know any better."

The newest family in town was ushered inside the store and the sheriff showed them to quarters in the back.

BILLY AND PATRICK rode slowly through the snow-covered trees. All of the hoof prints from yesterday were erased.

Riding in a wagon, they made slow progress. They did not find Tunstall's frozen body until midday. Climbing down, they heaved Tunstall into the back like a heavy log, The body had turned to stone overnight.

The funeral cortege of one decrepit wagon drawn by one sway-backed horse did not arrive in Lincoln until after dark. Unhitching the animal, they left the body outside to stay fresh.

Wednesday, Justice of the Peace John B. Wilson ordered an inquest into Tunstall's death and the two bullet holes in the body. Taylor Ealy's first official duty on his second day at his new home was to conduct an autopsy of the frozen body. The post surgeon rode over from the fort to assist after the body spent the day thawing.

The official cause of Tunstall's death was a gunshot wound to the face. His sidearm chambered three empty cartridges, proving William Morton's report that Tunstall had opened fire on the duly appointed posse.

The Reverend Dr. Ealy's second official function was to bury John Tunstall on Thursday, February 22nd.

Five men with picks hammered all night at the frozen ground between the back of Tunstall's store and the glasslike Rio Bonito.

"Deep as we're going to get till spring, boys," one of the broad shouldered ranchers said as he wiped perspiration from his face.

"Ain't deep enough," another sweating man protested.

"Tunstall ain't about to complain," the first man said firmly.

"Guess not."

Lincoln's womenfolk wore their best black bonnets under the blue, afternoon sky. Their men stood uneasily in the cool sunshine. Open palms rested on walnut grips of Colts, Remingtons, and Starrs where long coats were pulled back to reveal leather. The killing posse, Sheriff Brady, and Jimmy Dolan stood off to one side. Sean Rourke stood with the

House with Melissa leaning against him. Never before had they touched in public. Families who did business with Tunstall and McSween stood closer to the excavation behind the store. Patrick stood with these partisans, between Billy Bonney and Rob Widenmann. Dick Brewer slouched behind Billy. A tense peace prevailed under the narrow-eyed gaze of Company H of the blue-shirted 15th United States Infantry. Dolan had called out the troops from Fort Stanton during the night. The black faces of the cold soldiers matched the bonnets of the women.

Rev. Dr. Ealy read the Protestant graveside service while the Irishmen of the House looked on from under their wide brims. Mary Ealy's strong voice led the citizens of Lincoln in a hymn of mourning for the foreigner in their midst who did not know enough not to draw on a duly constituted posse. Jesse Evans and the Boys sang behind her like a dirty-faced heavenly chorus.

And above it all rang the clear tenor voice of Billy Bonney who loved to sing at church on Sunday mornings in the hard town of Lincoln, once known as La Placita del Rio Bonito.

While the mainly Catholic and Irish House prayed across from the mainly Protestant Tunstall–McSween store, the two brothers Rourke looked at each other over the open hole in the rocky sod. Each man waited for the other to blink and look away. Neither did. Sean wondered why his brother's eyes were so full of anguish. Each had been in the enemy's camp for little more than one month—hardly time to form bonds worthy of much grieving. When Patrick's gaze drifted down toward Melissa's eyes the color of the bright, mountain sky, only then did Patrick blink and look down at the clods of frozen mud soon to fall upon John Tunstall.

The voices raised on the banks of the Rio Bonito carried into the white hills above the hamlet. It echoed through the barren rocks and around smooth hills until snow-heavy trees smothered it into just another gentle breath of pine scented wind.

"MAYBE A WEDDING? Can't be church, can it?"

"I didn't think it was Sunday. Must be we lost count."

"Must be," the large black man nodded. "Sure it's Lincoln?"

"Sure only of that much," the thin white man smiled. "It's the day of the week I ain't swearing to."

Both men chuckled and spurred their horses through the little hills close to town. Their long, wool coats were blue. Blue trousers with a gold stripe on the outside of each leg were pushed down into knee-high cavalry boots. Each rider rode easily in his deep-seated McClellan saddle.

"Main road should be 'round them trees," the white man pointed. The older, black man followed silently between the hills.

The lead rider looked young with gray eyes, rosy cheeks and a red try-hard beard. His whiskers were thin and unconvincing. His narrow shoulders made him look like a boy ahead of the massive man close behind. The older man's face was clean-shaven except for a gray mustache. The road opened before them after an hour.

"There. Only another two miles west, Cyrus."

"Good eye."

"Could do it blind from here," the young man said cheerfully.

In the thin air, the two riders did not hear hoofbeats behind them until the lone horseman was nearly beside them. All three men reined in their mounts and squinted at each other beneath the high sun.

When Patrick Rourke exhaled at the two men in blue, his face was obscured by a veil of steam. His pale eyes were wide.

"Liam."

"Patrick? What's that on your face?" The pink-faced boy smiled warmly.

"A damn better beard than you sprouted, little brother."

Liam Rourke stroked his chin with his gloved hand. His cavalry gauntlet reached to the elbow of his government-issue greatcoat. Then he reached over to grab his brother's open hand.

Patrick looked across to the black man who appeared to be twenty years older than the youngest Rourke.

"This here is Cyrus Buchanan. He and I rode together on the trail of Chief Joseph. He's my friend."

Patrick's tired eyes nodded civilly toward the black man. The brother leaned over his horse's ears and extended a gloved hand. "Patrick Rourke, Sergeant Buchanan."

Cyrus took the hand into his yellow gauntlet.

"Patrick."

The middle brother eyed the blue uniforms, greatcoats, and military saddles.

"You mustered out yet?"

"Six weeks ago," Liam said, blowing steam toward Patrick. "They give us the clothes and tack 'cause it being hard winter still on the Canadian border. Got our civvies in the saddlebags. No use wearing out the knees in our own pants across seven hundred miles of open country."

"Guess not," Patrick said.

"Did Sean get the lawyer's letter and come home yet?" Liam sounded anxious to count heads.

"In town. We rode in together six or seven weeks ago." Patrick shrugged toward the east where the narrow road disappeared into a crease between gentle hills.

"And you?"

"Moved into Pa's."

Without asking about the soldiers' plans, Patrick smiled at his brother and reined his damp horse toward the west. As if answering the unspoken invitation, the men in blue fell into position on either side of Patrick. Riding silently while

the sun dipped toward the southwest, Patrick occasionally
glanced sideways just to assure himself that his long lost
brother was really at his side and not a mean snow mirage.

BONITA RAMOS HAD never seen the new deputy up close. She
pretended not to notice his disfigured cheek. But Sean could
feel the warmth of her gaze on the purple side of his face.
He had wondered how the dark-faced woman in her middle
thirties could regard herself as Melissa's friend when they
could never have shared a single conversation. Sean
reminded himself that he was again at the mute woman's
table for his evening meal in her tiny home and that she had
never uttered a word toward him either.

"Reverend Ealy planted the Englishman real pretty,"
Bonita said with little trace of Spanish in her accent. Her
Anglo mother had seen to that before her Mexican father
sent the white woman away twenty years ago.

"It was done proper," Sean said through the beans in his
mouth.

"Why did Mr. Tunstall try to shoot Mr. Evans?" Abigail
asked. Before Sean could swallow his food, he saw Melissa
touch the little girl's hand and gesture toward her plate. "I
just wondered, Mama."

Melissa tapped the plate again and Abigail looked disappointed as she studied the mule stew.

"Guess he didn't know no better," Sean volunteered. Pretending it was the beans that made him choke on his words,
he reached quickly for his coffee cup.

"But he lived here almost long enough to be American,"
Abigail argued softly. "He seemed like a nice man—for
someone what didn't do business with Mr. Dolan."

Sean shoveled some beans and chewed very slowly.

There was no more chatter until Bonita excused herself
and walked out into the chilly night. Sean lingered behind.
Abigail hugged him and climbed the ladder to the loft.

Melissa sat near the stove, beside Sean who took a pipe from his pocket. He struck a match on the side of the stove and blew smoke rings toward the ceiling. The silent woman watched his face. She sat on his left so he looked like any other man with a full beard ending beneath his gray eyes.

The woman watched him smoke peacefully. She could see that a hearty dinner, Bonita's lively talk, and a quiet pipe did not lighten the weight which he seemed to carry on his furrowed brow. When Abigail blew out the single lantern in the loft, only the red light flickering inside the stove's open door illuminated the couple's faces. An oil lamp on the dinner table was damped low and sputtered yellow.

Sean smoked for half an hour without words. Then he tapped his pipe on the side of the stove and looked hard into Melissa's beautiful eyes.

"Morton killed Tunstall in cold blood. Then Jesse killed him again. Just like that."

The part-time deputy sighed deeply, stood up, and touched Melissa's face before she had time to rise. His rough hand lay for an instant on her cheek with a touch as gentle as her mother's.

Stunned by the grief in the tall man's face, Melissa stayed seated until Sean reached for his hat and trail coat that hung from a peg beside the door. When Sean touched the heavy door, the woman stood, picked up the lamp, and walked slowly toward his side. She looked up into the good side of his face. Sean noticed for three weeks that she had a way of focusing only on the undamaged side as if the purple cheek were not there at all. She came close until he could feel her warm breath on his beard.

With Abigail sleeping in the loft, Melissa Bryant laid her hand upon Sean's, still gripping the cross-bar securing the door. She pulled his hand down to his side and lifted the lamp's glass toward her mouth. Melissa blew the lamp out. Then she reached up and removed Sean's hat.

*   *   *

AFTER FIVE EXHAUSTING days since Tunstall's murder, Patrick struggled to keep his eyes open. Liam and Cyrus continued to talk cheerfully as they passed a jug of sour mash whiskey between them. A fire roared in the hearth at one end of the large room of Grady Rourke's house.

At two in the morning, Patrick was fading fast. He turned to Liam.

"You're welcome to Pa's bed," Patrick said when he could sit up no longer, even without a drop of whiskey. "It'll feel good after sleeping on the ground for a month. Cyrus, you can bunk out here and I'll take the loft so you boys can talk all night if you want."

"I don't want to be no trouble, Patrick. I can sleep in the barn." The big man with sergeants' stripes on his sleeve looked at the two white brothers.

"My brother's friends stay in the house," Patrick said firmly enough to end the discussion.

"Thank you."

"Ain't nothing."

Patrick stood up with all of the energy he had left. He stumbled on the wooden ladder halfway up. The two retired soldiers heard snoring quickly reverberating from the ceiling beams. They never heard Patrick's boots bounce onto the floor.

"Is the house the way you remembered it?" Cyrus spoke over the mouth of a clay jug.

"Smaller, I suppose. But I ain't seen it in five years." He reached for the jug and took a swig without wiping the lip first.

"What do you make of your older brother riding with the men what killed that Englishman?"

"I don't know what to make of it. I ain't seen Sean since he went west in '68. I couldn't have been more than ten or eleven when he left. I don't know if I would recognize him if he walked through that door." Liam nodded toward the closed door beside the curtain full of night chill at the broken window. "But Patrick says it's so. He was part of that posse even if he didn't shoot him himself."

Cyrus shook his head and reached for the jug.

"It would seem, Private Rourke, that we rode into a hornets' nest." The middle-aged soldier was starting to slur his words. He squinted at Liam through the whiskey fog.

"We been through worse," the youngest Rourke said grimly.

Cyrus had the jug half way to his mouth. He stopped short and lowered the jug into his lap. His broad face frowned as memories erupted inside his whiskey-muddled mind. He looked up toward the billowed curtain where the night wind howled over John Chisum's cattle. Cyrus Buchanan listened as if the wailing outside sounded familiar.

"Yes," the older man said softly. "We seen worse."

SATURDAY THE 23RD, Alexander McSween awoke early and stood on the windswept porch at South Spring River Ranch when John Chisum rode up from inspecting his fence lines. The cattleman had been in the saddle since well before daylight.

"You're up early, Alex."

The lawyer watched Chisum dismount with the spry step of a cowhand half his age. Only his square face creased like an old cowboy's.

"I am. But John won't be. Can't stop thinking about him."

Chisum wrapped his reins around one of the vertical timbers holding up the porch roof. He removed his hat and wiped a handkerchief around the inside crown. Though the morning air was crisp, Chisum had broken a sweat during two hours of trotting.

"Yes, Alex. The report the men brought from town sure

don't sit easy: young John drawing on a dozen armed ruffi-
ans like Jesse Evans and his kind. Don't make sense."

"They murdered him. You know that." The lawyer
spoke with anger. Tunstall was a business partner, but
McSween had grown to like him in the sixteen months
since their first meeting in Santa Fe at the Herlow Hotel.
The lawyer never got rich off the Englishman after con-
vincing him to settle in Lincoln County. Tunstall paid him
for his counsel by crediting him with shares of the general
store ownership. The shares were to equal half of the
business by May—by which time Tunstall will have been
three months in the ground. McSween had always smiled
when Tunstall would launch into one of his soliloquies
about America where a man was limited only by the size
of his dreams.

"Yes," the rancher nodded sadly. Tunstall was Chisum's
partner in the town's only bank. "I'm sure they ambushed
him. John was a businessman, not a shooter. That story
about three empty cartridges in his handiron don't wash
with me. At least it don't sound like the House men know
you're down here."

McSween stepped into the morning sunshine. He turned
his face toward the red sky and closed his eyes. He let the
new sun warm his pale skin. Chisum waited for the lawyer
to collect his thoughts.

"I'm going to Lincoln tomorrow." McSween lowered
his gaze to Chisum who stood a head taller beside him.
"Dolan won't kill me. At least not on the main street and
not on a Sunday. That isn't his style. Bushwhacking suits
him better."

"Brady will lock you up as sure as you're standing here."

"I don't think so. He's got the horses for security. I'm
going to Lincoln. I want to see how many men will rally to
our side of the street if there's trouble. Will you ride in
with me?"

"Not yet." The cattleman spoke quickly as if he had

already mulled it over. "I'll send some of my boys with you."

McSween turned and held the door open for his host.

BY THE TIME Patrick awoke, it was Saturday afternoon. He could not remember sleeping so late or being so tired. His feet hurt from sleeping over twelve hours with his soggy boots on.

Liam and Cyrus were not in the house. Patrick found them outside where they were covered with sweat and grime. The gaping breaches in the fence around the house were closed by new posts and rails. Cyrus saw Patrick first.

"Good morning," the big man shouted as he walked up from the barn. "Did you catch up on your sleep?"

"Yes, thanks." Patrick held his hand up to shield his eyes from the sun. "Looks like you and Liam have been busy."

The sergeant still wore his field uniform with the sleeves rolled up. Sweat dripped into his friendly eyes.

"This ain't no one-man operation," the soldier said cheerfully. "We fixed the fence and Liam is down working on the barn where the wind stoved in the siding."

"I'm grateful." Patrick waited for Cyrus to come closer.

"The boy wants to ride into town to find your brother." Sergeant Buchanan appeared to expect an answer.

"He should see Mr. Shield, the other lawyer. He has Pa's will."

"I'll tell him. Will you ride in with him?"

Patrick saw Liam coming up behind Cyrus. "Afternoon, Patrick," the youngest brother waved. He wore his ragged civilian clothing.

"Liam. Thanks for the fence."

"Sure. Let them cows get their own house."

Patrick nodded.

"I'm going into town to find Sean."

"Cyrus mentioned that. You need to look up Mr. Shield in Tunstall's store. Sheriff Brady's men are keeping it closed, but the lawyer lives in the back."

"I'll do that. Will you be coming, too?"

Patrick studied the youngest surviving Rourke.

"No. I ain't been home for a week."

"I'll ride in with you," Cyrus offered.

"Good. I'd like the company."

"Sean's at the Wortley Hotel this side of town, on the left."

"All right. I'll just clean up first."

Patrick looked toward the west, then back toward his brother.

"You ain't got more than four hours of daylight left. You could wait till tomorrow."

"No. I ain't much for Sundays. Them cityfolks will be going to church and all. I'll go today."

"Whatever," Patrick sighed. "But it'll be quieter there tomorrow. The House men probably don't shoot folks on Sunday."

Chapter Nine

ALL OF LINCOLN COUNTY'S SADDLE HORSES SEEMED TO BE tied up at either the Wortley or Ike Stockton's saloon further down the street. The ranch hands on Chisum's huge spread and men from smaller ranches throughout the Pecos Valley were paid on Friday. By the time Liam and Sergeant Buchanan rode into town late Saturday afternoon, February 23rd, half of the cowboys were already broke again and the other half were well on their way. Easy women who usually lived in sutlers' wagons near Fort Stanton began arriving in Lincoln on Thursdays to service the hungry men on Saturdays.

The two riders tied up to the hotel. Cyrus wore his blue cavalry blouse and Liam wore the ragged uniform of a cowpuncher. The sergeant hesitated outside in the bright chill. He looked into Liam's face with its boyish beard.

"What is it?" Liam was anxious to enter.

"The hotel's probably just for white folks."

"In Lincoln? There's more Mexicans in this town than *Anglos*." Liam smiled cheerfully. "It's more likely they won't let me in."

Cyrus shook his head, not very convinced. He outranked Liam by two stripes in the Army, but he deliberately fell in behind the white man as they approached the doorway.

Several men with cow muck on their boots turned around when the door opened. They quickly sized up the two new

men and then returned to their business of visiting in the
open area or leaning against the long bar. Others came and
went through the hallway leading to the cantina. More than
half of the faces were Hispanic.

"Like I said," Liam smiled. "Only your coin has to be the
right color on Saturday night."

Cyrus nodded, gradually becoming more comfortable.
The night clerk shuffled toward them.

"Buenos dias," the little man said showing more black
spaces than teeth.

"Good evening," Liam said. "We're looking for Sean
Rourke."

"Sí, señor, he's in the cantina—through that hallway."

"Thank you."

Liam led Cyrus into the shadows. Cigar and pipe smoke
filled the hallway and the cantina was packed with loudmen
and the kind of women who do not require their men to have
clean fingernails. Only one of the women in the room was not
dressed in chorus-girl costume and did not have a face caked
with grease paint. Her beautiful face was clean. When she
glanced toward the hallway, Liam was struck by her incredibly violet eyes. She stood between two men sitting at a large,
round table. One man was Jesse Evans. The other had a disfigured face and he did not look up as the pocket-heavy
cowboys came and went during their night on the tiny town.

"There," Liam gestured with a cock of his head. "That's
my brother."

Sean did not look up until he felt two men standing
beside him. When he did, it took a moment for him to recognize the brother who was a pimple-faced boy when last he
had seen him. The oldest brother stood. Without a word, he
stepped forward and wrapped his long arms around Liam.

"Sean," Liam said softly. He separated from Sean's
embrace and looked into the burned face. Enough sunlight
still poured through the windows to brighten the ghastly
purple wound. Liam concentrated on Sean's clear, pale eyes.

He did not remember the flecks of gray in his brother's hair and whiskers.

"Liam. Damned good to see you. When did you get into town?"

"Yesterday. This here is Cyrus Buchanan. We rode together up north."

Sean looked at the faded stripes on the black man's blue shirt and quickly extended his hand.

"Sergeant. Thanks for keeping an eye on Liam here."

"Didn't have to do much of that. The boy's a fine soldier."

"Retired soldier," Liam said eagerly. "Gentleman farmer now."

"Oh?" Sean's face became serious. "You've been out to Pa's?"

"Yes. Staying with Patrick."

"Oh." Sean turned back to the five men sitting around him. "This is Jesse Evans and a few of the men who ride with him. And this is Melissa Bryant, a friend of mine."

Melissa nodded and said nothing. Jesse Evans smiled and made half a salute with a wave of his hand toward Cyrus.

Sean pulled out two of the empty chairs and gestured toward Liam and Cyrus. No one raised an eyebrow when Cyrus sat in the company of half a dozen white men. He was beginning to like Lincoln's easy ways.

"What'll you boys be having?" Jesse sounded cordial. Melissa leaned toward Liam.

"Maybe whiskey," Liam smiled.

"Same," Cyrus said firmly.

Melissa turned and pushed through the crowded hallway.

The smoke in the cantina burned Liam's eyes. He reached into the pocket of his long duster and pulled out a black brick of tobacco. During the long chase of Chief Joseph's band through the cold northland, he had given up smoking and took to chewing to keep his throat warm. He bit off a chaw and handed the rest of the wad to Cyrus who did likewise.

"You learned some nasty habits in the Army, little brother." Sean was grinning and his good cheek bulged with his own chaw.

"Seems so," Liam chuckled. "Done worse than this even. But you remember how it was."

Sean nodded silently. He remembered.

"The boy says you was in uniform?" Cyrus looked at the good half of Sean's face.

"The gray," the older brother said with almost an apology in his voice.

Cyrus looked into Sean's weary eyes.

"Soldiers is soldiers," the black man said.

Sean nodded. He liked the company his brother kept.

Melissa returned with two shot glasses. Cheap liquor dripped from her fingers. She laid a glass in front of Liam and Cyrus.

"Thanks, ma'am," Sergeant Buchanan said warmly. The woman nodded and walked to another table.

"She don't say much," Liam noted toward Sean.

"No. You going to stay with Patrick?"

"For a while, I suppose. Till we sort out Pa's business."

"We can do that now that you're home."

"That's what Patrick said. How come you ain't living at the ranch with us?"

Sean looked down at his empty glass. He shifted his chaw from his live cheek to the dead one, which bulged wrinkled and blue.

Liam felt a slap on his shoulder. He looked sideways to see Jesse Evans pulling his hand back and smiling broadly.

"Because the company's better at the Wortley, boy. Ain't that so, Deputy?"

Liam looked at his brother.

"Deputy?"

"Yes. I needed the work. Our brother runs Chisum cattle on Pa's land and I work for the sheriff."

"I wouldn't have figured you for a lawman, Sean. Guess

times change." There was a twinkle in Liam's blue eyes.

"Yes."

"You boys come to town in time for fireworks all right," Jesse Evans slurred his words merrily. "We fought the Revolution all over again this week, boy."

Liam glanced toward his brother for an explanation.

"An Englishman was killed by a posse on Monday. Nasty business." Sean was talking to his empty glass but loud enough for Liam to hear over the cheerful noise surrounding them.

"Were you there?"

Sean did not look up.

"Reckon so." Sean raised his empty glass and held it airborne. In a moment, Bonita Ramos took it out of his hand and left a full glass. Lowering the glass to the wet tabletop, the older brother faced Liam. "You been to the lawyer's?"

"Not yet. My letter was from a Mr. McSween."

"He ain't around just now," Jesse answered for Sean. "He's on his way to jail or maybe he's already feeding the coyotes beside the road to Mesilla." The blond man laughed, heartily amused.

"McSween's partner is Mr. Shield," Sean said over Jesse's loudness. "His office is across the way in Tunstall's store. Tunstall is the man the posse killed."

"Does Shield have Pa's papers?"

"Yes."

"You seen Pa's will?"

"Yes. What did Patrick tell you?"

"Nothing. Just that you wanted to stay in town."

Sean nodded and sucked down his sour mash in one gulp. He raised the empty glass again. The half-Mexican woman replaced it within half a minute. She paused only long enough to smile warmly at Cyrus who returned the courtesy with a face full of grin.

"Patrick and I saw the will when we rode in five weeks ago." Sean swigged his whiskey and laid the dirty glass on the table before he looked hard into Liam's wind-burned face. "Pa left everything to you and Patrick. Cut me out. He ain't had no cause to do me that way."

Liam looked stunned.

"Why?"

"Must have had his reasons. But that don't have nothing to do with you and me. Blood is blood."

"What about Patrick? He said you ain't talking to him."

"I ain't ready for that yet. Besides, there's two sides in this town. Jesse Evans here and the Sheriff is on the side of the House—the mercantile across the street. Patrick took up with Tunstall's side of the street and McSween and Chisum. Chisum cattle are grazing Pa's land. You stay with Patrick and you've chose sides, Liam."

"But we're kin." With only one whiskey in him, Liam was already having trouble following the argument, if an argument it was. "Besides, I ain't got any money to move into town. We don't get our government script for another month, if then."

"You can work for us," Jesse answered for Sean. "Sheriff Brady can always use another gun." He looked across the table toward Cyrus. "Even a black one."

Liam looked down at the soggy table. He blinked as the memory of Indian blood running across the high plains swept through his mind like a river of red.

"I seen enough trouble to last me, Sean. I come home to settle up Pa's affairs and to make something grow. I want to plant or ranch. I want to do something what does no harm." Liam blinked suddenly moist eyes. "I ain't about to hurt nobody no more."

Sean laid his large hand upon his brother's shoulder.

"That's all right, boy. I come home for the same thing. I truly did." The blue side of Sean's face twitched. "But I just ain't got no place to do it right now. Pa seen to that."

Cyrus studied the youngest brother's anguished face. All winter in a cavalry saddle had reddened his face and hard liquor made it even redder. The big man in Army blue pushed his empty glass away.

"If we go across the street, Liam, maybe you can see that lawyer and we can get home before midnight."

"Yes. We better go, Sean."

"All right. Is the sergeant living at Pa's, too?"

"Just till I move on," Cyrus answered.

Sean nodded as Liam and Cyrus stood. Just as they pushed their chairs under the table, Bonita and Melissa came over to stand beside the table. Liam looked into the silent women's wide blue eyes and he remembered the color of slow moving water in the Red Fork of the Powder River in the Bighorn Mountains. Melissa was paralyzed by the strange and terrified look in Liam's eyes. She stood beside him and inhaled the cloud of whiskey fumes pouring out of him as he stood transfixed by her eyes.

The liquor running through Liam's brain carried him to the Red Fork. In a heartbeat, the white-washed adobe walls of the cantina evaporated. He saw only Melissa's clear blue eyes and the cigar smoke halo around her long black hair smelled suddenly like sulfur smoke. The black hair was on the ground everywhere.

In the warm saloon heated by warm-blooded men, loose women, and blazing pine in the fireplace, Liam felt cold. He shivered. He felt the dawn chill of the 25th day of November 1876. Like tonight, it was a Saturday. Colonel Ranald Mackensie's eleven hundred troopers of the 4th Cavalry were storming down upon the Cheyenne village of chiefs Dull Knife and Little Wolf. Forty of four hundred Cheyenne were slaughtered. When the soldiers found blood-soaked uniforms from George Custer's last battle concealed in the village, two hundred lodges were burned.

The white men laughed during the night when the temperature plunged below freezing and eleven Cheyenne infants froze to death at their mothers' breasts.

"Liam?"

The brother shuddered when he felt a hard hand on his arm. He broke his stare from Melissa and turned.

"Sergeant Buchanan. Sir."

"It's all right, boy. It's all right. We have to go."

"Yes. Yes," Liam stammered. His shaking hand raised his hat to his brow. "Yes."

The two men pushed their way through the crowd toward the hallway and the street. Sean Rourke watched his brother's back as he shuffled at the black soldier's side. Liam only came up to Cyrus Buchanan's massive shoulders. By the time they walked outside, the bustling dirt street was dark under an overcast and starless sky.

"Ain't it funny?" Jesse Evans laughed loudly across from Sean.

"What?"

"Niggers is welcome where you ain't."

SUNDAY MORNING CAME on an ill wind driving sleet which slashed across the Sacramento Mountains. Liam slept off his whiskey until seven o'clock. By the time he found the hot coffee pot on the hearth stones, Cyrus and Patrick had already worked an hour in the barn, shoring up siding that the bitter wind had loosened during the night.

"Then what did Shield say?" Patrick was bundled in his fur trail duster and a woollen scarf, which pulled his hat brim down over his ears. Cyrus worked in shirt sleeves and no hat.

"The lawyer told the boy that your daddy had the right to cut off Sean so long as Mr. Rourke had his mind when he wrote the will. The lawyer says he knew your daddy and his mind was sound when he wrote it."

"Sean took it real hard, Cyrus."

"Yes. We seen him at the Wortley. He talked like he might come 'round in time. But everyone talked about taking up sides like it some kind of war in that town."

"And Sean thinks I've taken the Englishman's side 'cause I had to continue Pa's lease of the pasture to Chisum."

"Seems to be."

Patrick covered his face when the barn door opened to let in a wave of sleet. Ice pellets bounced across the dirt floor like tiny wet marbles. Liam had to use both hands to close the heavy door when he entered.

"Got your beauty sleep?" Patrick smiled.

"Says the man who slept through Saturday," Liam laughed. He held a cup of coffee which was already cold just from the walk to the barn. "Need a hand?"

"Sure." Cyrus pointed toward a pile of barn siding in an empty stall. Half a dozen stalls were filled with the saddle and pack horses.

While Liam walked toward the stall, the door flew open again. Both brothers thought the wind had done it. But Billy Bonney led an icicled horse into the barn, dropped the reins, and pulled the doors shut.

"I knocked," Billy said where he shivered. His horse turned his mousey brown face to lick his sides near the saddle where chunks of sleet dangled from his winter coat. "Mind if I keep my mount out of that weather?"

"Not at all," Patrick said cordially. "Liam, this is Billy Bonney. He worked for Tunstall at the store till Brady closed the place. Billy: my brother, Liam, and Sergeant Cyrus Buchanan, late of the U.S. Cavalry."

Billy took off his snow-covered hat.

"Liam. Sergeant Buchanan."

"Mr. Bonney. Call me Cyrus. I'm retired now."

"Cyrus." Billy turned toward Patrick. "You might want to come to town today, Patrick."

"In this weather?" The howling wind nearly drowned out his voice. Slits between the barn's siding acted like a huge musical instrument. Each crack resonated with its own tone and the wind moaned through the west wall like a wood-wind orchestra.

"What could be that damned important, Billy?"

"Mr. McSween's come to town. And Justice Wilson— Justice of the Peace—is going to hold a meeting about Mr. Tunstall's death."

"Murder, you mean." Patrick put down his three-pound hammer.

"Yes, murder. Wilson and McSween are having a meeting this afternoon. Going to form a posse to hunt down Tunstall's killers."

Patrick thought of Sean who rode with the killer deputies.

"A posse to hunt down another posse? What about Sheriff Brady?"

"Brady ain't invited. Just boys from the right side of the street. You saw what them others did to Tunstall. You have to come."

"It ain't my fight, Billy. I have a ranch to run."

"You won't have a ranch if Jimmy Dolan and his kind have their way. John Wilson is all that stands between us and a war in the middle of town."

"Who's the law in Lincoln? Brady or Wilson?"

"Both," Billy sighed with fatigue borne of his ride through pelting sleet and snow. "If them people can let Jesse Evans kill Tunstall, none of us is safe. You have to come."

"But it's Sunday, Billy. Can't it wait till tomorrow?"

Billy heard Chisum's cattle complaining outside about the snow falling on their backs and the sleet stinging their eyes.

"When Brady and Dolan send Jesse and the Boys to steal them steers and drive them down to Seven Rivers where they hide the cattle they rustle, you won't have no money to keep this ranch, Patrick. Joining us will give you the guns you need to protect your Pa's livestock. You need our guns; and we need yours. And Liam's gun and the sergeant's."

"Where you going to meet? Can't use Tunstall's store if Brady has it locked down."

"No. We're meeting at McSween's house next door.

Brady ain't locked down McSween's place. And Mrs. McSween ain't back yet."

Patrick walked over to Liam. He had to raise his voice slightly to be heard over the wind.

"Liam? You interested?"

Liam glanced over to Cyrus who slowly shook his head as if he knew the answer.

"No. I ain't lifting my iron against this town. Or against Sean, if he's riding with the sheriff."

"All right. Then you and Cyrus can stay here. I ain't got no choice." Patrick faced Billy at Liam's side. "Let's go up to the house and put some hot coffee in you. Then we'll ride down to Lincoln."

"Good. McSween will be glad to have you."

"Maybe. But I ain't raising my weapon against my brother."

Billy showed his squirrel teeth. The nineteen-year-old clerk pushed back his long coat to reveal his handiron on his hip.

"Your brother don't talk like he's still your kin."

BILLY AND PATRICK never spoke during their grueling ride back to Lincoln. They never looked up from under their hats for five miles. They kept their chins inside the collars of their coats to keep the sleet from cutting their faces. The horses obediently followed the wagon road into town without help from their motionless riders.

Patrick was surprised that the paddock surrounding McSween's large adobe compound was full of horses. No one saw them ride past the Wortley on their left. McSween's home was the next large structure on the same side of the street. The next building further down was Tunstall's store where behind it, fresh snow covered the little mound of rocks piled over the dead Englishman's body. At least a dozen horses stood rigidly in a row. They all faced away from the wind blowing hard out of the west.

Inside, a stone hearth warmed just over a dozen men. Cigar smoke swirled toward the ceiling. Patrick guessed who Alexander McSween was by his face. There were only three pink, smooth faces in the crowd and they were the only unarmed men present: Justice Wilson, the lawyer, and a stranger. McSween wore better clothes. All the other armed men wore cowpuncher uniforms of baggy trousers shining from wear inside the knees and sweat-faded shirts.

After brief introductions of Patrick Rourke, Justice Wilson called the late afternoon meeting to order.

"Men, John Tunstall was bushwhacked in cold blood. We don't know for sure who done it. But we know Sheriff Brady's posse went after him to serve the attachment writ. I'm prepared to deputize what men among you is willing to serve the law of New Mexico Territory. We ain't no vigilantes. Whoever takes the oath will bring in Tunstall's killers to stand trial fair and square. I warn you: There's hell to pay for those among you what take the oath. These here arrest warrants are for Jimmy Dolan, Deputy Morton, and . . . Jesse Evans and three of his Boys."

A dangerous murmur rumbled through the company of smoking and chewing men.

"Whoever can follow the law and can swear not to become a mob, stand and raise your right hand."

Patrick found himself standing beside Billy Bonney. Every man was up and every hand was raised in the smoky cloud.

"Do you swear to uphold the law and to defend this territory from enemies of the people? So help you God?"

Fifteen throaty voices mumbled, "Yes." A few voices firmly replied, "Damned yes."

"Then you're deputies. We'll call ourselves the Regulators." John Wilson looked pleased with himself. He had formed a posse and named it, all in one breath. "Alex?"

The soft-looking lawyer walked to Wilson's side. McSween put his thumbs in his vest pockets.

"Boys, you are now the Regulators. You are all that stand between law and anarchy. Do your duty! Justice Wilson will now sign arrest warrants for the killer or killers of our esteemed friend, John Tunstall, subject of Her Majesty the Queen."

Several armed men spit wads of chew on Susan McSween's floor to seal their oath.

One by one, the Regulators picked up copies of Justice Wilson's warrants, took a swig from one of several clay jugs, and marched headsdown into the blizzard. McSween lingered to visit with Patrick Rourke.

"I knew Grady well. He was a good man."

"Thank you, Mr. McSween."

"I hear that Sean hasn't taken well to the disposition of your father's estate."

"No, sir. He ain't."

"I'm sorry, Patrick. I suppose your father had his reasons."

"Nothing I can figure. Sean was a soldier and my father was proud of him. Pa were a soldier in Mexico in '47."

"Yes. Decorated, I hear."

"By the President himself. I don't understand it. Billy brought me out, you know. I ain't going after no man who didn't shoot Tunstall. Doc Ealy says Tunstall was shot twice. There were a dozen men in the Sheriff's posse."

"How do you know that?"

"I just know it. I was riding with Tunstall into Lincoln."

"Did you see him murdered?" McSween stepped closer.

"Not exactly. I just know how many there was."

"Well, you heard Justice Wilson. The Regulators aren't vigilantes. They are only to arrest the killers, not be judge and jury. But remember this," McSween's whiskey breath was close to Patrick's face, "everyone in Brady's posse is at least an accessory to assassination, whether someone pulled the trigger or not. The Regulators' job is to bring them in. You're a lawman now, not a jury."

"Or hangman, neither."

"No. Billy says you're living at your Pa's."

"Yes."

"Good. We'll just send word out to you when we're ready to ride after the weather breaks. You better get on home before you lose the daylight. I'm going back down to South Spring River."

"Chisum's?"

"Yes." McSween paused to listen to the howling wind.

"Today?"

"Guess so."

"You could spend the night with us, Mr. McSween. Then get an early start tomorrow. It's a long ride for one day. Especially in a blizzard."

"Thank you. I'll take you up on that. I'll ride out with you in a few minutes. I need to talk with Doc Ealy for a minute."

"Fine. I'll wait and we can ride out together."

"Thank you. I won't be long."

McSween walked over to the man in bankers' clothes whom Patrick had not seen before. The lawyer pulled a folded document from his breast pocket inside his black waistcoat. The physician read the two pages carefully. Then, he looked over his steel-framed spectacles, dipped a pen into the inkwell on the desk, and signed the papers without ceremony. He had witnessed the Last Will and Testament of Alexander McSween.

Patrick turned toward Billy.

"The man says we're lawmen." Patrick spoke with a tinge of disbelief in his voice.

William Henry Bonney smiled his buck-toothed grin.

"Sure we are," the clerk said cheerfully.

* * *

PATRICK RODE HOME beside McSween in gathering darkness.
The damp chill in the air matched the feeling in the pit of his
stomach. The riders reined their mounts to a slow walk
westward.

On the far side of Lincoln, half a dozen riders rode hard
toward the southeast. Deputy William Morton led a remnant
of his posse into the sheltering veil of high-country night.

Chapter Ten

ALEXANDER MCSWEEN EXHALED A LONG CLOUD OF STEAM ON the crest of a small hill. The snow had crystallized from yesterday's sleet, which froze during Sunday night. The lawyer felt a wave of relief sweep the cold out of his bones. The afternoon sunshine glistened down the hillside all the way to South Spring River Ranch. Lincoln and its killing law had spared him one more time.

"It's starting to look like home to me."

Liam nodded. Steam rose from the perspiration inside his shirt under the comforting weight of Patrick's furry trail coat. But his lips were too cold to move. Frozen breath clinging to his bald beard encircled his mouth. The ring of white frost looked as if he had fallen face dawn in a cat's milk bowl. The patchy beard did not add anything to his twenty-one years.

"Chisum will be glad to have one of the sons of Grady Rourke riding his fence line along the Pecos. You'll see."

The two riders spurred their weary horses down the glasslike hill toward the ranch house. By the time they tied up near the front porch, two armed men were standing sentry beside the doorway. They smiled up at McSween when they recognized him. The horsemen dismounted stiffly. The icy wind had driven the blood out of their knees miles earlier and each man had to walk with his knees slightly flexed.

"Boys, this is Liam Rourke, late of the United States Cavalry and the surrender of Chief Joseph up north."

The cowhands patted Liam on the back as if running starving Indians to ground were heroic. He winced.

McSween and Liam were standing palms-out in front of the hearth when John Chisum entered the greatroom of the house. The lawyer made the introductions.

"Chief Joseph, you say? That was grand work, Mr. Rourke. Your late father would have been proud of you."

"I suppose so, Mr. Chisum."

"John. We don't stand on formality at South Spring. You're in need of work?"

"Yes, sir. Until my father's affairs are settled."

Chisum glanced at McSween for news from town.

"His brother Patrick signed on to our posse yesterday. Justice Wilson named them the Regulators. Nice ring, don't you think?"

"Indeed. Well, we can always use another hand, Liam. And another sidearm." The cattleman eyed Liam's Army-issue, 1873 Colt .45 revolver. "Yes, we surely can. Glad to have you with us as long as you like."

Chisum extended his hand which Liam accepted. The rancher turned to McSween.

"When will the Regulators ride?"

"Within the week."

"Warrants?"

"Signed and sealed by Justice Wilson."

"Good. Maybe now we'll see some real justice."

When Chisum faced Liam, he saw that the retired soldier had turned around and was looking into the crackling fire.

SEAN ROURKE WALKED under the purple sky toward Melissa's cottage. Smoke swirled from its stone chimney and Sean could smell the pine resin on the cold air. He had crawled out of the woman's warm bed before daybreak so he would be gone when Abigail came down from the loft. He approached the front door to return for midday supper with mother and daughter.

"McSween was in town yesterday."

Melissa nodded over her plate of stew. She did not have to be at the Wortley until late afternoon for the dinner shift with Bonita Ramos.

"Rumor has it that Justice Wilson formed some kind of posse to hunt down Tunstall's killers." Sean toyed at his food with a wooden spoon. Abigail watched him closely.

Melissa laid her rough hand on his. Sean looked up and saw the concern which tightened the corners of her beautiful eyes. He was slowly learning to read her mind. No other woman in his past had spoken to him like this woman who never said a word.

"They say Patrick got swore in with McSween's bunch. I don't know about Liam and the darkie soldier."

Melissa nodded and withdrew her hand.

"Has Bonita come by today?"

"We ain't seen her," Abigail answered for her mother.

"She weren't at the Wortley this morning either."

PATRICK AND SERGEANT Buchanan heard the buckboard crunching over the frozen snow at two o'clock. They walked out of the barn into blinding sunshine. They glanced at each other's sweating face when they saw Bonita Ramos rein her horse to a stop.

"Patrick. Mister Buchanan. Thought you might want some real food. You'll have to put it on the fire. It probably got froze again on the ride out here."

Patrick stood with his mouth open. He reached up to take her gloved hand, but she hesitated long enough for Cyrus to step forward and grab her middle. The big man eased her down to the ground so softly that her boots did not make the hard snow crackle. She leaned over the buckboard and lifted a large basket from the back.

"Can you tie up my horse, please?"

Patrick took the long reins and led the animal and buckboard to one of the newly planted fence posts. He wrapped the leathers three times around the frosted wood.

"Thank you."

"Would you like to come in?"

"Sure. What about the sergeant?" She smiled up at Cyrus. She presumed that he slept in the barn.

"Mr. Buchanan lives in the house with Liam and me."

"Oh. Is Liam here, too?"

"No, ma'am. My brother rode over to South Spring River this morning, early. Looking for work so we can keep Pa's ranch till the estate is settled up."

"I see. You know Chisum?"

"Not really. But Mr. McSween went along. Said he could get Liam on."

She nodded and her face clouded for an instant. She brightened quickly when Patrick gestured toward the house. The woman followed in step between the two men with Patrick leading.

Bonita opened her basket and spread several covered plates upon the table. The two men sat down at opposite ends. Their hostess edged toward Cyrus who watched patiently.

"Did both of you sign up for McSween's posse?"

Patrick was surprised by the casualness of her tone.

"No, ma'am. Just me. Cyrus here and my brother Liam have had their share of scraps already."

"In the cavalry, I hear."

"Yes'm," Cyrus smiled.

"Please call me Bonita. Everyone else in town does." She put three plates on the hearth stones close to the fire that Patrick had stoked when they entered the house. The front window was still covered with fading curtains holding back the cold breeze. "There. That won't take long."

Bonita sat down at the table.

"It must be lonely out here for two bachelors."

"There's not much time to think about it," Patrick said slightly uneasy. He was not accustomed to discussing such things with women. "I found the ranch beat up by the weather. It's been almost like building it from scratch."

"Your Pa built it?"

"Yes. I can't hardly remember the time. I weren't but six or seven. Liam was just a baby. I suppose Sean would remember." Patrick's face looked distressed as he thought of his estranged brother.

"Sean seems to be taking up with Melissa these days." Bonita showed a slight smile.

"The girl what don't talk much?"

"She don't talk at all. She ain't said a word since the Apaches done her over back in '70. There was a raid on the fort. Her ma and pa was killed. They left her with a child, Abigail. But she loves that little girl like any mother."

Patrick and Cyrus nodded thoughtfully. They could not imagine; and they did not try. The white man was not yet comfortable in the woman's cheerful company.

"You with the House or the dead Englishman?"

The woman did not blink at the important question.

"I work with Melissa at the hotel. The hotel is House property. Melissa is House property: old Mr. Murphy and Jimmy Dolan they always looked after her, what with her being an orphan and all. For me, it's just work. I can sweep, or I can whore." She smiled her attractive, crooked smile. "I sweep."

"I didn't mean no harm, ma'am. It's just I got made Chisum property 'cause of Pa's grazing lease. Chisum is with McSween and the House ain't. I didn't mean no harm."

"Stew should be warm enough." Bonita stood and walked to the hearth. She put the tip of a finger into one of the dishes.

Patrick could watch her from his seat. But Cyrus had to turn and look over his shoulder. When she bent over, he turned back to Patrick and grinned broadly. Patrick nodded.

Bonita laid a plate in front of each man. Then she went back for her own.

"Now you boys tell me if my cooking is as good as yours."

"Don't need to taste it, ma'am," Cyrus said cheerfully. "It even smells better."

"Thank you, Sergeant. But the proof is in the tasting." She looked into his eyes closely.

"Yes'm."

FRIDAY NIGHT, MARCH 1st, Liam was exhausted. During his first four days on the Chisum ranch, Liam had worked harder than he had in months. He joined a gang of hands digging holes in the frozen ground for fence posts and he had driven cattle between snow-covered pastures, which were ten miles apart. The bunk house was warm and comfortable. Sleep had come almost instantly after drinking a quart of water so cold his throat burned. He had forgotten how winter wind can dehydrate a man. But sleep would not come on his fifth night of being a hired hand.

The large cabin was dark except for bright red embers in two stone fireplaces. A dozen men snored around him with the rumble of a steam engine taking the high ball signal up a grade. Liam wrapped a wool blanket around his shoulders and he stood in his long woollies at the window.

Though only half a moon hung in the sky, it cast enough light from a clear sky to illuminate the dry winterscape of Chisum's empire. Liam rubbed fog from the window clouded by his warm breath. He blinked.

A figure walked from the shadows toward the bunk house. Liam thought it might be a bear standing upright. In the moonlight, the distant shape did not have human form.

Liam could not take his eyes from the window. He glanced toward the mantel above the nearest hearth. A lever-action Winchester rifle hung on wooden pegs. In his mind he calculated how much time he would have to dive for the ever-loaded weapon if the bear charged through a window or the unbolted door.

Wiping the window again with the heel of his hand, Liam exhaled so hard that he fogged the wavy glass completely and had to wipe it a third time.

The bear stopped in a wide clearing ten yards from the cabin. The moonlight fell coldly upon a human form. Like Liam, the body was wrapped in a blanket that dragged across the fresh powdery snow. A wide path trailed behind the figure into the darkness. Against white snow glistening in pale light, the body cut a sharp outline against distant hills. When it pulled the blanket away from its face, Liam's voice came to his throat in a stifled yelp like a puppy stepped-on. He looked quickly over his shoulder to see if he had awakened anyone. The train sped on in the cabin uninterrupted.

Looking back to the window, Liam watched the shape. He saw a woman with long dark hair. Her face was lost in shadows.

Liam's eyes were wide. He could not blink and his eyeballs began to hurt as they dried.

The long-haired woman reached into her blanket and pulled out a short stake. Even in the fragile moonlight, Liam could see a tuft of what he knew to be hair waving from one end of the stick, thick as his forearm. Reflexively, Liam stepped back from the window when the woman placed the post in the snow and leaned upon it with all her weight to drive it into the frozen earth. The post was erect and knee-high when she straightened her back. Liam finally blinked painfully when the woman seemed to look clean through him with her large, black eyes. Then she turned and walked back into the night. Her long robe moved from side to side in the path it had already cut.

When the woman was absorbed by the night, Liam could clearly see the spirit post and its moon shadow upon the snow. He recognized the Cheyenne spirit post and he knew that the hair blowing gently in the night breeze was the hair of the woman's dead child.

"Spirit Keeper," the boy at the window sighed, fogging it completely for the last time.

Liam returned to his still warm bunk. Looking up at the ceiling, he decided that he was dreaming. He wanted to go outside to urinate. His bladder had awakened him from a nightmare, he thought. He smiled with certainty that he would find only new snow beyond the window come morning.

But he could not bring himself to climb out onto the cold wooden floor. He closed his eyes and waited for sleep to return and to push out of his mind the memory of Red Fork and brown babies frozen to their mothers' breasts.

Liam awoke to the sound of groggy men shuffling through the bunk house. Some cursed the icy floor as if the discomfort of cold splinters piercing stocking feet were deliberate. Others dropped heavy boots onto the floor as they dressed in dirty clothes that had been folded within their bedrolls to keep the outfits warm.

The newest man rubbed his eyes, felt the intense pressure in his bladder, and stumbled out of bed. He could hardly open his eyes to the blinding daylight outside. Wearing boots and his longjohns, Liam could not wait to dress before making some yellow snow. But before such certain relief beyond the corner of the cabin, he paused and looked away from the sun to where his nightmare had stood. He saw three cow hands standing closely together. Liam joined them.

The three men made room for the new man so all four could examine the strangely painted post sticking in the snow. But there were no footprints leading to it from the nearby pines. No snow had fallen for two days to cover tracks. Liam shivered this Saturday morning. But not from the cold.

SEAN ROURKE COULD sense that Abigail's cheerful face looked at him differently. The sun was never quite peeking over the eastern mountains each morning when he slipped silently out of Melissa's soft, warm bed of deep goose down. The hand-me-down mattress from Lawrence Murphy—founder of the House—was the little home's one luxury. If the little girl heard the door creak open after she blew out her oil lamp, or heard the door close softly before dawn, she never said a word. But Sean felt something different in her eyes when she opened the door at midday on Saturday, March 2nd.

"Mama ain't back yet. She had to buy flour at the House for hot cakes."

"I can come back."

"No. Mama said for you to wait. She won't be but a minute."

Sean was not quite comfortable when he hung his coat on the peg beside the door. He had never been alone with the eight-year-old before.

"Does Melissa talk to you?" Sean was intrigued.

"Not really. I just know."

He nodded. Sean had the same sensation with the soft-bodied woman. He was grateful when Melissa opened the door five minutes after his arrival. The tall man took a heavy basket from her arms.

Melissa had flour on the flatiron griddle within ten minutes. She had also bought a fresh tin of maple syrup shipped in from the East. Sean regretted that he had not thought to buy it for her. When the three took their places at the table, Sean felt as if he finally had a family. The feeling comforted him as much as Melissa's cooking.

"Dolan says that Justice Wilson deputized Dick Brewer

yesterday to lead them Regulators going after Tunstall's killers."

Melissa looked up at him. Her eyes were fearful.

"I ain't worried. I didn't shoot no one out there. Besides, I suppose I'm part of Jesse's gang now and Sheriff Brady's camp. And I live in Jimmy Dolan's hotel. I'm as safe as I can be. Don't you worry, neither."

The woman nodded without much conviction.

"I'm sorry I didn't think to get the maple syrup. I'll get a quart today."

Melissa shrugged toward the new tin.

"That's all right. An extra won't go to waste." Sean smiled toward Abbey who grinned back at him with eyes he had not seen before.

BY SUNDAY, CYRUS Buchanan had waited a week to see Bonita Ramos again. He fought the urge by pounding fence posts into the ground and by nailing patches onto the weather-beaten barn. When that failed to clear his mind of the woman's presence, he cursed John Chisum's cattle for leaning too hard against new fencing, which would not set firm until the earth finally thawed.

"You're like an old woman," Patrick had said good-naturedly. "You'll be giving me your boot if you don't ride into town and make some time, Sergeant Buchanan."

Patrick never used the big man's former rank except for conversations of serious gravity involving Tunstall's murder or whiskey and women.

"If that's an order," Cyrus laughed.

"And so's a clean shirt."

"Yes, sir. With my respects, sir." The soldier's laughter filled the house and he hummed the cavalry tune "Garry-owen"—the 7th Cavalry's marching song—when he pulled his scrubbed blouse from a chairback pushed close to the hearth to dry. He took a wire brush to his cavalry-issue floppy hat and whisked the dust out of the crown.

"Have a good campaign," Patrick waved as Cyrus opened the door.

"Just going to church," the soldier said as he closed the door behind him.

JOHN CHISUM AND Alexander McSween assembled two dozen men around the large dining table in the big house. Everyone except Liam went into the kitchen for thirds of the midday Sunday supper.

When the last cowhand finally pushed his plate away clean enough to put back into the cabinet, the lawyer stood up at a corner of the long table where Chisum presided at the head. McSween waited for all eyes to look up.

"Boys, it's time we brought John Tunstall's killers to justice. We all know it was Bill Morton's posse who gunned down the only honest shopkeeper in Lincoln. Tomorrow, the Regulators will ride. I've sent word to Dick Brewer to lead you."

Everyone looked at McSween as he sat down. The eyes around the table were narrow and hard.

Only Liam was not thinking of high-country justice. He thought instead of two mornings in a row, pulling spirit posts out of the snow. Saturday after midnight, the Spirit Keeper had pressed her nose against the glass window. Liam alone saw her last night. No foot prints marked the mourning mother's coming or going.

PATRICK WAS NOT surprised when Cyrus did not ride home Sunday night. Monday morning, he awoke alone in the house for the first time since Liam had returned from the Army. He got up early and was busy pushing steers away from the fence when two riders came hard down the lane.

"Is Cyrus all right?" Patrick demanded instinctively.

"Cyrus?" Billy Bonney asked as he dismounted beside a winded Dick Brewer.

"Yes. He rode into town yesterday."

"I wouldn't worry none," Billy smiled. "He won't freeze in Bonita's room."

"I suppose not," Patrick said, wondering how the youth knew. "What brings you out so early?"

"The Regulators is riding," Dick Brewer answered quickly before Billy could. "Tomorrow. We need to know if you be with us?"

"Come in out of the cold," Patrick said to change the subject, even for a moment. Billy and Brewer tied their sweating horses to the new fence rail. Steam floated on each animal's back from the canter to the ranch. The three men walked inside where the room was comfortable although the fire was little more than red embers.

"Coffee might be warm," Patrick said.

"Thanks," Brewer said.

"Sheriff Brady is going to get his comeuppance, if I have any say in this business." Billy sounded genuinely angry.

"Come on, Billy. One night in the poky ain't done you no harm." Dick Brewer was overly cheerful. "You got a hot breakfast you ain't had to pay for."

Billy was simmering where he sipped his lukewarm coffee.

"Jail?" Patrick tried to follow.

"Brady arrested me yesterday just for asking him to make me a deputy to go after Morton's posse of bushwhackers. All I wanted was to be legal all 'round. I figured that Brady's warrant and Justice Wilson's would make me legal and proper four square. But he locked me up last night just for asking. He'll get his, you'll see."

"Ease off, Billy," Brewer's voice was calm and father-like. "You got Wilson's warrants and that's enough by me. Brady don't mean no harm to you."

"Well, I mean harm to him."

"I don't want to be part of no lynching," Patrick said firmly. He was not drinking coffee and both of his hands were free to gesture forcefully. "I ain't no vigilante. Like McSween said."

"Don't worry, Patrick. We ain't either. Billy'll cool down." William Bonney did not look cool to Patrick's eyes. "Besides, if you ride with us tomorrow, you can be sure that the law is rightly served."

Patrick thought of his brother Sean.

"The law serves who pays the most." The middle brother did not want to be a Regulator, oath or no oath.

"Well," Dick Brewer grinned, "we ain't being paid nothing to go after Morton's posse. We're volunteers. You better come, too , if you're worried."

Patrick looked into Billy's fiery eyes filled with blood. There was no choice.

"All right. I'll ride with you. But we ain't no assassins."

Billy put his coffee cup down and did not say a word.

"Well then," Brewer said softly, "we'll ride over here in the morning. Bring a good horse. The darkie can come if he wants."

"He ain't about to leave Bonita's for no posse," Billy smiled for the first time. "I sure wouldn't trade her bed for no horse."

Dick Brewer handed his empty cup to Patrick and led Billy back into the sunshine. Patrick stood in the doorway and watched them ride off at an easy trot. He closed the door and set the cup down.

Alone in Grady Rourke's house, Patrick stood quietly and looked at the portrait of his uniformed father and his Confederate brother.

SHERIFF WILLIAM BRADY paced the floor of his adobe home four miles east of Lincoln before daybreak Tuesday, March 4th. His roundly pregnant wife, Bonifacia, and their eight children slept peacefully all around him, surrounded by the one thousand acres that he had earned for them. His house looked like the barracks the former, brevet major remembered from his Civil War days when he chased Indians instead of Rebels.

Brady could feel trouble coming the same way his wife's back—weakened by too many babies—could forecast rain. So he touched his wife's face, whispered in her ear, and stepped quietly into the calm darkness.

Morning twilight turned the southeastern sky a hard pink in the cold, thin air by the time the sheriff rode into Lincoln. Even in the fragile light of dawn, the single street showed dark clods of freshly turned earth within pale, dried ruts from yesterday's wagon wheels. Brady rode to his adobe courthouse next to Ike Stockton's saloon on the lightly settled, south side of the street—the House side.

"Looks like a stampede tore up the street," Brady said as he entered his cramped office. He hung his coat on a peg and adjusted his Peacemaker low on his hip. With his gloves off, he rubbed his chapped hands together near the pot-bellied stove.

"Dick Brewer rode out around midnight with maybe ten men." Deputy George Peppin handed the sheriff a hot cup of coffee.

"Regulators?"

"Yes, Sheriff. Stopped at Justice Wilson's on the way out of town."

"Damn." Brady wrapped his red fingers around the hot tin cup. "McSween still down at South Spring?"

"Far as I know." Peppin had his boots on the sheriff's desk. Brady was too preoccupied to care.

"Which way they ride?"

"East."

"Any word from Morton?"

"None for two days. He'll stay scarce once he learns Brewer's gang is on the loose."

"What about Jesse?"

"He ain't gone no place. His Boys will take care of the captain. He ain't worried." The deputy scraped his spurs across the desk and Brady winced. "Heard you arrested young Bonney."

"For a night only. Wanted me to countersign Wilson's warrants for Morton, Jesse, and Jimmy. For God's sake!"

The sheriff had not taken a seat. He paced nervously. The stove brought beads of sweat to his cheeks around his wide mustache. He spoke to the fogged window.

"Take a message, please, George."

The deputy set his feet on the hardwood floor, took a sheet of paper from the desk drawer, and licked the tip of a pencil.

"Ready, Sheriff."

"Get this to the telegraph office as soon as you see a light down there: 'A. A. McSween, Widenmann and others have collected a well armed mob of about fifty men and are getting more to join them. They defy the law. They threaten the lives and property of our best citizens. I cannot serve any legal documents or carry out the law if I am not assisted by the military. Please see His Excellency Governor Axtell and ask him to obtain an order from General Hatch to the Post Master of Fort Stanton to protect me in the discharge of my official duties.' Signed, William Brady, Sheriff."

George Peppin scribbled for another moment to catch up.

"Fifty men, Sheriff? I ain't seen but a dozen at most." The deputy suppressed a tight smile.

Brady paced to the window where morning light pushed back the last of the shadows.

"They'll be fifty by the time Brewer gets to South Spring River and takes on Chisum's little army."

Deputy Peppin's face hardened at the sudden picture in his mind.

"Yes. Who should I telegraph this message to?"

"Wire it to Governor Axtell for countersignature, with instructions to send it on to President Rutherford B. Hayes."

Chapter Eleven

THE RANKS OF THE REGULATORS DOUBLED WHEN DICK Brewer's posse reached John Chisum's spread Monday night. Patrick Rourke rode grimly with them. Billy Bonney and Rob Widenmann joined ten other Chisum men who rode out with Brewer Tuesday morning. Sunday, Brewer had spoken with townsfolk who were too afraid to ride with the Regulators but hated the House for its usury. With lowered eyes and raspy whispers, they told Brewer to burn daylight for Roswell to the west.

Liam Rourke made excuses and stayed behind at South Spring with a few hands too old to ride through the mountains in the late-winter cold. He had begged Patrick to stay with him at the ranch. But the middle brother rode out to protect Sean if he were found with Morton's fugitive lawmen. Liam was beyond exhausted. All night he had waited at the bunk house window for Spirit Keeper to come for him out of the ground and its fires below. But she did not come for the first night in four.

After the Regulators thundered down the stage road to cross the frozen Rio Hondo for Roswell only six miles to the northwest of South Spring, Liam sleep-walked to the barn where he stacked hay to keep from falling down between the dozing horses. In the house, Alex McSween and John Chisum smoked expensive cigars and sipped brandy when they spoke confidently about justice certain and righteous.

When Liam's head touched his bedroll Tuesday night, he did not remember closing his eyes. The spacious cabin was chilly with more than half of the bunks empty. Red embers glowed in the dying fireplaces when he awoke three hours before dawn. Sitting up in bed, he gathered his wits to put his feet down on the cold floor to throw fresh logs into the hearth. He knew that the cold had awakened him until he saw the woman's face in the frosted window.

ALL DAY WEDNESDAY, Liam watched the road where snow was finally melting into stinking brown puddles of mud and manure. He looked for Patrick with the same pursed brow that Patrick had worn when he stood on Grady Rourke's porch waiting for Liam to ride home from Chief Joseph's surrender. That morning, the spirit post behind the bunk house had toppled over with a warm breeze blowing from the south. Locals enjoyed what they called false spring.

Liam slept fitfully Wednesday night, but Spirit Keeper did not come with the encouraging warm spell.

By midday Thursday, March 7th, Chisum's vast herd of steers had turned from brown to coal black as they wallowed like pigs in the newly soft earth. The split-eared animals did not look up when two dozen weary men on horseback rode slowly down the muddy hillside toward the ranch. Dick Brewer rode in the lead beside three men whom Liam had never before seen.

The three men were the only riders without iron bulges under their long dusters. Their hands were bound with coarse hemp to their saddle horns.

The Regulators dismounted under the watchful eyes of Alex McSween and John Chisum. Six possemen, two at a time, helped the three prisoners from their saddles. All of the riders were caked with sweat and mud.

"Welcome to South Spring," Chisum said coldly in the comfortable air. Deputies William Morton, Frank Baker, and William McCloskey did not return the cattleman's contrived civility when they were pushed stumbling onto the low porch. A Regulator behind each prisoner pulled off each captive's muddy hat as if they were in the presence of royalty.

"Inside," McSween ordered. Sheriff Brady's men were led into the house. Their weary faces had the gray pallor of condemned men.

"Take the ropes off them," Chisum said. Dick Brewer obliged, one at a time. When Patrick walked in, Liam stepped close to his brother who smelled of horse sweat and man sweat.

"Four of them got away," Patrick said softly. "We chased them for five miles before we run them to ground. Sean weren't with them." Liam looked relieved, although his eyes were sunken into black wells on his lightly bearded face. Patrick was surprised by Liam's gaunt face. "You all right?"

"Just tired. I ain't up to ranching yet."

Patrick pulled a chair from under the long table. He looked to Chisum who nodded. Patrick slumped down hard.

"You, too," Chisum said to Morton and his two men. "You'll be guests here till Deputy Brewer escorts you back to Lincoln to stand trial for murdering John Tunstall."

"In cold blood," the lawyer interrupted before Chisum had finished his greeting.

The prisoners sat down close to Patrick. Liam took two steps backward to give Chisum speeching room.

"Tunstall drew on us, Mr. Chisum. That's a fact." William Morton spoke respectfully but firmly. "You weren't in town for the inquest. Tunstall fired three rounds at us on the road to Lincoln. His iron had three spent cases in it. Tell him, Mr. McSween."

Morton's voice was tired but confident. Facts were facts.

"Tunstall wouldn't draw on an armed mob in the middle of nowhere. He was a businessman, not a shooter." McSween spoke with emotion. He owed his livelihood to the dead Englishman after the House had fired him as their attorney. And he had grown to like the soft-spoken foreigner who loved Americans.

"That ain't so, Mr. Chisum." Morton addressed the man in charge. "Tunstall drew and fired. We was trying to serve lawful process attaching Mr. McSween's property by writ of attachment. We fired in self-defense. Pure and simple."

Morton was not pleading. His voice was calm and clear. Only the two prisoners beside him appeared to tremble and their ashen faces twitched in the company of twenty armed men.

"Judge Bristol will decide, gentlemen." Chisum was coldly formal. "A jury of twelve good men and true will decide if Mr. Tunstall was murdered."

A poisonous murmur went through the Regulators surrounding the sitting prisoners. Chisum looked over to Dick Brewer. At his side, Robert Widenmann played with his revolver.

"When can you take these men to Lincoln?" Chisum knew it could be a two-day ride through rugged country if the weather turned.

"We rode hard after Roswell, Mr. Chisum. The horses could use a day or two of decent forage. Two days for sure. Saturday, I'd say."

"Well enough. Put these men in the bunk house and post a guard. Don't tie them up, just watch them. And let them stop at the privy on the way." The rancher faced Morton. "I'll send hot food down to you shortly."

"Thank you, Mr. Chisum." Morton sounded reassured by Chisum's measured tone. He had expected to be left dead on the trail just as he had left John Tunstall almost three weeks earlier. "Thank you."

"We'll see, boys. . . . Take them out, Mr. Brewer."

The assembly separated to let Dick Brewer lead the three men from the house. Then they fell in behind with their hands resting on their revolvers at their hips where their trail dusters were pulled back.

Rob Widenmann twirled his piece toward his holster. He missed on the first pass and hoped that no one noticed.

FRIDAY MORNING, THE 8th of March, Cyrus Buchanan met Sean Rourke on the side porch of the Wortley. Both men had come out early to tend to their horses. Sean had returned to the hotel by first light; Cyrus had left Bonita's small room for breakfast of sourdough hot cakes and bitter coffee in the cantina. The two men leaned on the fence rail of the Wortley's paddock. The air was cool but comfortable. Most of the snow was gone, having been trampled into the softening ground by a dozen horses.

"I heard Justice Wilson's posse went out after that Englishman's killers."

"That's what Bonita said." Cyrus looked at Sean's mangled face. It was nothing new to his soldiers' eyes.

"Did Patrick ride out with them? Dolan said he joined McSween's men the other day."

"I don't know. I ain't been back to the ranch in four days."

Sean smiled and squinted into bright sunshine. He could hardly fault the big man for enjoying some female comfort. Sean had not spent a night in the hotel in weeks. He faced the former cavalryman who still wore his blue blouse and stripes.

"I rode with Deputy Morton's posse when Tunstall was shot."

Cyrus looked strangely saddened. Liam Rourke's friends were his friends, and Liam's brothers were nearly his kin from the bonds formed by men at war, even a pathetic, ill-matched contest like chasing the Nez Perce band of survivors. A flash of memory washed over the black man as he listened to what amounted to Sean's confession to a virtual stranger.

The cavalry veteran thought of September 30, 1877. He road in file beside Liam when Colonel Nelson Miles attacked one thousand seven hundred Nez Perce led by chiefs Looking Glass and Joseph. Beside Snake Creek in the Bear Paw Mountains, thirty miles south of the Canadian border, one hundred twenty-five troopers of the 7th Cavalry fought hand-to-hand in Chief Joseph's final stand. Sixty soldiers were killed or wounded. Liam's blood and Sergeant Buchanan's blood was on the sand. Joseph laid down his weapons forever on October 5th. A stray bullet killed Looking Glass the same day.

"It ain't my business, Sean. I just rode along with Liam 'cause I ain't got no better place to be. When the passes open in the mountains, I'll head west. California, maybe. Liam and me, we looked out for each other for going on two years. I ain't coming between his brothers. And I ain't riding in no man's posse. I done my share."

The soldier could not help but focus on Sean's battle-scarred face. It looked to Cyrus as if the white man had already seen one fight too many. Sean had replaced his winter furs with an ankle-length, canvas duster.

Sean felt the tall's man's gaze and he turned toward the peaceful livestock. "Just thought I would mention it, Sergeant. Patrick and I have taken up opposite sides in this bad business. Maybe young Liam won't have to make the choice."

"Liam rode down to Chisum's spread with the lawyer, McSween, last weekend."

Sean lowered his face until the shadow of his hat hid the grief welling in his eyes.

"So."

"I'll be riding back to your pa's as soon as I saddle up. I can tell Patrick anything you want me to."

"Tell him it's time we went to see the lawyer to settle Pa's business. If McSween ain't here, his partner is."

*   *   *

FRIDAY AFTERNOON, THE looks on the faces of Dick Brewer's Regulators were too much for Deputy William Morton. During the two days of his captivity, he never complained and he never whimpered. John Chisum admired that in a man. So when Morton asked to see one of New Mexico Territory's wealthiest men, Chisum walked alone to the well guarded bunkhouse.

"I don't mean no trouble, Mr. Chisum."

"You and your two men ain't trouble, Deputy."

"I would like some writing paper and an inkwell. Brewer says we're leaving for Lincoln tomorrow." The lawman blinked quickly toward the low ceiling. "I would like to take care of some business before we leave."

"Can you read and write?"

"Yes, sir."

Chisum looked at the prisoner's weary face.

"You'll be safe with Dick. He ain't no hot-head."

"It ain't Brewer I'm worried about. It's them others. I seen the white eye."

"Let me get your paper. I won't be but a minute."

Morton paced the bunk house while his two deputies stared at the hearth.

Chisum returned in five minutes with paper, ink, and pen. William Morton turned a cracker box over near his bunk. He wrote a long letter to his family attorney in Richmond, Virginia. He expected to die on the road back to Lincoln, he wrote.

SATURDAY, LINCOLN BUZZED with excitement. Governor Samuel Axtell rode into town and set up territorial government in Alexander McSween's empty house. Within three hours, the harried chief executive issued a formal proclamation declaring the commission of Justice of the Peace John Wilson to be null and void, along with his arrest warrants for William Morton and his posse. With a stroke of the pen, the lawfully deputized Regulators became outlaw vigilantes. Sitting in the fugitive McSween's home, Governor Axtell also declared that the only law in Lincoln County was Judge Warren Bristol—who had ordered McSween's arrest at Christmas—and Sheriff William Brady.

The sun was halfway between noon and the western ridges when the Governor climbed into his buckboard, tossed a blanket over his knees, and ordered his driver to whip the team toward Santa Fe.

SATURDAY AFTERNOON, WILLIAM Morton handed his one letter to John Chisum for posting. Then his hands were bound and two Regulators pushed him up into his saddle. His deputies, Frank Baker and Bill McCloskey, were shoved onto their mounts beside him.

"Don't waste daylight," John Chisum waved toward Dick Brewer who sat his horse beside Billy Bonney. Patrick Rourke sat pensively behind Billy. Liam watched his brother from the ranch-house porch. The younger Rourke and Chisum were the only unarmed men in the company of two dozen Regulators.

"We'll have these birds in Sheriff Brady's cage by sundown," Brewer smiled as he pulled his rested and well fed horse toward the dirt road. Chisum waved with his hat and watched the Regulators disappear over the muddy hills.

By the time the little army had covered twenty miles, they were strung out along the road for half a mile.

The mounted men rode double-file westward along the still frozen bank of the Rio Hondo. Patrick Rourke rode in the rearguard of fifteen men. Half a dozen Regulators with their three prisoners were out of sight ahead. Billy Bonney and Dick Brewer trotted on either side of the prisoners riding three abreast.

GET FOUR BOOKS TOTALLY *FREE*—A VALUE BETWEEN $16 AND $20

PLEASE RUSH
MY FOUR FREE
BOOKS TO ME
RIGHT AWAY!

Leisure Western Book Club
P.O. Box 6613
Edison, NJ 08818-6613

AFFIX
STAMP
HERE

Twenty-five miles from town, the troop rode into Black-water Canyon, a frozen riverbed surrounded by low hills.

Patrick Rourke's heart jumped into his throat when he heard an echoing volley of gunfire rolling over him from the west. He and the Regulators around him spurred their mounts into full gallop toward the shots. Rounding the canyon's sides still covered with light snow, they skidded their animals to a halt near a cluster of mounted men.

Dick Brewer's startled horse still spun in circles. Three horses were riderless.

Patrick kicked the sides of his horse and eased up to the empty saddles. The wind left his chest in one long spasm when he saw Billy standing over three bloodied men. William Morton and his two deputies were dead. Morton had nine holes in his body.

Smiling up at Patrick with a boyish grin, Billy Bonney pushed his warm and empty revolver into his holster. "Leave them," Billy said sourly. "Like they done Mr. Tunstall."

BY ONES AND TWOS, the Regulators trickled into Lincoln on Sunday and Monday.

"Ain't found them," was their uniform answer to questions on the street and at Ike Stockton's saloon.

Monday, March 11th, a buckboard chugging slowly through thawing mud turned heads on the single street. Sheriff Brady looked across the street from his courthouse window. He hoped to see William Morton climb down for a drink and a shave. Brady sighed when the wagon driver helped his fare step into the mud.

Susan McSween had come home.

PATRICK FOUND CYRUS waiting for him when he returned to the ranch. The hearth stones were warm and the coffee was hot. The cavalryman appeared rested, fed, and at ease.

"Did you find Bonita?" Patrick hung his duster on the peg beside the broken window where the curtain strained to keep out the evening wind.

"I did. Did you find Sheriff Brady's men?"

"No."

"How's Liam?"

"Not much of a rancher. He looked tired."

Cyrus waited for Patrick to pour his coffee and set his chair close to the fireplace.

"I seen Sean in Lincoln this morning."

Patrick nodded and sipped his coffee. His dirty face was tense and haggard.

"Did he say anything?"

"He said you and Liam should go with him to one of the lawyers to take care of business."

"Yes. Sean's right. I can ride to town tomorrow to tell Billy. When he goes back to South Spring, he can fetch Liam."

"I can go back." Cyrus tried to stifle his grin.

"I'll go with the buckboard. We need pantry stores anyway."

"All right. I wonder if Bill Morton's men will come in by then."

Patrick raised his cup, which concealed most of his face.

"Maybe."

SEAN ROURKE STOOD ankle-deep in mud at the center of the hotel paddock. The air was warm enough for him to work without a coat as he brushed his horse with a curry comb. The animal enjoyed the attention. He closed his eyes and stretched his neck while his companions looked on from a distance.

Patrick rode past the Wortley and did not see his brother in the corral. Two adobe buildings further east, the middle brother pulled up rein on his buckboard at Tunstall's store.

He expected to see Brady's men guarding the place. But they were gone.

Instead of Billy Bonney behind the counter, Patrick saw a broad-boned woman with plain and rather unpleasant features.

"May I help you?"

"I'm Patrick Rourke. I come for supplies and to see Mr. Shield."

"Yes. You're a friend of Mr. Chisum."

"Not exactly. He runs his herd on our pa's land. I'm glad you're open for business."

"Sheriff Brady doesn't stand up to me. I sent his thugs home and the sheriff let them go. I'm Sue McSween. Alex is my husband."

"I saw him at South Spring."

"That's what Billy said. Thank you for standing with him." When her angular face opened with a pleasant smile, the thirty-three-year-old woman did not look as hard as her first impression.

"Billy said your brother, Liam, is down at South Spring River and your other brother is with the House."

"Yes, ma'am."

"How's that?"

"Mr. Shield didn't say?"

"He doesn't break his clients' confidences, Mr. Rourke."

"Oh. Well, our pa cut Sean out. So he moved into town. Took a room down the street."

"I see. Did David show you your father's will?"

"No. But he read it to us."

"You haven't read it yourself?"

Patrick hesitated. He remembered to remove his hat. Sue McSween looked at him closely.

"Can you read, Mr. Rourke?"

Patrick shrugged.

"You ride with the Regulators, Mr. Rourke?"

"Yes, ma'am."

"You didn't find Deputy Morton last week?"

"No."

"The Regulators are disbanded, you know."

"Disbanded?"

"Yes. Governor Axtell threw Justice Wilson out of office and revoked his arrest warrants for Mr. Tunstall's killers."

"I didn't know that."

"If the Regulators ride again, they're vigilantes. Judge Bristol will hang them."

Patrick's perspiring face looked troubled. He reached into his duster's deep pocket.

"This here's the list of supplies we need."

"Is the soldier still at the ranch?"

"Yes."

Mrs. McSween studied the long list of groceries printed in large letters.

"How much corn whiskey?"

"Whatever the list says."

"It doesn't say how much." She pushed the list toward him on the counter. The writing was upside down for Patrick. He glanced at it with a blank expression.

"Oh, just make it a gallon jug. I'll return the jug."

"That will be fine." She looked at the young man's kind but dirty face. "Mr. Rourke, I could teach you to read."

The rancher looked down at the counter top.

"I'm afraid I ain't got time, ma'am. I have a ranch to run. I just come in for flour, sugar, and some bacon. And whatever else Sergeant Buchanan wrote there."

"I'll keep the offer open, Mr. Rourke. While I'm getting your things, Mr. Shield is in the back. He's not with anyone, if you want to go in."

"Thank you, ma'am."

David Shield looked up when Patrick knocked on the door frame of his open door.

"Mr. Rourke? How can I help you?"

The lawyer stood and shook Patrick's hand.

"I just come in for supplies. My brother Liam is back from the Army. He's down a South Spring. When can the three of us sign whatever we need to settle up the ranch?"

"Any time, Mr. Rourke. There are documents of administration to sign. Nothing complicated. We will admit the ranch to probate. Whenever Judge Bristol comes to town, he'll review the paperwork and sign the estate deed conveying the land to you and Liam as common tenants. Each of you will then own what the civil law calls an undivided one-half interest in the land and outbuildings."

"Do we have to all be here together?"

"That would be best."

"All right. I'll get my brothers. Liam is nearly sixty miles away. When do you want to see us here?"

"Oh, let's see." Shield looked at the calendar on the wall. "How about April 1st, in three weeks? The judge should be up on the 2nd or 3rd since the local Grand Jury meets on the 1st. Say two o'clock?"

"That's fine with me. I'll talk to Sean on my way out. We'll get word to Liam. Maybe Billy can give Liam the message when he goes out there."

"That's a good idea. I'll mention it to Billy."

"I didn't see him outside."

"No. He rode down to San Patricio. That's about ten miles south of here. He'll be back in a day or two. Quite a few of the Regulators are camped down there. You might wish to keep that in mind if it gets too close in town."

"Thank you."

"Deputy Morton hasn't come back yet, you know."

"I know. Thank you, Mr. Shield."

"Any time, Mr. Rourke."

Back at the counter, Patrick put twenty dollars gold in Susan McSween's hand in exchange for several sacks of supplies. He had to make two trips to his wagon.

After securing the stores in the buckboard, Patrick left the wagon and walked two hundred yards down the street to

the Wortley. The Mexican at the desk told Patrick that
Sean was not in. With a trace of a smile, the little man told
Patrick the directions to Melissa's home. He returned to
the almost-spring sunshine for the short walk east.

Abigail opened the door when Patrick knocked. Hearing
his voice, Sean pushed back from the table and went to the
door. Instead of inviting his brother inside, Sean stepped
outside and closed the door.

"I been to the lawyer." Patrick saw no room for idle conversation on Sean's face.

"And?"

"He says the three of us should come over April 1st to
sign some papers."

"I'll be there."

"Mr. Shield will send word to Liam."

Sean nodded. Patrick looked uncomfortable standing
with his hat in his hands.

"Do you live here?"

"My new family lives here."

"Oh."

"Anything else?"

"No."

"Deputy Morton ain't come back yet. Did the Regulators
find him?"

"I don't know."

"Didn't you ride out with them Chisum vigilantes?"

"Yes. I did. But the bunch I was with didn't see no
deputies from Brady's posse. Didn't see Jimmy Dolan neither. Dolan came out to Tunstall's spread the day the
Englishman was killed."

"Jimmy wouldn't be out with Morton now. He broke his
leg on the 13th here in town. He'll be laid up in Santa Fe for
months. I hope Bill Morton gets off so light, if Chisum and
McSween's men find him."

Sean squinted into Patrick's eyes. The middle-brother
blinked first.

"I see," Sean said softly. Any words on their way up and out were stopped short when he remembered John Tunstall lying dead in the snow. The older brother sighed and looked up at the violet and unseasonably warm sky. "Maybe Morton and his men will turn up now that the thaw has set in."

"I suppose." Patrick put on his hat. "I best move on before I lose the daylight."

"Yes."

"I'll see you, Sean."

"April first."

Sean watched his brother walk slowly down the muddy street. He saw Patrick shake his head as he walked away.

ALTHOUGH CYRUS BUCHANAN was good company, Patrick spent two weeks thinking about his brothers: Sean who had Tunstall's blood on his hands and Liam who rode fence lines at South Spring.

Every second or third night, Cyrus rode alone into Lincoln to take comfort from Bonita Ramos. If he encountered Sean in town, he never mentioned his name to Patrick.

The early spring thaw lingered and cold, dry air was replaced by gray and soggy skies. The Rourke ranch floated in a sea of mud. Its suction on his boots forced Patrick to stop and rest when he walked from the barn to the house.

When Cyrus stayed gone for two nights in a row, Patrick could stand the oppressive silence of his father's empty house no longer. His horse was already saddled Thursday morning, March 28th, when Cyrus drove a buckboard down the lane. Bonita rode at his side.

"I'm going to ride over to see Liam. The three of us need to be in Shield's office on the first. I ain't heard from Billy that he got word to Liam."

"It's muddy," Cyrus said. "Better take a full set of horseshoes with you and extra nails."

"I have all that. The mud will probably pull the old boy's shoes off before we get ten miles."

"Probably."

Cyrus stood beside the buckboard. His round face looked sheepish when he glanced up at the woman who sat patiently with a blanket over her skirt.

"You can keep the house warm till I get back, if you don't mind." Patrick held back a smile.

"I could do that," the sergeant grinned.

PATRICK RODE SLOWLY for two full days. By the time he reached the Rio Hondo, the ice had broken and the river was flowing fast with melt water. His horse limped on sore, bare feet across the river's rocky bottom. Two full sets of horseshoes were buried somewhere in fifty-five miles of tarlike mud.

Liam was in the bunk house when Patrick arrived after dark on Friday. Patrick was stunned by his brother's face. His pale skin seemed to hang loosely around his sunken eyeballs. Liam looked diseased although he protested his fitness for ranch work.

"But you look like hell."

"I haven't been sleeping. I'm damned glad you're here. There's something I want to show you after the others bed down."

"What?"

"I can't say. But you'll see it outside before morning."

Dick Brewer greeted Patrick warmly and invited him to the big house for dinner Saturday evening.

Liam spent the entire night standing close to the window of the hired hands' cabin. Whatever Liam had expected never came. But he waited all night anyway. After two days on horseback, Patrick had to sleep and he left his brother alone at the window.

Saturday, Alexander McSween and half a dozen Regulators sat around John Chisum at the large table. That Governor Axtell had revoked their commission as lawmen did not trouble anyone. Patrick struggled to keep his eyes open when the lawyer stood up to address the assembly.

"Boys, Sheriff Brady and the governor have tried to make all of us into outlaws. Right here and now, I am making a pledge to you. John Chisum is my witness. I'm offering five hundred dollars to the man who kills William Brady."

Patrick Rourke sat with his mouth open.

Chapter Twelve

PATRICK AND LIAM SLOSHED UP THE TRAIL AN HOUR AFTER midnight, Sunday morning. A dozen sleeping cowhands did not stir when the brothers crept out of the bunk house five hours after dinner. Chisum's regular stockmen and the few Regulators among them had talked loudly near the fireplace before finally turning in. Their cheerful banter sounded like small boys laying secret plans to saw the legs from church pews. They spoke merrily of assassination and of spending the five hundred dollars on the desperate needs of lonesome men.

Liam was eager to ride all night. But his brother and Patrick's horse were still sore from their drive to South Spring. Patrick was amazed by Liam's determination to spend the night on horseback. Although his face looked wasted and sickly from fatigue, Liam appeared to Patrick to be a man who did not want to sleep. When Patrick was a small boy, he had worn his boots to bed to keep himself awake all night so his nightmares filled with Grady Rourke's terrible voice would not come in his sleep. Trotting through nighttime hills twenty years later, Liam now wore that same scared-animal look in his hollow eyes. Patrick had long since banished those memories from his mind.

When Patrick's horse began stumbling on rocks under his tender, unshod feet, the two brothers walked their horses by hand, leading them by the reins for an hour of rest. Then they took saddle until Patrick's horse tripped in the dark and skinned his brown knees.

An hour before sunrise, Patrick's horse went down for the last time and refused to rise. The brother cursed the animal, removed his battered saddle, and threw it atop Liam's. The former-cavalryman brother grieved for the old horse whose great heart Patrick had broken. In the cavalry, a man's horse is the one soldier whose courage never falters. Liam kept his mourning to himself. The brothers walked on in silence and led their surviving horse by hand.

At eleven o'clock Sunday morning, they shuffled into Grady Rourke's barn. Liam pulled both saddles from his animal's back. He stood for a long time gently rubbing the patches of bare horse skin where the saddles had abraded the hair away. Patrick sat on an overturned water bucket. He wondered if he would be able to extract his swollen feet from his wet boots.

"You shouldn't have talked to your horse like that, Patrick." Liam spoke to the raw, red wounds on his mount's back and flanks.

"Huh?"

"Nothing. We can go in now."

The brothers found Cyrus and Bonita sitting at the table. She had prepared one of her plain but inviting meals. Cyrus sat with his suspenders dangling at his sides. He wore his Army trousers but his faded red woollies covered his shoulders.

"Late breakfast?" Patrick said cheerfully as he led Liam through the door. His weary, thirsty voice was a raspy whisper. Cyrus had not heard the men approach until the door opened.

"An early dinner," the ex-sergeant smiled.

"Good to see you, Cyrus." Liam's voice was little more than a weak breath.

Cyrus stood when he saw Liam. His kind face looked suddenly troubled.

"You all right, boy? You look like wolves drug you home."

"I ain't slept well." Liam almost fell into a chair near the blazing hearth. Patrick slumped into his father's rocker.

"I guess not," Cyrus said as he laid his large hand on Liam's sweat-soaked shoulder. "You sick?"

"No. Tired. Tired like after Bighorn."

Cyrus nodded. A picture flashed instantly into his mind. Their troop had gotten to General Custer. But too late by a day.

Patrick collected the last of his strength. He had been in the saddle for three days.

"Bonita? You going to town today?"

"Yes. After I clean this up."

"Will you see Sean? I think he's living with Melissa."

"I could."

"You need to get a message to him. McSween's men are riding to Lincoln today or tomorrow. They're gunning for Brady."

"The sheriff? Are they crazy?"

"Crazy with greed maybe. McSween offered five hundred dollars to the man who kills Sheriff Brady. I just can't ride another minute."

The woman looked at Patrick's exhausted face and at what was left of Liam's emaciated cheeks.

"I'll find him and warn the sheriff."

Patrick looked up so slowly that Bonita thought she could hear the bones in his neck grinding against themselves before he whispered toward her.

"Don't let our brother get hurt."

"I won't."

"AIN'T YOU GOING to church?"

Sean Rourke wore his one clean shirt. Morning sun poking through holes in an overcast sky made the starch

sparkle. Melissa smiled and shook her head, No. She pulled
Sean by the hand into her tiny home.

"Where's Abbey?"

Melissa pointed across the street as she closed the door.
When Sean sniffed the freshly ground coffee in the cozy air,
she poured him a cup.

"Thanks."

Sean looked at her. The woman's hair was pulled back
and tied behind her neck. Sunday morning daylight coming
through the windows glowed on her rosy cheeks. She
looked remarkably beautiful. Sean's eyes kept focusing on
her cotton blouse as she hovered near the pot-bellied stove
where the coffee pot perched. Her breasts looked somehow
rounder. Still standing in his open duster, he reached out and
put his hands around her waist to pull her closer.

He looked down into her dark blue eyes that were a color
he could never describe. Once, he had traveled from the
gold fields to San Francisco. He had stayed until the heavy
yellow dust in his pockets ran out at the gaming tables and
the whore houses. Looking at Melissa's face, he remembered the Pacific Ocean in the bay at sunrise. Her eyes were
that shade of blue.

Pushing her to arm's length, he studied her radiant face
and searched her eyes for the source of the strange warmth
that he felt radiating from her face.

Melissa Bryant smiled and placed his open palm on her
long skirt, flat against her belly. She carefully watched him
as he stood there thinking hard.

Sean pulled his hand away as hard as if she had laid his
bare fingers on the red-hot stove lids.

"My God, woman!"

He pushed her away by the shoulders and she nearly toppled over a chair. He had to instantly reach out to grab her
before she fell backwards into the wood pile.

The pain in the silent mother's eyes wrenched the tall
man's heart.

"I'm sorry, Melissa." He stepped toward her and she stepped backwards, avoiding the chair. With her back against the wall, he put a hand as gently as he could upon each side of her frightened face. Then he pulled her to his chest. "I'm sorry, Melissa. Forgive me."

The woman sniffed once and stepped out of his embrace. She stood two steps in front of him. The good side of his bearded face was full of anguish.

"I love you. I would give my soul to hear your voice, even once." He turned his back to her and faced the hot stove. "But I can't be no father." He sighed and turned back to her. Sunshine fell on his destroyed cheek and her eyes narrowed for an instant. Her eyes locked onto his sad, gray eyes. "I ain't never had nobody to teach me."

Melissa raised her left hand that would have touched the wounded side of his face for the first time. But before she touched him, Sean stepped aside and marched quickly toward the door. He opened it to the gray morning and spoke over his shoulder as he walked outside.

"I ain't had nobody to teach me."

BY SUNDAY AFTERNOON, early spring rain whipped across the high plains of Lincoln County. It blew across the Sacramento Mountains and drove sideways across the last of the snow.

A dozen cowhands and Regulators rode slowly with their faces down inside their collars. Rain stung the eyeballs of their horses. Alexander McSween rode beside Billy Bonney at the head of the miserable troop. When they reached the hamlet of San Patricio ten miles from Lincoln, the vote was unanimous to camp there for the night until the weather broke. After hot biscuits and coffee, Billy agreed to ride ahead into town to alert other Tunstall loyalists that the Regulators would ride in on Monday, April 1st.

*   *   *

BONITA RAMOS WRAPPED a shawl over her head against the
rain. She knocked on Melissa's door at five o'clock in the
evening. Abigail opened the door and invited Bonita inside.
She found Melissa sitting in the shadows.

"Where's Sean?"

The mute woman shrugged. When a single tear rolled out
of her eye, the other woman removed the shawl from her
shoulders soaked to the skin.

"You told him?"

Melissa nodded.

"I see."

Melissa covered her wet cheeks and red eyes with her
hands. Bonita shook her head. She had seen the same
expression on Melissa's face the last time she learned that
she was with child.

Bonita sat beside Melissa for an hour. Neither woman
spoke a word. Abigail puttered quietly in the loft where she
lived with cheerful stuffed animals of calico. Before she
went outside into the twilight drizzle, Bonita wrote a careful
note on a scrap of paper.

"Give this to Sean, please, if you see him before I do."

SHERIFF BRADY WAS surprised to see Sean Rourke filling the
courthouse doorway. Sean was equally disquieted by his
strange and sudden need to smoke with William Brady.

"It'll be nine when the next one comes in the fall," the
sheriff smiled through blue pipe smoke. "Each time, I
expect my wife to make me sleep in the barn 'till death do
us part.' But it must be the Mex in her or something. I don't
think she'd mind a dozen little ones." He blew a smoke ring
which hung in the thin, humid air of a rainy Sunday. "My
constitution might not be able to handle it, though."

Sean smoked peacefully. The soles of his muddy boots

were close to the soles of Brady's boots in the center of his battered desk.

"You got a girl in mind?" The sheriff squinted through the smoke toward Sean's thoughtful face. Like everyone in Lincoln, Brady knew very well where Sean had been sleeping since his second week in town.

"No. Must be my age. But I been thinking of children, for some reason."

"Well, your folks raised three boys. Two soldiers and one rancher. That ain't bad." Sean was still uncomfortable in spite of Brady's genuine courtesy. The only real bond he had with the man was the two dollars a week he paid for part-time deputies—hired at Jimmy Dolan's whim—and the blood of John Tunstall soiling both of their souls, even though neither of them had pulled the trigger. Dolan ran Brady and Brady sent Dolan out to challenge the Englishman; Dolan then sent William Morton up the trail with Jesse Evans; and Sean was there when Evans did Dolan's dirty work. There was something sickening about propping his feet up on Sheriff Brady's desk. Sean was startled when Brady laughed out loud.

"Sean, I think it's just the springtime in the air. Yes, sir! You got the itch just like all the barnyard this time of year."

Brady's voice and face were too full of good cheer for Sean to take offense. He just pulled his feet from the desk, tapped his pipe on the side of the stove, and stood. The sheriff stayed seated and chuckled softly. In the evening twilight illuminated only by the open door of the stove and a single oil lamp, Brady's hard face softened with the tranquility of a man who would leave nine children behind to carry on his name—such as it was. Sean put his warm pipe into his duster's pocket.

"Maybe it is just the weather, Sheriff. I don't know what got into me. But I'm grateful for your time and the smoke."

Brady nodded and pulled the pipe out of his black mustache. The waxed ends curled up when he smiled warmly.

"You know, Sean, nobody taught me neither. About fathering, that is. My wife and I learned together. And we done all right." He nodded thoughtfully. "We done all right."

Sean paused at the open doorway.

"Thanks, Sheriff."

Brady waved with his pipe and blew another smoke ring.

When Sean returned to the Wortley Hotel after dark, the clerk was surprised to see him.

"We are still holding your room, *señor*," the Mexican grinned. "But you never use it."

"I will tonight, Raul."

"*Sí.* Bonita left you this."

Sean took the scrap of paper. He looked at the upside-down letters and pushed the note into his pocket with the warm briar.

"*Buenos noches, Señor* Rourke."

THE RAIN STOPPED during the night. The ground was a river of mud by sunrise Monday.

The Regulators broke camp before first light and reached the Rio Bonito by daybreak. Rain made the thawed river run high and they made camp on the north side across from town, just opposite the back of John Tunstall's store. Between the swollen river and the store, the mound of earth above Tunstall's grave had been washed flat with the muddy paddock.

Billy Bonney reached Tunstall's store by seven o'clock. He opened the door and expected to see Alex McSween. Brady's deputies had not yet taken up their posts at the front door.

"They're camped across the river," Susan McSween said sleepily to Billy as she fired the stove. "Don't know when they'll cross with the creek so high."

"Where's Brady's men?"

"They won't trifle with me," the woman said acidly. "Brady won't send them back here."

Billy suppressed a smile. The plain-faced, plain-talking
woman could stare down Brady's whole posse as far as
Billy was concerned.

BY NINE-THIRTY IN the morning, Sean stood in the hotel's
paddock and curried his well-rested horse who was getting
fat on rolled oats and clean water. The animal closed his
eyes, lowered his head, and dozed on his feet while his
master brushed him. Sean kept an eye on the muddy street
for his brothers due in town to meet with David Shield. The
river fog lying across the Rio Bonito concealed Shield's
brother-in-law, Alex McSween, and his little army camped
on the far side just behind the hill above the north bank.

On the east end of town, twenty men summoned for jury
duty milled around the adobe courthouse. They did not know
that the first day of the new session of court had been delayed
for a week. Sending them home was the sheriff's job.

At ten o'clock, William Brady and three deputies walked
out of the House on the west end of Lincoln. The sheriff
carried a written order proclaiming the new date for
convening court. When a fourth House man joined them,
Brady walked up the center of the main street beside
Deputy George Peppin, George Hindemann, Jacob "Billy"
Mathews, and Jack Long.

The four men passed Tunstall's store. Sue McSween
glared coldly at them from the window. Directly across the
street, former Justice of the Peace John Wilson was working
in his garden. Too anxious for spring to wait until the last
danger of frost, Wilson scowled at Brady and turned his
back on the four House men.

Brady stopped at his courthouse, informed his veniremen
to come back next Monday, and nailed his order to the
adobe wall. Then he turned to walk back to the House where
he belonged, along with Dolan's stock of flour barrels,
salted pork, and bolts of calico.

Sean looked east from the hotel corral where he whispered sweet nothings into his horse's ear.

Sheriff Brady and his men walked west in front of Tunstall's store. Sue McSween was gone from the window when Brady looked her way. Without blinking, he lowered his face to keep from tripping face down in fresh manure. He never heard the explosions beyond his left shoulder.

Sean's horse spun around and bolted with the other animals to the far corner of the paddock. Sean dropped to his knees and crawled through wrist-high muck to a water trough where he crouched.

A fusillade of small arms fire erupted from an adobe wall adjacent to the Tunstall compound. The Regulators across the river heard the gunfire carried on the wet morning air.

William Brady went down instantly. He was dead before he could close his mouth around a clod of horse droppings. George Hindemann dropped bleeding badly beside him. The two other House men hobbled into the shadows between the few buildings on the south side of the street. They fired blindly toward Tunstall's paddock as they ran. Across from Tunstall's, a stray bullet caught John Wilson in the back pocket of his trousers. He fell face down and cursing into his new garden.

In half a minute, the hail of bullets stopped.

With a shout, Billy Bonney jumped from behind the low wall. He limped badly and his left leg was stained with blood. He dropped to his good knee beside Brady's body. Five Regulators squatted beside him. Billy picked up Brady's rifle, waved it in the air, and retreated into Tunstall's store. He left a trail of muddy blood in the street.

Six Regulators huddled breathlessly in the deserted store: Billy, John Middleton, Jim French, Fred Waite, Henry Brown, and Frank McNab. Only Billy was wounded. Outside, George Hindemann bled to death.

The street cleared quickly when the gunfire started. Townspeople ran for cover and stayed hidden. Sean stood up behind the water trough. He wiped green manure from his bare hands to his trousers. Then he plunged his raw hands into the ice cold water until all of the muck dissolved. Wiping his hands on his muddy duster, he pulled his Peacemaker, opened the gate, and spun the cylinder. Putting the handiron back in its holster, he started across the street.

Sean stopped beside Sheriff Brady and Hindemann. He knelt in the impression made by Billy's bloody leg and felt Brady's throat for a pulse. He felt none. The other man lay face up, staring into the purple morning sky. There was no need to touch him.

Standing, Sean stepped onto Tunstall's front porch and pushed open the door. He took care to leave his duster flopping across his holstered weapon.

"This ain't your fight, Sean Rourke," Billy said calmly. He sat in a plain wooden chair. His bloodied hands tied a knot in a piece of dress fabric which he wrapped around his left thigh. The boy's fair-skinned face was more pale than usual. His bluish lips seemed slightly shrunken from shock and made his front squirrel teeth protrude even more. He looked pained and frightened.

"That was cold-blooded murder, Billy."

The wide-eyed Regulators behind the counter trembled visibly. When Sean looked hard at them but did not push his duster away from his holster, the men side-stepped like a muddy chorus line toward the hallway leading to the back room. When the last of them disappeared, only the sounds of their boots running across the hardwood floor filled the storefront where Billy nursed his leg.

"Not much of an army," Sean said coldly.

"If you come here as a House man, then let me stand up and fill my hand fair and square." Billy glared up at the tall man in the doorway.

Sean stepped inside and closed the door behind him.

"Fair and square like you done Brady?"

"Who's talking?" Billy frowned. "I seen you with Morton and the rest."

Sean's brow pursed above his nose.

"What about Morton?"

"When Morton done Tunstall. I was in the trees above the road. I seen it all." Billy paused to take a deep breath when he twisted a stick which he had passed under his tourniquet. "And Patrick, too." He looked up with narrow eyes.

"Patrick?"

"Patrick was with me in the woods. We both seen you riding with Morton's gang when he did Mr. Tunstall. We seen it all."

Sean's broad shoulders dropped as if from a physical blow. His jaw sagged and the good side of his face twitched.

"I ain't no House man." Sean stepped closer to the sitting man. The teenager's trousers on the left side were soaked in dark blood. "You're going to bleed to death in that chair."

"Maybe."

"You need to get up to Doc Ealy's."

"I can't walk." For the first time, Billy's voice betrayed the slightest whimper. He did not flinch when Sean extended his hand. A trace of William Brady's blood was dry and brown on his fingertips. The large hand grabbed Billy's upper arm and pulled him out of the chair. When Billy stood, he left a puddle of blood on the coarse wood.

Sean came around to Billy's side and lifted the wounded man's left arm until it was around his shoulder. Billy had to stand almost on tiptoe to reach.

"Come on, Billy."

The boyish gunman hesitated, grimacing with sudden pain radiating up his spine.

"But you're one of Brady's deputies."

Sean looked down into Billy's tortured eyes. He looked more like a hungry urchin than ever.

"I am. And you're my brother's friend."

Billy blinked and leaned on the big man who held him erect all the way to Taylor Ealy's house.

BEFORE NOON, A buckboard crossed a shallow ford in the swollen Rio Bonito. Alexander McSween and his wife rode back into Lincoln. Their wagon left deep ruts in the soft street. They looked neither to the left nor to the right when they passed William Brady's body, which still lay facedown in the mud. For nearly two hours, no one had come forward to drag the town lawman out of the soggy dirt. He lay where he fell. Neither his wife nor their eight children knew yet that, in an instant, they had become a widow and orphans.

When the spring sun stopped and hovered in the southern sky at noon, a blue line of sweating men road two abreast into Lincoln from the west. Twenty-five troopers from Fort Stanton had answered Sheriff Brady's Sunday call for the Army to keep order if the Regulators rode across the river.

Their white officer, Captain George Purington, dismounted ahead of his double column of black cavalrymen of Company H, 9th United States Cavalry. He stood beside Brady's riddled corpse, which was beginning to stiffen and rise out of the mud on rigid elbows. The soldier looked up at his weary men.

"Clean this up."

Chapter Thirteen

ARMED SOLDIERS PATROLLED the single street when Patrick and Liam rode sleepily into Lincoln on Monday afternoon. A provost guard blocked entry to John Tunstall's store and Attorney Shield's office. When Liam briefly stated his military pedigree, the black cavalryman at the door cheerfully spilled a quick story of assassination and anarchy. But the street was quiet.

The brothers turned and led their horses by hand down the street and tied them at the Wortley Hotel. Inside, nervous men packing sidearms filled the boarding house. Sean looked up from Jesse Evans' table when his brothers entered. Patrick paused to look for Melissa and Bonita. He saw neither through the dense fog of tobacco smoke.

"What the hell is going on here?" Patrick still looked tired when he spoke. Sean looked closely at Liam who looked worse than tired.

Without rising, Sean studied his brothers and addressed them collectively.

"We won't being going to the lawyer today. Billy Bonney killed Sheriff Brady this morning. Deputy Peppin has taken his place as sheriff. You remember Captain Purington from when we rode in?"

Patrick nodded.

"Peppin ordered Purington to arrest McSween and that other one of your chums who fancies himself a shooter.

What's his name? He plays with his handiron."

"Rob Widenmann?"

"That's the one."

"Are they in jail?" Patrick's narrow eyes scanned the table where Jesse Evans and his Boys sat in front of half a dozen empty shot glasses per man. "The House men will kill them for sure in there."

"That's what McSween said," Sean said quickly before Jesse could take a breath. "So Purington has the bunch of them under guard in a wagon to take them to the fort for safe keeping. Has Mr. Shield and Mrs. McSween, too. They'll all be gone within the hour, from what I hear."

Liam seemed unsteady on his feet. Sean pulled a chair for him from another table. The oldest brother still had not stood up. Liam slumped heavily into the seat while Patrick remained standing, hat in hand.

"Is Billy dead?"

"Not yet," Jesse interrupted. "They say he took a round and someone carried him to Doc Ealy's. Doc ain't saying. Billy's hiding out somewhere in town." The gunman, called Captain by his friends, smiled. "We'll find him." He glanced at his men who sat red-eyed and full of cheap whiskey. "There ain't no rush."

"How's Melissa?" Patrick asked. There was no point in whispering in the noisy saloon.

Sean looked down at his own neat row of empty glasses.

"All right, I guess."

"Well, then. There ain't no reason for Liam and me to stay, is there?"

"None that I can see. Pa's ranch is yours anyway—yours and Liam's. Signing them papers ain't but for finishing it up legal-like. Peppin says the judge'll be in town next week. You can come back then." Without thinking, Sean lifted an empty glass to his lips and licked out the last drops. "I'll be right here."

Patrick shrugged and lifted Liam bodily out of his chair.

The two brothers pushed their way through the cantina.

Standing in the mud in the last of full afternoon daylight, they paused to watch a parade pass. Blue shirts and black faces on horseback led an open wagon toward the west. Three glum men and one plain-faced woman sat in the back. Looking up, Patrick remembered a woodcut illustration in a book about the French Revolution.

As a misty spring darkness fell softly around them, Patrick and Liam rode slowly out of town to the ranch. By the time Cyrus Buchanan's welcoming light in the window greeted them, Billy Bonney mounted a horse in the Tunstall store's paddock. Wincing from the pain beneath clean bandages on his leg, he spurred his mount out of Lincoln toward the southeast and the Regulator's hidden camp at San Patricio. There, Billy could take comfort from his own kind.

SPIRIT KEEPER CAME to Liam three nights in a row. But she left no spirit posts behind. Liam wondered if she were satisfied by merely making moccasin footprints in the thawed ground visible with daybreak.

In the churning cesspool of steer hooves from Chisum's cattle, Patrick never noticed human footprints in the black ooze.

Thursday morning, April 4th, Cyrus heard the floor boards creaking in the single greatroom of the ranch house. With only one eye open, he watched the shadow of a figure block out the red embers in the dying hearth. When the front door opened, a gust of wind carried enough moist, piney scents for Cyrus to know that dawn was an hour away. He climbed out of his bed roll and walked in stocking feet to the closed door. Opening it, he saw Liam's thin frame silhouetted against distant mountains beneath sparkling stars.

"Liam?"

The youngest brother neither startled nor turned around.

He just stood in the cool breeze and watched the spruce trees against the sky. The wind could be heard in the mountain air. Midnight advection fog climbed the mountains and kept the air humid enough for sound to carry for a mile. So Liam and Cyrus could hear the wind rustling the treetops and growing from the gentlest whooshing sound into a chilly blast in their faces.

"Liam?" Cyrus in his red woollies laid his large hand on the young man's bony shoulder.

"She's come for me, Cyrus."

"Who's come for you, boy?"

"A Cheyenne spirit-keeper."

"Here? Impossible."

"She left spirit-posts every morning down at South Spring. I seen them with my own eyes." Liam's voice was a whisper full of pain and resignation.

"With hair on them?"

"Yes. Every one. Her child's, must be."

Cyrus squinted into the darkness. They both looked west where the sky was purple-black. Behind them, beyond the house, the sky was dark gray with stars still shining. The retired sergeant could not doubt the sign. He had seen them over the years near bodies of frozen Indians whose hard bodies were flecked with red gouges where lead bullets had pecked at them like sculptors' chisels on dry stone.

"So that's what eating at you?"

Liam nodded without turning his face from the mountains.

"What does she want with you?"

Liam laughed out loud before he answered with his voice cracking from grief.

"Mackensie's raid, maybe? I don't know."

"Impossible." Cyrus tried not to sound impatient. "That's nine hundred miles from here, boy."

"There ain't never been born no Indian woman who could walk nine hundred miles just to make you touched in the head."

Liam faced his friend for the first time.

"I seen her sign for the last three days."

Cyrus looked down at Liam and then up toward the last of the night.

"Maybe she's done with you. Maybe she ain't coming tonight. It's almost daybreak anyway."

Liam shivered in his white longjohns and bare feet.

"She ain't done."

WHEN TAYLOR EALY shouted at Sean to never darken his doorway again, the tall man left the physician's home at ten o'clock, Thursday morning. The physician-preacher would not permit such words to be uttered under his roof where his beautiful wife cuddled in bed with their two small daughters. The six-month-old baby still suckled.

Sean shuffled back to his table at the Wortley. Melissa Bryant waited on tables but her eyes never stopped when her gaze passed over him. He sat with Jesse Evans. No one sat with them. Sean leaned forward so he could speak in subdued tones to the captain. He asked for and received the outlaw's word that Sean's question would be kept in confidence and that Jesse would ask no questions.

Sean was surprised when Jesse's cheerful face became serious. The look in Jesse's eyes made Sean believe that his secret was safe. Sean wondered if perhaps murder does create a peculiar brotherhood. Jesse never once glanced over toward Melissa as Sean spoke.

"Roswell, Sean. You need to go to Roswell."

"Roswell? There ain't nothing there."

"Nothing more than two, maybe three, cabins. I know." Jesse spoke softly and earnestly. "There's a doctor who lives just off the main road. Lives in a bark hut. You'll see it from the stage road. White folks won't go near him. He ain't quite right. They say he's from New York. Done opium or something and rotted out his mind. But the Indian Agency lets him see to the reservation when the cholera's up. Maybe they figure it'll take him, too. But some of my boys has taken womenfolk down to him when they was in the family way. He's got an herb tea the Apache taught him. He ain't no butcher like up in Albuquerque or Santa Fe. Just that there concoction." Jesse smiled for the first time, only for an instant, until the expression on Sean's face made him serious again. "The tea will fix your problem."

"You sure?" Jesse lifted his shot glass as if making a whispered toast.

"I know it for a fact."

PATRICK RODE BESIDE Billy Bonney in warm, noontime sunshine. He had resisted, but Billy made his case that John Chisum expected all of the Regulators to ride no matter what Governor Axtell had done to their commissions. Sheriff Brady's assassin had pointed to Chisum's cattle which were keeping Grady Rourke's estate out of bankruptcy.

Billy's invitation was just as well for Patrick. He had endured Liam's morose distemper since Brady's death Monday. Escaping from Liam's black mood was worth thirty-five miles in the saddle. Riding southwest from Lincoln, Billy and Patrick met a dozen Regulators riding south out of San Patricio. They all followed the Rio Tularosa. Dick Brewer, twenty-seven, took the lead.

Rumor had it that some of William Morton's possemen who killed John Tunstall were in the area. So Patrick went along, expecting nothing but a respite from Liam's depression. Cyrus stayed behind with Liam.

By noon, the hills opened on rocky farm land, hardly worth tilling. The riders looked down on the Mescalero Apache Reservation. Joe Blazer's sawmill stood near the Indian Agency building. Both were rundown and weather-beaten.

During the Civil War, Joe Blazer had been a dentist and

some people called him Doc, whenever they ventured this far into the outback to his business known as Blazer's Mill.

While the Regulators shuffled around the sawmill and ate lunch at the Indian Agency, a lone rider approached from the opposite direction. Dick Brewer pointed and smiled. Andrew Roberts rode closer to the mill. Roberts had been in Morton's killing posse in February.

"Like I said," Billy grinned toward Patrick through his crooked teeth. The men took up position inside the sawmill.

The Regulators waited inside until Roberts dismounted and tied his horse to the hitching post. Then, one by one, the gunmen came outside. Each pulled his long duster from his handiron. Patrick did not touch his weapon and remained in the shadows of Doc Blazer's office in the sawmill.

When Andrew Roberts stood beside his horse and looked up at men facing him, it was too late to retreat.

"You're under arrest, Andrew Roberts," Dick Brewer called. His right hand rested on the walnut grips of his holstered sidearm.

"Says who?"

"We have warrants for Morton's posse signed by Justice Wilson."

"He ain't justice no more. Not in Lincoln County. You're the outlaws now; not me."

"Lay down your piece," Brewer ordered.

The odds were fourteen to one, not counting Patrick who had not come out. Roberts lowered his hand and smiled.

The out-numbered House man cleared leather in a heart beat. He cracked off one shot as he dove headlong into the sawmill office. Behind him, Dick Brewer rolled his eyes, sighed once, and fell backwards. Roberts' bullet had blown his forehead off and shreds of his brain ran red and gray down the white-washed wall of Blazer's Mill.

As Roberts rolled into Doc Blazer's office, Patrick charged past him into the sunshine. Each man was so surprised by the other that neither popped off another round.

Patrick rolled in the moist earth until he felt far enough away to jump to his feet and run for a safe corner of the mill.

For ten minutes, the Regulators peppered the dentist's office with gunfire. Roberts kept up a brave volley from inside. When the barrage of small arms ended, Roberts lay in a pool of blood and intestinal juices, fatally gutshot. Brewer was dead and Billy Bonney was slightly wounded in the arm, four days after taking his leg wound in Lincoln.

When Patrick stood up in the silence, he felt a splinterlike sting on his left arm. Raising his hand to his shoulder, it came down bloody. A ricochet had creased him between the elbow and shoulder. The wound was not serious. Pain was quickly replaced by white-eyed anger. He stood shaking in the sun beside two dead bodies. Patrick wished that one of the bullets had ripped out Billy's throat. But the boy gunman just laughed at Patrick's side. A fierce light seemed to burn in Billy's pale eyes.

It was almost midnight Thursday when Patrick rode home alone. By the time Cyrus met him at the door, his left arm was badly swollen. Brown, dried blood caked to his shirt. Cyrus was aghast.

"Dick Brewer's dead along with one of Morton's men. Down south of here at Blazer's, near the Indian Agency.

"You're hurt."

"Just grazed. Damned Billy won't be happy till I'm in the ground beside Tunstall."

Cyrus stood aside so Patrick could come in out of the pitch darkness. Blinking at the bright fireplace, Patrick looked for Liam.

"Where's Liam?"

"Outside, by the well."

Patrick tossed his duster onto a chair.

"What the hell is he doing outside at midnight?"

"Waiting."

*   *   *

WORD OF THE Blazer's Mill shootout went mouth-to-ear throughout Lincoln by Friday noon. Passersby on the dirt street spoke in hushed voices of yesterday's deaths of Dick Brewer and Andrew Roberts. They spoke as people do in a sickroom. The war between the House and the Regulators was a contagion not fit for public discussion among decent people.

Jesse Evans brought word to Sean of Patrick's wounding at the mill. Jesse knew no more than escalating rumor—and that he was glad that he had not ridden out with Roberts.

Sean had not stood outside Melissa's doorway since Sunday. He half-remembered arguing with her, if a man can argue with a mute woman. He thought of the physician in Roswell who had a potion for ending pregnancies. The picture rattled around his mind like a vague pain: the kind that cannot be located with precision, yet prevents sleep none the less. The counsel of Jesse Evans and the memory of the hurt in Melissa's breath-taking eyes tumbled together inside Sean's head in a single tangled mass of grief. Sean already regretted knocking on her door.

"Mama can't come out now," Abigail said without any hardness in her voice.

"She didn't come to work today."

"No. She's sick."

"Sick?" The coming of spring would bring with it the diseases and infections that the mountains' hard winter had put to sleep for five months. "How sick?"

"She throws up every morning. Today it just started later than usual. She said it would stop in another few weeks."

"Did she eat something what went bad?"

"I don't know. I ain't sick. Must be different."

Sean felt people watching him from the street and stores.

"May I come in, Abbey?"

"What if you get sick?"

"I'll take my chances."

"All right."

The little girl opened the door wide and Sean walked inside as he removed his hat. Melissa sat head-bowed at the little table. Her face looked gray.

"Abbey said you was sick."

Melissa looked toward her daughter and shook her head when the child was not looking at her. The mother waved quickly as if to say Nothing Serious.

"Good," Sean said slightly breathlessly. "Good. I'm sorry to bother you. But I can't find Bonita. It's Patrick, my brother."

Melissa's face perked up. She wiped her mouth on a napkin and pulled her long black hair from her face. The open door on the stove cast a red glow upon her moist cheeks that gave the illusion of health.

"You heard about the sawmill yesterday?"

The woman nodded.

"Patrick got wounded." Sean choked on the last word.

The sickly woman stood up and went quickly to his side. She touched his drooping shoulder covered by the threadbare duster.

"Jesse told me. He don't know how bad. I can't go to him just now. I thought maybe that . . ."

Melissa stopped him short with her index finger across his bearded lips. She pointed to the wall and Abigail followed her finger to a heavy blanket on a peg. The child took the blanket from the wall and handed it to her mother. Melissa picked up a basket from a corner and pushed a pile of bed linen inside. Then she kissed Abigail on her forehead and opened the door. She waited for Sean who stood with his chin on the collar of his dirty shirt.

In the early afternoon daylight streaming through the open door, Melissa saw a tear roll down the purple side of the big man's face.

*   *   *

"My name is Lieutenant Colonel Nathan Augustus Monroe Dudley. Effective this date, Friday, 5 April 1878, I hereby take command of Fort Stanton, by order of the War Department. Captain Purington is hereby relieved of duty for transfer elsewhere at the Army's pleasure. We wish him well. Dismissed!"

The colonel took off his steel spectacles and two lines of black troopers fell out of formation and returned to their duties that included keeping a loose guard on Alex and Susan McSween, Robert Widenmann, and David Shield. He walked beside George Purington.

"Our job is fighting Indians, not keeping the peace in some rat-hole hamlet." Lt. Colonel Dudley's breath already smelled of alcohol in the middle of the afternoon.

"With my respects, Colonel, Governor Axtell ordered me to respond to Sheriff Brady's request for assistance."

"I know that, Captain. But we weren't ordered to impose martial law. Without it, we are doing nothing but exposing these troops to a potentially hostile situation. Africans or not, these are good men who don't get paid to be civilian deputies."

Captain Purington stopped walking across the open parade ground in the center of the fortress which had no stockade walls.

"Colonel Dudley, it's all your problem now."

The senior officer surveyed his new command. Not far away, Alex and Sue McSween strolled the campground like they were on a picnic safely removed from Acting Sheriff George Peppin's men.

"Thanks, Captain. Makes me wonder who the hell I offended in the War Department."

"Colonel, they must have been mighty important."

The retiring commanding officer had to smile. Colonel Dudley did not.

*   *   *

PATRICK ROURKE SAT alone on the front porch of his father's
home. He wore shirt sleeves in the unseasonably comfortable afternoon sunshine. One sleeve bulged where a clean
bandage was wrapped around a poultice of pine tar that
Cyrus had made to draw out any infection in the surface
wound. Armed with a soldier's knowledge of battle dress-
ings, the ex-sergeant hoped to see what the Army surgeons
called laudable puss within a week. Inflammation would
mean that the flesh wound was healing. A clean wound
would be a sure sign of deep rot with blood poisoning certain to follow.

Liam had been working on fence repairs since before
daylight. He had not slept more than an hour after Patrick
returned from the sawmill. Cyrus helped him dig post holes
in the thawing earth. The big man never strayed far from
Liam, whose eyes were only thick black circles of thinning
skin. Only Patrick saw the buckboard approaching at four
o'clock. He squinted down the lane to make out its single
driver.

Patrick could see the sky reflected in the driver's incredibly blue eyes even before he recognized Melissa's pale face.

Chapter Fourteen

LIAM SLEPT IN THE BARN FRIDAY NIGHT SO MELISSA BRYANT could have his bed in the bedroom, which had a door. The woman's eyes reflected her relief when Patrick took off his still-bloody shirt to show her his minor wound. But she silently changed the brown bandage anyway since infection can come quickly to a wound made by a dirty lead bullet on an arm born to work in a barnyard.

Melissa tore the linen in her basket into neat strips of white muslin, which she piled atop the bureau in front of the portraits of Sean and Grady Rourke. From the bottom of the basket she retrieved a covered plate overflowing with fresh meat and biscuits from the Wortley's kitchen. Cyrus recognized the taste of Bonita Ramos' cooking. Melissa nodded when he asked if Bonita had sent the meal that was set in front of the three hungry men.

Patrick had insisted that she not drive the buckboard back to Lincoln after dark. So Cyrus bedded down in the great-room and Patrick took the loft. Only Liam did not eat their first real meal since leaving South Spring River Ranch. He pushed his meat and potatoes from one side of his plate to the other like a small boy stacking his food to make it appear that half had been eaten. "It's all right," Cyrus gently told Melissa when Liam took four blankets and trudged alone into the darkness toward the barn. "He ain't himself right now."

The oil lamps were extinguished well after midnight.
When Cyrus and Patrick heard the woman close the bedroom door, they laid awake for a long time—Cyrus by the
hearth and Patrick beyond the top of the wooden ladder.
Each man stared at the ceiling and tried not to think of
Melissa undressing under their roof. Each felt ashamed
and each knew that the other did not nurse such sordid
longings.

Alone in the dark barn, surrounded by the earthy and
musty smells of dozing horses, Liam's nighttime thoughts
were also filled with images of a woman. But his wore a
blanket brightly colored with Cheyenne medicine hexes.
Although the fifth night of April was comfortable, especially inside the now tight barn warmed by five horse
bodies, Liam did not strip down to his woollies. He only
removed his boots before climbing into his heavy blankets
on a bed of hay.

Liam's empty stomach churned as if looking from side to
side for food. At two o'clock in the morning, one of the
horses whinnied when the growling of Liam's narrow belly
disturbed its horse dreams. The man opened his eyes and
blinked. He pushed his curly blond hair from his forehead.

He was not surprised to see dark eyes shining down at
him from five feet away. Sitting up, he pulled his single, top
blanket to his chin to keep out the night chill blowing in
through an open side door. He had slept with three blankets
under him since cavalrymen know that bodies sleeping on
the hard ground loose heat into the Earth rather than into the
air through the top blanket.

Liam's eyes were already adapted to the dark and he
could see Spirit Keeper clearly. Four of the horses in their
stalls slept silently, standing upright with one rear hoof
cocked against their other back foot. The fifth horse from
Melissa's wagon was too tired to sleep standing after drag-
ging its feet through five miles of mud. So he slept on his
side with his feet straight out in front of him like a colt. The

weight of the animal's body on his lungs made him snore like a grandfather.

Spirit Keeper faced Liam for a long time, perhaps an hour. The longer he looked at her, the clearer her features became: dark skinned, black eyed, and hair flowing to her waist in back. Liam was surprised at how young she was. While he sat transfixed, she opened her robe which was long enough to reach the dirt floor. She pulled out a spirit post.

The woman slowly knelt on both knees. She leaned forward, put her hands together, and began to scrape out a small trench as long as the sacred post. Liam could hear her moaning softly as she peeled back each layer of the hard ground. In the dark, he imagined that he could see her fingers bleed. When the hole was two feet long and six inches deep, she laid the post into the tiny grave and carefully adjusted the hair bound to the top of the post. Pushing the soil on top of the stick, she whispered unintelligibly.

In the cavalry, Liam learned that many of the Indian Nations believed that hair was the visible extension of the human soul since both grow every moment of life. Some medicine men would let their hair grow until it dragged across the ground to show the power of their souls. Keeping the hair of a dead loved one was a special honor. It comforted the soul of the dead. And attaching a dead child's hair to a spirit post was the most sacred rite of all—done usually by the grieving mother.

Liam had only two close friends in the Army. One was Sergeant Buchanan. The other was a skinny cavalryman from back East. Being raised in a tenement slum, the second soldier had a strange respect for the Nations he was paid to destroy. He studied their ways and spoke of such things to Liam around many campfires. From him, Liam learned that those Nations that scalped their enemies did not always do the ugly deed for the coups hanging on a lodge pole. Many did it to keep part of their defeated foe's soul as the ultimate battle trophy. Liam's friend's soul now dangled from a Sioux pony's war bridle.

When Spirit Keeper's little ceremony was finished, she stood and wrapped her blanket around her shoulders. Even in the dark, Liam could see perspiration glistening on her prominent cheeks.

"What do you want with me?" Liam asked. Although his lips moved, he did not hear his own voice and the horses around him did not stir. He still sat cross-legged under his blanket.

Spirit Keeper made a fist, which she beat gently against her breast in time to her heart.

Liam bowed his head and closed his eyes. His breath came in slow, shallow movements. He seemed to sleep sitting up, as peacefully as the horses around him. When he opened his eyes and looked up, Spirit Keeper was watching him closely. She cocked her head slightly to one side. Moonlight glinting off puddles of melted snow cast its coldly white glow through the door and upon her face. Liam was mesmerized by the pale light on her dirty cheeks. She was not only young; she was beautiful. The man let a weak smile cross his silent lips.

Then Liam reached under his bed of hay and pulled out his heavy revolver. Looking up into the old soul shining out of her young eyes, he slowly pulled back the hammer which clicked into the cocked battery with a cold, metallic sound.

The smile slowly evaporated from Liam's lips as he raised the weapon with his right hand and laid the muzzle against his temple. He was surprised that the steel felt so cold against his skin.

"YOU AIN'T WELCOME here." Lt. Colonel Dudley spoke on whiskey vapors over his plate of cold hash. "I have Sheriff Peppin's word that you will not be molested. There ain't no evidence that you played any role in Sheriff Brady's assassination. I can't say the same for William Bonney or the Regulators. You, your wife, Shield, and Widenmann are free to leave."

"Peppin will murder us like he did Tunstall." Alexander McSween was perspiring heavily in the office of Fort Stanton's new commanding officer. "I demand that you keep us here for our own protection."

Colonel Dudley pushed his breakfast away and stood up behind his desk.

"This is a United States Army post, Mr. McSween. When you commit a crime against the United States of America, I shall take you into custody until a United States Marshal rids me of you. Until then, the War Department has no jurisdiction in civilian brawls. You may leave after you have taken breakfast in the mess if you don't mind eating with darkies. If you don't leave by ten o'clock, I shall have a company of troopers escort you off post and dump you by the side of the road. Your choice, sir."

"I demand protection, Colonel. At least for my wife."

"Sir, I remind you that you were born in Canada. I don't even know if you are an American citizen. Either way, this interview is terminated." The slightly inebriated officer squared his shoulders. "Orderly!" A black private threw open the door. "You are dismissed, Mr. McSween. Orderly, show our guests to the mess tent and have the First Sergeant hitch up their wagon. They will be leaving directly."

"Yes, Colonel. This way, sir, if you please."

"Our blood is on your hands, Colonel." The lawyer slowly buttoned his black frock coat with some ceremony. He pulled on his short gloves like gauntlets.

The colonel smiled sourly.

"I shall try to live with that, Mr. McSween."

When the door slammed, Colonel Dudley stood red-faced for a moment. Then he sat down, opened a desk drawer and brought out a bottle.

*   *   *

Patrick and Cyrus watched Melissa putter about the tiny kitchen and pantry. Both men noticed her rosy face and the slightest bulge at her waist. They glanced at each other until she turned around with a tray of biscuits and hot gravy. The silent woman set the platter down and bent low near the hearth for the coffee pot. The two men waited for her to sit and serve herself before they reached for the plate. All three turned around with their mouths full when the doorway opened to a clear and bright Saturday morning. With gravy trickling down his chin, Patrick stood with his mouth open when Liam entered. He walked slowly. His feet never completely left the floor as he approached the table. Liam was nearly bald.

"Jesus Christ, boy," Cyrus shouted. He wiped his mouth with the back of his sleeve.

Liam stood emaciated and trembling slightly. His scraggly beard ended at his ears. Where his shoulder-length hair had been, raw stripes criss-crossed his scalp like a bloody field newly plowed. The top of his head was brightly white above his tanned and wind-burned face. Faint trickles of blood erupted from his dry shave by a hunting knife sharpened on an oiled stone.

"My God, Liam," Patrick whispered. "What in the name of Heaven?"

Liam pulled out a chair and sat down heavily. Melissa's blue eyes were wide. But her beautiful face showed no terror. That corner of her mind that had been brutalized eight years earlier instantly sensed the presence of another tortured heart. Instead of fear, she was overwhelmed by a brooding sense of kinship—to what, she had no clue.

Melissa stood and took two steps to Liam who sat, head bowed. Beside him and without a word, she put a hand firmly on each of his shoulders. She touched him as gently as she would cradle Abigail after a bad dream. Cyrus and Patrick both stood at their places and looked down dumbstruck.

Liam felt Melissa's hands. When he looked up into her face, his gray eyes were dry and empty. He looked sideways to Cyrus who bent slightly forward when Liam's pale lips moved and his words came out softly.

"Spirit Keeper is done with me, Sergeant. All she wanted was my soul and I gave it to her. I'm free now."

The smile that spread across Liam's gaunt face was terrifying. Melissa raised her hand to his cheek and she pushed his face against her soft chest. Liam was still smiling when tears rolled down his face.

SAN PATRICIO WAS not even a hamlet. A cluster of clapboard and adobe shacks nestled together against winter's howling wind and summer's ferocious heat. As hard-faced men with heavy handirons rode into the camp beside the swollen Rio Hondo, the bivouac of Regulators almost made a town out of the widening in the dirt road.

By Sunday afternoon, Alex and Susan McSween and their company increased the population to nearly fifty. Billy Bonney and John Chisum were there to greet them like returning heroes. But warm welcomes were muted by the sober remembrance of Dick Brewer only three days dead.

Susan McSween should have been uncomfortable in the company of so many desperate men. But they were like an army and the Regulators regarded her husband as their general. If San Patricio were to become a sovereign country, the austere and aristocratic John Chisum would become its Secretary of State.

With Lincoln and its House men only twelve miles up the road, San Patricio became a tiny garrison. Pickets were posted around the camp in case George Peppin might lead a posse to disband the Regulators once and for all. By Governor Axtell's proclamation, they were now vigilantes and nothing more.

A few Hispanic families called the San Patricio settlement home. They did not welcome these narrow-eyed shootists. The white men packing Colts and Remingtons on their hips steered clear of the Mexicans and their Catholic hovels. Regulators stayed close to the adobe home commandeered for their field headquarters.

Alex McSween's pink face continued to wear the wrinkled brow of man uncomfortable in his new element. Firearms did not fit well into the lawyer's soft hands. He sat uneasily at John Chisum's table. Billy Bonney looked like a pimple-faced boy beside Chisum's square jaw and leathery face. The grown men tolerated the teenage firebrand in their midst since he had been close to John Tunstall. Also, like McSween, he had walked both sides of the street in Lincoln and he knew the House.

When Billy had first arrived in Lincoln in the fall of 1877, his first job had been as a field hand for William Brady. Across Billy's lap was Brady's rifle, taken from his corpse heavy with Billy's bullets. Now Billy was a known killer: he had killed a man in Arizona only eight months before he shot Sheriff Brady. It had been Dick Brewer who hired Billy away from Brady's ranch to work on Tunstall's Rio Felix spread. By this April 7th at San Patricio, all but Billy were dead.

"How long do we just sit here?" McSween sounded nervous. His eyes twitched from the sweat running down his forehead.

Chisum took a long drag on his pipe. The cattle baron was calm and dignified.

"Until the time is right for us to take Lincoln back."

BONITA RAMOS TOLD Sean that Melissa had returned to town Sunday evening. He waited until Monday morning to knock on her door. As he walked up the street, he could feel the town's ragamuffin children pointing from the shadows at his disfigured face. His pace quickened.

"How's Patrick?"

Melissa nodded and forced a smile. Then her face darkened.

"And Liam?"

The woman lowered her face and shrugged. She shook her head. They were alone since Abigail was across the street in a one-room schoolhouse with ten other children ages six to thirteen. The big ones helped the little ones.

"Is he sick?"

Looking up, her expression was difficult to read.

"The soldier and Patrick will take care of him. He ain't much more than a boy."

Melissa nodded. She agreed.

Sean sat for half an hour. He sipped hot coffee and avoided Melissa's penetrating eyes. They haunted him as much as the memory of Grady Rourke who would not stop invading the tall man's fitful sleep. He did not look at her until his tin cup was empty.

"Melissa, I need to get away from here for a while."

Instantly, her eyes filled. Sean continued before they could spill over into his heart.

"I want to take you with me, if you'll come. Abbey can stay with Bonita. She's a good woman and I think Abbey likes her." Melissa nodded. "Maybe we could take the buckboard over to Roswell. Jesse says it ain't as high as here and spring will come earlier down there." His brow pursed slightly when he looked into her face. "Will you come with me, Melissa Bryant?"

Blinking her moist eyes, she reached across the table and touched his hard hand. Sean Rourke wished that his heart would stop.

FOR THE WEEK after Melissa left Grady Rourke's ranch, Liam recovered his strength, if not his mind. For the first time in five weeks, he slept without dreams or demons. He was back on his feed and Patrick wondered if they would run out of flour and bacon before week's end. When Liam cleaned his supper plate before the other men, Cyrus would silently shovel food from his plate into Liam's.

Liam's bald head scabbed over into rows of grotesque black crust. During meals, he wore his floppy yellowed, cavalry hat so Patrick and Liam could eat.

While Liam worked on a new garden plot close to the fenced-in graves of Grady and Shannon Rourke, and three infants too new to have been given names at all, Cyrus and Patrick would speak in hushed voices in the privacy of the barn. Cyrus explained to Patrick the ways of the Cheyenne. When the soldier spoke of campaigns and bloodied grass, his words came in clipped and carefully chosen sentences. His stories of the cavalry felt incomplete to Patrick. But he asked no questions and ex-Sergeant Buchanan offered no answers.

THURSDAY, APRIL 18TH, Cyrus saw the buckboard first. He called to Liam and Patrick who came up from the barn. Bonita Ramos drove the two-horse team and Abigail Bryant sat at her side. The child was bright-eyed and happy.

The three men greeted their guests in warm sunshine. Patrick lifted Abigail out of the wagon and Cyrus put his large hands around Bonita's waist. Cyrus noticed baskets and blankets in the back of the buckboard.

"On a picnic?" the soldier asked.

"We come to stay for two weeks," the little girl replied cheerfully. "Uncle Sean said it was all right."

Patrick glanced at Liam and then toward Bonita.

"Sean and Melissa have gone down to Roswell for a few days."

"Oh." Patrick looked thoughtful. "Do you need a place to stay? We have room, I suppose."

For her answer, the dark-faced woman leaned over the wagon's side and pulled out two of the baskets. Wonderful vapors drifted from the food inside. She handed two baskets to each man and half of the blankets to Abigail. Bonita took the last of the blankets in her arms.

"I thought you lived at the Wortley?" Patrick struggled to make sense of the unannounced visit.

"I had a room there and a shack in town. But the House is out of business and Jimmy Dolan sent word down from Santa Fe to move the help out. He's up there with his leg broke."

"What do you mean out of business?" Cyrus looked as confused as Patrick.

"Closed up yesterday. Dolan just sent word down to lock the doors and be done with it. The House ain't in business no more after yesterday. Ain't that something?" Bonita did not sound too disappointed.

"What will you do when you go back to town? Where will you work?" Cyrus was already feeling a vague sense of trouble. A woman—and a child—had just shown up on his doorstep, which was not even his.

"Maybe Tunstall's store will open again. Maybe Jimmy will keep the Wortley open and let me come back. I'll worry about all that when Melissa and Sean come back next week."

Cyrus shook his head as Patrick led the way toward the house. He was already figuring where the menfolk would sleep: perhaps one in the greatroom and two in the barn. The thought of sleeping in the barn made Patrick look at Liam's covered head as they walked into the house.

Bonita looked at the morning's dishes still laying on the table. Longjohns of white and red were strewn over the backs of several chairs. Abigail giggled as Patrick quickly gathered up the underwear.

"A woman's touch for a few days won't do no harm in here, Patrick."

"I suppose not." He sniffed the baskets of food. He had not been hungry when she rode up the lane.

"I'll fatten the lot of you up by the time Melissa gets home."

Patrick heaved the longjohns up into the loft. He and Cyrus removed their hats in the house. Liam did not.

Bonita looked at Liam. Although his face had filled out, his eyes still had a sickly blankness to them. The light behind them that the woman remembered seemed extinguished.

When Liam felt her eyes looking at him, he reached up and removed his hat too.

Bonita and Abigail stepped back and gasped. Liam only smiled, except for his eyes.

Chapter Fifteen

THE ROUGH TRAIL WAS NARROW AND BUMPY FOR NEARLY SIXTY miles on the south bank of the brown waters of the Aqua Negro creek. Where the thawing ground completely absorbed the stream, the trail continued eastward for another six miles.

The rocky trail ran parallel to the main stage road, twenty miles to the south which skirted the north bank of the fast-running Rio Hondo.

Sean drove the wagon on the grinding trail to avoid packs of Regulators who might be prowling the main road, which led westward to San Patricio.

The buckboard bounced to the crest of a dry hill over-looking two shanties perched precariously beside the Rio Hondo.

"Roswell," he sighed in comfortable, early spring sun-shine on Wednesday, April 24th.

Melissa's eyes widened at the dismal landscape. The expression on her silent, sweating face asked if the rock farm down the hill was the end of seven days of tooth-rat-tling trail?

Sean pointed to a shack of peeling pine timbers that stood five hundred yards away from the two main buildings, which sat side-by-side. The lone structure had a paddock beside it. Two mules stood motionless in a corner.

"A friend of Jesse lives in that one. Jesse said we would

be welcomed. We can stay the week, he said."

The woman shrugged, wiped her brow, and rested her hand on Sean's knee. A flick of the reins moved the team down the hill. Sean stopped at the white-washed, bark hovel.

He lifted Melissa from the wagon when the cabin door opened. A man came out, so filthy and grizzled that Melissa inched slightly behind Sean.

"Jesse Evans sent us."

The man stepped into the bright afternoon sunshine. Although he was a white man, his face was blackened by the high desert sun and wind. He did not wear a hat. Looking closer at his sweating cheeks, Melissa saw brown, irregular patches of skin cancer. His face looked worse than Sean's.

"I see," the dishevelled man said. "Jesse ain't sent nobody during the winter. You be the first this year. I'm Hansen."

"First name or last?"

"Don't matter out here."

"I'm Sean Rourke. This here is Melissa."

The man with one name gestured with his right hand as if he were tipping an imaginary hat. He squinted toward the couple and studied Sean's face so long that Sean felt uncomfortable.

"You Grady's boy?"

"Yes." Sean sounded surprised.

"Your father came down here over the years. Twice, maybe three times."

Sean felt suddenly sickened. He already longed to leave.

"Soup's hot. Unhitch the animals and put 'em in with mine." Hansen turned his back on his guests and shuffled inside. Melissa looked up at Sean. She waited for him to unhook the two horses and lead them inside the fence. The gate was secured by a leather thong. The horses dropped their faces toward sparse scrub grass. Two mules only

flicked their pointed ears in the horses' direction, but did not
go over to investigate.

"SONSABITCHES!" JIMMY DOLAN shouted over a telegram on
his sickbed in Santa Fe. "Sonsabitches!" Acting Sheriff
George Peppin shouted in William Brady's old chair.

"Sonsabitches!" Billy Bonney began shouting half a
mile from the Regulators' headquarters at San Patricio. He
skidded his winded horse to a halt so hard that the animal
tossed a shoe with the curved nails still attached. The horse
hobbled under saddle into a paddock full of Regulator
mounts.

John Chisum and Alex McSween came out into the
Thursday afternoon sun. Sue McSween kept close to her
husband. Rob Widenmann came out with his shiny, oiled
Peacemaker drawn and cocked. Looking up at the lawyer,
Billy continued a little jig in the mud with his breathless
chorus of "Sonsabitches, Mister McSween!" Widenmann
put his piece to leather when he recognized Billy.

"What the hell's got into you, Billy Bonney?" Chisum
demanded, completely out of patience. Three weeks of
beans, flour tortillas, and rancid alkaline water had blown
the starch and dignity out of the cattleman during hourly
trips to the privy.

The teenage killer stopped twirling and wiped an oily
glaze of sweat onto his filthy sleeve.

"The Grand Jury, Mr. Chisum! The Grand Jury down in
Mesilla done ex-honored Mr. McSween there. I slipped into
Lincoln this morning and got it straight from the telegraph
operator."

"Exonerated, you mean?" McSween asked, stepping
slightly in front of Chisum.

"That's what I said, ain't it? They threw out the case
agin' you on old man Fritz's business." Billy slapped his
dusty hat on his frayed knee. "And damn if they didn't 'dite

Jesse Evans and three of the Boys for bushwhacking Mr.
Tunstall. Jimmy Dolan got 'dited too."

"Indicted, you mean?"

"Yes, sir." Billy paused and caught his breath. Wiping his
face again, he seemed to puff out his narrow chest against
his suspenders. "And I'm famous now, too. Old Judge Bristol done indicted me for doing over Sheriff Brady and his
deputy. Seems the judge also made John Copeland sheriff
and fired Peppin." Billy was beaming to the little crowd of
men who gathered around him. "Hell, Mr. Chisum. We're
all famous now. The judge indicted the whole damned lot of
us for killing Andy Roberts at the sawmill."

Billy exhaled a long breath and closed his cracked lips
over his buck teeth. His bulletin had exhausted him more
than his break-neck gallop to San Patricio. A murmur simmered through the assembled Regulators—itinerant
farmers, mainly, and hired hands masquerading as gunfighters.

"Well," John Chisum said gravely. He was more concerned about diarrhea than politics. "Well. Congratulations,
Alex."

Chisum screwed his hat on and pushed through the
throng toward the nearest out house.

Susan McSween squeezed her husband's arm.

"Thank God, Mac."

SATURDAY MORNING AFTER three nights sleeping in Hansen's
back room, Melissa awoke in a soggy pool of perspiration.
Sean stirred in his longjohns. Half of his body was wet with
the naked woman's night-sweat.

First light drifted faintly through the glassless window
above their narrow bed. A blanket hanging limply from the
doorway separated them from the dark-faced man who slept
on the dirt floor in the shack's one main room. Even through
the cloth door, Sean could smell Hansen's sleeping body.

Melissa lay on her back. Her eyes were closed tightly and she breathed in short, shallow breaths through her wide-open mouth. While his mind struggled to waken, Sean propped his head on his hand and looked at the woman. Dawn made her moist body glisten. He studied her ample breasts and the new roundness of her belly that rose and fell with each labored breath. Sean sucked in his wind at her breath-taking beauty.

Then Melissa jerked upright with her eyes still closed. She grabbed her shining midsection and doubled over against Sean. She groaned softly from deep inside. It was the first sound Sean had ever heard from her.

"Melissa?" He leaned over her and pulled the matted hair from her face. She softly whimpered and rocked against his thigh. In the light of a new day, Sean could see that her face was flushed. Her breath came more and more rapidly in short, weakening pants. When Sean touched her side, he was stunned to feel how cold she was even though the stuffy room was warm and she was bathed in sweat.

"Hansen!"

Sean jumped out of bed and threw the blanket out of his way at the door.

"Hansen!"

"What?" The man on the floor rolled over and belched.

"Wake up, damn you." Sean shook the sleeping man. He could hear the cot in the back creaking as Melissa shivered.

"What the hell?" Hansen opened his eyes and labored to focus in the grayness. "What do you want?"

"Melissa is sick. Real sick." Sean was panting almost as fast as the woman.

"All right, all right." Hansen sat up and rubbed his eyes. When he stood up, he passed gas like an old cow. "Let's have a look."

Sean put a hand on the man's wet shoulder.

"Let me cover her first."

Hansen blinked and looked up at the tall, frightened man.

A genuine smile crossed his face, which softened in the half light. He touched Sean's arm.

"My boy, I'm a physician. I've put my fingers in white ones, black ones, Indians, and Mex ones where their husbands ain't even poked. Let's have a look."

The sudden expression of compassion on the stinking man's face made Sean release his tight grip.

"That's better. Bring the lamp."

Sean carried an oil lamp and followed Hansen into the room.

The round man laid his palm on Melissa's face. He gently pushed her over onto her back. He placed his hand on her bare abdomen below her navel and pressed gently. The woman exhaled hard with a little yelp. Then he pushed her smooth thighs apart and lowered the lighted lamp. When Hansen put his dirty hand between her legs, Sean grimaced at the semi-conscious woman's violation. The physician sniffed his fingers for only an instant.

"Ain't no discharge yet. Probably by tomorrow. Sponge her down from the basin and keep a blanket on her. Her body temperature will be low for a few days. Very dangerous, but she's young and strong." He raised the lamp and saw pained outrage in Sean's scarred face. "I was a surgeon in the war. I've seen it all and smelled it all." He shrugged. "Human women, birthing cows, ovulating mares: they're all the same to me. I've had my hand in them all, up to the elbow sometimes. I don't see their sex, Sean." His sun-baked and malignant face looked strangely comforting. "Just keep her warm."

Hansen shuffled out into the main room and Sean bent over Melissa who had drawn her legs up to her breasts. She cried softly with her eyes closed. Sean took a rag from the basin and began to wash her trembling back.

The physician returned with a bottle of clear liquid.

"This is mineral oil. Force-feed her as much as she'll keep down. Make sure she's awake so you don't choke her.

The oil will coat her stomach and bowels so she don't spit up her mucous membranes."

Sean looked sickened when he took the heavy bottle. He nodded and Hansen went outside to the privy.

For three days, Hansen had graciously fed Melissa tortillas made from a special tin of corn flour. The men ate from another tin.

The physician had laced Melissa's corn flour with the very bottoms of corn stalks grown in a large garden beside the paddock last summer. Corn grown in the blistering New Mexico sun has high concentrations of nitrate in the lower stalk. In Melissa's beans, he had added finely chopped rye grass and lamb's-quarters leaves from a patch of sweet soil in a low area where sparse rain collects in the spring. Fast-growing rye and the weed concentrate nitrate.

Toxic levels of nitrates can kill livestock. The most common symptom of nitrate poisoning in the barnyard is miscarriage of calves and foals in the spring. Hansen carefully measured the dose to be strong enough to pass through Melissa's placenta, but not powerful enough to kill her.

Hansen returned to the gurgling sound of the mute woman vomiting mineral oil.

JESSE EVANS CLIMBED down from his lathered horse on Monday morning, April 29th. Two of his Boys were at his side.

"Doc Hansen," Jesse said as he wiped trail dust from his eyes.

"Captain. Long time."

"Ain't needed the recipe for a long time. Guess I'm slowing down."

"Maybe. Your friends are still here. The woman ain't doing real good. She's pretty well stove up in the gut."

"You didn't kill her, did you, Doc?" Jesse smiled.

"Ain't killed one yet. She passed the fetus yesterday.

She'll be back on her feed in a week or so."

"Good. Now, where's Sean?"

"In the privy." Hansen's malignant facial lesions sweated in the spring sun although the morning breeze was chilly. "He ain't much of a doctor, I'm afraid."

Sean walked toward the four men. He stopped for a moment and then continued when he recognized Jesse. He did not know whether to thank the outlaw or kill him where he stood.

"You look like hell," Jesse said warmly, putting out his hand. Sean did not take it but toyed with his hat instead.

"Ain't slept since Wednesday. Melissa's got the gripes something fierce." Sean's wasted face was gray and anguished.

"I seen it before," Jesse said softly. "She'll bounce back. Mine always did after the hard days."

Sean nodded and looked at the ground.

"I need you to ride with us, Sean. I'm sorry." Jesse sounded like he meant it.

"I can't leave Melissa. Not like this. She ain't woke up for two days."

"Like I said, it won't wait. I done for you." Jesse's face hardened and he shrugged toward the physician. "Now you have to do for me."

Sean was boxed. The sensation caused him to make fists at his sides.

"Just one day at most, Sean. Doc'll tend the girl, won't you, Doc?"

"I suppose."

"I could stay and do it," one of the Boys said as he licked his sweating lips. "Yes, sir. I'll doctor her fine."

When Sean's hand moved sharply, Jesse grabbed his wrist hard.

"Easy." Holding Sean's arm, Jesse looked at his man. "You keep that mouth of yours shut, boy."

Sean relaxed and Jesse released his grip.

"The Regulators is riding this afternoon. Jimmy Dolan has a man among 'em who got word to town. We got our own bunch in Lincoln, but we need your piece to be sure. Won't take long. Just want to scare them vigilantes off, is all. Few hours maybe." Jesse looked quickly toward the squalid hut. "I done for you."

Sean sighed and shook his head. His pale eyes were sunk into black pits.

"Doc?"

"Don't you fret. I'll take good care of her. Ain't I already?" Hansen smiled, but not the kindly way he usually did.

"Sure. All right, Jesse. Let me see Melissa first."

"Fine. Don't take too long."

Sean waved with the back of his hand when he went inside.

"She really going to pull through, Doc?"

"I think so, Captain. She's still heaving blood, though, from both ends. But she don't really know what's happened to her. She ain't got her head back yet. Don't keep Sean too long." Hansen looked troubled.

"I won't. He'll be back by sundown."

The sun was not yet high in the clear southern sky.

"Good."

Sean returned. His handiron was strapped to his side. He wore his duster in the cool air.

"Let's get on with it," Sean said firmly.

"You got it," the captain nodded cheerfully. He and his men mounted while Sean walked to the paddock where his saddle sat on the fence.

THE HEART OF the defunct House's enterprise for rustling John Chisum's cattle was a place known as Seven Rivers. Sixty miles due south of South Spring River Ranch, Seven Rivers marked the rich farm land where the Pecos River joins the Rio Peñasco. Not a town but a settlement of small ranches, Seven Rivers centered on Robert Beckwith's spread. When Jesse Evans' Boys rustled Chisum cattle to sell them for the House to the Indian Agency, the Beckwith ranch was the stolen steers' first stop. It was on Beckwith's property that Chisum's brother found a pit full of buried, jingle-bobbed steer ears.

When Jimmy Dolan announced the demise of the House on April 17th, the cattle rustling industry at Seven Rivers ended with it. During the twelve days which followed, the suddenly destitute ranchers formed their own little army and proudly named it the Seven Rivers Warriors.

At first light on Monday the 29th, thirty-five Warriors rode toward Lincoln to proclaim their loyalty and their guns to the new sheriff, John Copeland, to help arrest Sheriff Brady's indicted killers: the Regulators.

Ten of the Seven Rivers Warriors had ridden in Bill Morton's posse which murdered John Tunstall.

Sean Rourke and Jesse Evans with his two men rode into the Seven Rivers Warriors' camp, eight miles south of Lincoln at evening twilight. Sean recognized Deputy Billy Mathews and former sheriff, George Peppin, among the mob of armed men.

As the sun set over the Sacramento Mountains to the west, three more riders ambled up the road to Lincoln. On Jesse's command, the Warriors took horse and disappeared into a stand of pines along the trail. There was no dust from the muddy road. When the travellers reached the Warrior's position, they trotted out from both sides of the trail. The three new men were surrounded before they could draw their sidearms.

"Frank McNab!" George Peppin called. "Don't drop them reins."

Before McNab's horse could stop spinning with fear, his two companions bolted ahead into the darkness, leaving McNab behind.

"We got the general," Jesse laughed loudly.

Frank McNab was the new field leader of the Regulators, nominated after Dick Brewer died at Blazer's Mill.

"Captain," McNab said with his voice trembling. He dropped his reins and Peppin grabbed them to steady the terrified prisoner's mount. McNab raised his hands, palms out. "I ain't holding, Jesse."

"No you ain't, Frank."

Jesse Evans smiled broadly, pulled his revolver and blew McNab from his horse.

"For the love of God!" Sean shouted behind Evans.

Jesse looked over his shoulder and glared hard at Sean.

"Ain't you ever been in a war before, Sean Rourke?"

A dozen Warriors laughed and dismounted. They led their horses one hundred yards further toward Lincoln and tied their animals to the trees. Then they set about building small fires for the night. When the whole band moved toward the campsite, they left Frank McNab alone and dead on the road, just as John Tunstall and William Morton had been left before him.

After hot coffee and dried, jerked beef beside the trail, a dozen Warriors remounted and started northward.

"You come, too, Sean," Jesse ordered.

Sean walked closer to the outlaw who stood holding his animal's leathers.

"For how many more murders, Jesse?"

Jesse's face opened into a narrow grin, nothing resembling a smile.

"However more it takes. You're in it now, Sean. Mount up."

"And if I don't?"

Jesse thought about the question for a long moment. His blue eyes looked down toward Sean's right hand resting on the walnut grip of his holstered handiron.

"I'll send a few of my Boys to look after the dumb girl for you."

Sean blinked and moved his hand away from his side. With his head bowed, he walked to his horse and climbed up heavily. He spurred at the walk toward Jesse who mounted his own horse.

"That's better," Jesse said with that same hard grin.

Half of the Seven Rivers Warriors mounted and the rest stayed behind. They reached Lincoln well after dark and marched straight for the House. Jesse and the rest slept on the floor. Sean sat in a chair, smoked his pipe, and watched the fire in the hearth until morning.

Tuesday morning, the Warriors poured coffee and twirled their loaded cylinders. When daylight was bright enough, Jesse looked across the street toward Alex McSween's adobe compound. When one of the Warriors pushed the front shutters open, a volley of gunfire raked the House windows.

A hail of lead crossed the dirt street from both directions. Regulators had taken up positions in McSween's abandoned home during the night. While the armies blazed away, Sheriff Copeland rode hard out of town toward Fort Stanton.

Bullets chipped away at the adobe House and the McSween home for half the day. Although cussing from both strongholds rang eloquently across the deserted street, no one was hurt in either fortress of two-foot thick, baked mud.

The ineffective firefight continued past noon. Hungry men in both camps loaded and fired mechanically. They seemed to enjoy the noise.

Sean remained in the rear of the merry assembly. He never unholstered his weapon.

Firing slackened when a bugle call rang down the street.

Fourteen black cavalrymen slowly rode in single file down the center of the street. No one fired from either position. Sheriff Copeland rode at the end of the column.

"You all come out now," Copeland shouted. "One more round from any of you and you'll pay hell to the War

Department." Copeland screamed like a drowning man.

One by one, the Seven Rivers Warriors and the Regulators emerged into an overcast afternoon. The street was nearly obscured by a stinking cloud of sulphur.

Sean came out last, with Jesse Evans at his side. Jesse's fair complexion was bright red from excitement. Sean's weathered face was darkly grim.

"Real easy now," Copeland shouted. "We ain't here for no picnic."

Within two minutes, a dozen men stood on either side of the street with the cavalry mounted between them. Copeland looked down at George Peppin.

"George, you mount up your people and come back to the fort with me." Then the new sheriff turned toward the Regulators. "And you boys just git. Mount up and ride out of here. I don't want to see nothing but dust. Go on now!"

"Where's Frank?" one of the Regulators shouted across the street.

"Ain't coming," Jesse Evans called back.

The Regulator drew his pistol half out of his holster.

"How much lead can you carry and still walk, boy?" Copeland shouted hoarsely.

The Regulator let his weapon slide back to his side.

"Now mount up, the lot of you." Copeland rode to the front of his column of troopers.

The milling armies shuffled toward their corrals. Through the clearing smoke, Sean looked across the street. His blurry eyes met Patrick and Cyrus. The brothers turned their backs on each other and found their nervous horses and mounted.

"Sheriff?" Jesse said from horseback beside Copeland. "This here is Sean Rourke. I promised him he could ride back to Roswell. He's one of us."

Sean appreciated the gesture, but his skin prickled at the thought of being one of Jesse's Boys.

"All right," Sheriff Copeland said. "You ride east and

don't turn around till you get to that stinkhole. Billy Mathews? You ride with him as my deputy."

The Seven Rivers killer and lawman nodded and
mounted.

"Thanks, Sheriff," Sean stammered. His eyes burned
from the gunsmoke.

"Go on now." At Copeland's nod, Jacob Mathews rode to
Sean's side.

Sean pressed the sides of his horse and trotted toward
the far end of town. Out of the corner of his eye he saw
Patrick and Cyrus riding slowly westward. Neither brother
spoke across the terrible killing space that separated them.

WHEN MELISSA BRYANT awoke Tuesday morning, she
needed half an hour to collect her wits. When she could
finally sense the world around her, she felt weak and cold.
But she was fully conscious for the first time in a week.
Her hands moved down her naked body and stopped at her
stomach.

She felt starved and tender. Pressing on her belly, she
experienced penetrating pain, which radiated down to her
toes. Melissa turned her head and labored to focus on a
figure beside her cot. The form was bent over and busy.

In the morning light, she concentrated hard. Just before
her terror engulfed her entire body like an ice-water wave,
she remembered the foul-smelling man named Hansen. She
recognized him from behind.

Squinting, she saw his wrinkled hands with their black
fingernails gathering scraps of white cloth. Looking closer,
she saw that the linen was stained brown with blood. In full
possession of her weary mind for a moment, she pressed her
belly again and felt the pain. She watched the man and his
bloody rags. Pain and blood; blood and pain. She forced her
brain to make sense of it. Then she remembered vomiting
until she thought her spine would rupture.

She would have called for Sean, but she remembered that she had no voice—only pain and blood and a feeling deep inside which no woman could explain to a man, even if she had a voice.

Hansen picked up a bottle of amber liquid and sucked it hard. He swayed slightly when he put it down to fold his rags. He did not turn around when Melissa silently put her bare feet on the dirt floor.

The round man saw a blinding white flash behind his eyeballs. He felt like his sweating head had plunged into a kettle of boiling water.

Hansen stumbled slightly when he turned slowly around. He blinked at an incredibly beautiful and naked woman standing an arm's length away. Then he tasted blood, warm and coppery.

The dark-faced man lowered his arms to steady himself. His eyes fluttered slightly and the vision of the woman felt like a dream. When his right arm would not come down, he looked at his armpit. The handle of a carving knife protruded at an odd and amusing angle.

The blade severed his aorta and each round of blood surging from his heart poured into his lungs instead of riding up to his brain.

Hansen raised his chin and looked at the woman who seemed to hover just above the dirt floor like some glistening, naked bird.

With his last breath, he laughed out loud.

Chapter Sixteen

CYRUS BUCHANAN SPOKE TO HORSES AND HORSES SPOKE TO him. If a cavalry horse went lame, even the white officers of the black regiment would lead the animal to Cyrus so he could lay on hands like some prophet of old. "Frying pans," stripeless troopers would say to describe those huge black hands. Cyrus would touch the shoulder or haunches of the nervously pawing animal and black horse-eyes would blink only once into the trooper's black man-eyes. Then the horse would sigh a long musty hay-breath, lower his weary neck, and give himself completely to the tall man's kneading fingers. "Sergeant Buchanan's hands just know," General Custer said before taking his trusted mount from Cyrus and trotting off to Little Bighorn.

Neither horses nor Chief Crazy Horse nor Chief Joseph frightened Cyrus Buchanan. Boy soldiers, even white ones—especially the white ones—would drift close to the quiet sergeant after their first battle as if Cyrus radiated a kind of gravity. Liam Rourke first met him that way: so terrified that his new blue trousers were as wet as the fresh blood on the prairie grass. They would come casually, one by one, as if by accident. And they would ask where courage comes from since the sergeant's supply seemed deep and sure. He would smile the way he put horses to sleep and he would say to them as he had said to teenage Liam: "Do the Lord know your name, boy?" Those who understood would

222

ride hard the next day; those who did not understand would ride slowly.

Only children scared Master Sergeant Cyrus Buchanan. He did not speak to them and they did not speak to him. Then Abigail Bryant came to Grady Rourke's ranch.

Like the horses, the little girl blinked only once at Cyrus and he blinked back. For two weeks, she was his small, bright-eyed shadow. When fences went up in spring sunshine, Abigail held the big man's hammer. She needed both hands.

When the loving attention of Bonita Ramos could not ease the child's homesickness for Melissa, Abigail would sit cross-legged by the crackling hearth while Cyrus told nighttime tales of Sioux and Cheyenne children who could close their eyes, hold their breath, and become red-winged hawks when the new Moon was just right. His stories rode clouds of pipe smoke and Abigail watched the smoky words rise toward the darkened ceiling as if the deep and gravelly voice somehow made magic. When her chin would finally touch her nightgown collar, Cyrus would carry her to Bonita's bed like some terribly fragile treasure. An hour later, Bonita would leave the sleeping child but would be beside her when she awoke in the morning and asked for Cyrus.

Cyrus and Bonita slept together in the main room with Patrick in the loft. Abigail returned Patrick's cheer and kindness with a child's careful civility. Liam slept with the horses in the barn. The thin man who never removed his hat frightened her, so he kept his distance.

Liam would join the sudden family at the table where his appetite returned and was rewarded by Bonita's cooking. His face lost its carved-out look. But his gray eyes were still dull like something important behind them had been removed against his will.

When Abigail would allow, Cyrus tried to keep close to Liam as he had done in many cavalry skirmishes with the last of the prairie Nations. It was hard for Bonita not to resent the divided attention.

"He don't need no nursemaid, Cyrus."

"Soldiers take care of each other." His whispered words carried a sharp edge.

"You ain't soldiers no more."

"It don't change once you've seen the elephant"—what soldiers call their first battle when other words are too painful.

In the middle of the second week, Bonita became ugly.

"You poke me but you talk to him."

With Liam in the saddle chasing Chisum cattle out of their new garden, she did not have to lower her voice.

"The boy ain't right no more, woman. I need to keep an eye on him."

"He ain't no boy. He's a grow'd man. Besides, he's got Patrick and Sean, when he comes back from Roswell."

Cyrus tossed the empty bucket down the well and wiped his brow when the rope snapped taught like a hanged man. His eyes flashed when he turned to face her. Abigail was in the barn brushing the horses with Patrick.

"That scar on my side? A Nez Perce bullet did that last August by the Big Hole River in the Montana country. We was detached to Colonel Gibbon's white troops. Old Looking Glass hisself attacked us. Thirty of our men was killed. Thirty-nine was wounded. Them white boys left me for dead; left me face-down in the blood of eighty-nine dead Indians. Only young Liam over there rode back for me. Bullets was still flying when he come back for me. No other white man on God's Earth done that." His angry face softened. He gently touched Bonita's face with his leathery palm. "He come back for me. Now he thinks he ain't got no soul. All the power I poured into that boy got cut out by some Cheyenne ghost or something. I have to go back for him like he done for me."

Bonita kissed his hand that lay lightly upon her cheek.

"I'm sorry, Cyrus. You done right by Liam. But you don't believe that Injun magic do you?"

Cyrus looked away toward the garden where Liam listlessly waved his coiled rope at marauding steers with floppy, torn ears.

"That boy believes it. Either he shaved his own head or a real spirit-keeper come and done him. I ain't saying which." He looked down at the woman who loved him like no other in his forty-odd years. "Whatever done him, he's broken." He touched his chest. "Broke inside. I seen that look on soldiers before. Then they die."

The tall man turned quickly and hauled on the well rope like the water bucket were filled with liquid lead. Bonita touched his arm and walked back toward the house.

WEDNESDAY, MAY 15TH, marked the end of Abigail Bryant's third week without her mother. Even when Cyrus was at her side on his hands and knees in the vegetable garden not yet greening, each puff of spring wind made her look past him toward the lane. April's mud was beginning to turn into brown powder as the thin mountain air and bright sun dried the countryside. She searched each brown dust devil for a buckboard and bright blue eyes.

The little family had settled into an easy routine during the nearly three weeks since the shooting fest across Lincoln's only street. With the Seven Rivers Warriors back on their end of the Pecos and the Regulators in their San Patricio garrison, Patrick decided that the fragile peace was prime time to ride into town for another month's worth of supplies. Billy Bonney had ridden out to the ranch on Monday to announce that with the House doors closed tightly, Tunstall's store had been allowed to reopen by Sheriff Copeland as the only mercantile in town. He even suffered Sue McSween to run the place in spite of her tart mouth, so long as her husband stayed at San Patricio.

Patrick stood in the paddock at midmorning and tightened the leathers on the single horse secured to Bonita's buckboard. Abigail had begged to go along, but Bonita thought the risk too great if the conflict should flare.

Looking again around Cyrus, Abigail was the first to see the lone rider leading a little dust cloud down the lane. She had also first spied Billy two days earlier. Before Patrick could look up, Abigail was running break-neck toward the rider and shouting "Sean! Sean!"

Patrick threw the wagon's reins over the fence and walked to where Sean stopped his sweating horse and dismounted slowly. Sean's face was haggard from lack of sleep. Dust caked his face with a dull brown patina except for his eyes that became wet when Abigail jumped into his arms.

"Where's my mama?" the child demanded, finally breaking down into a little girl's whimpering.

Sean ran his gloved hand through her long black, Apache hair.

"She's in Lincoln, Abbey."

"Home? Without me? I want to go to town with Patrick."

Sean pushed her to arm's length but held her shoulders firmly. Patrick saw terrible grief in his brother's wornout face.

"Abbey, your mama is fine. She's been a little sick, is all. But she'll be just fine real soon. You have to stay here until she's well. Please."

The child lowered her face and tiny dust clouds burst where her tears fell between her shoeless feet. Cyrus led Bonita toward Abigail. When Cyrus touched the girl's shoulder, she turned and buried her wet face into his belt.

Sean straightened his back and looked at the group around him.

"Where's Liam?"

"Riding the fence line," Patrick said. "He'll be back by supper."

Sean nodded.

"You've planted Ma's garden?"

"Yes. A little early, but Abbey couldn't wait." Patrick glanced at the grieving child.

Sean looked up at the perfect sky. He blinked perspiration out of his eyes.

"If the weather holds, it'll be all right." Sean lowered his face toward his brother. "We need to talk. Maybe Bonita could take Abbey to the garden for a little while."

Abigail gripped Cyrus tighter. Her hands could not touch against his wide back.

"I'll take her," the sergeant said. "Come now, girl."

The brothers and Bonita watched Cyrus lead Abigail by the hand up the hill.

"Where's Melissa?" Bonita asked softly.

"Jail," Sean sighed. "She done killed a man in Roswell. Deputy Mathews took her in last week."

"My God!"

"Murder?" Patrick whispered.

"Yes. A doctor. She was sick and he hurt her, I suppose."

"Where were you, Sean Rourke?" Bonita spoke through clenched teeth.

Sean glanced at his brother.

"I had to go to Lincoln for a day."

Patrick said nothing.

"Let me take care of my horse and we'll talk."

Sean led his mount into the paddock where the buckboard horse stood dozing in harness. He unsaddled and turned the animal out to nibble the new spring grass poking through the dried mud.

The brothers and Bonita walked into the house. Sean took off his hat and slowly looked around. It seemed smaller with the clutter of three men, the woman, and a child.

"Glass ain't come in yet?" Sean asked, looking at the faded, torn blanket covering the front window.

"No. What about Melissa?" Patrick watched his brother with hard eyes. He saw a murderer of John Tunstall, and maybe, of Frank McNab. Patrick forgot about William Morton, the dead deputy.

Sean sat down and rested his battered hat on his dusty knee.

"Coffee?" Bonita tried to sound civil.

"Please." Sean took the warm cup and closed his eyes when he wet his throat. "Thanks."

Patrick and Bonita pulled chairs close to him.

"Melissa put a butcher knife through the doc. Mathews was riding with me from Lincoln a week ago. He arrested her, took her to Lincoln—I went, too—and the new sheriff locked her up till Judge Bristol comes up in two months."

"Two months!" Bonita's eyes were wide. "Abbey won't last another two months with her mother locked up."

Sean sighed so deeply that the chair creaked.

"It looks like she's got a home here with all of you." Sean's voice was pleading. "I just come by to tell you. I'm going back into town to stay close to Melissa until I can figure all this out."

"This ain't Abigail's home," the woman argued. "Home is with Melissa."

"What's Sheriff Copeland's take on this? It sounds like self-defense to me." Patrick sounded earnest, like he was trying to make sense of it.

Sean swallowed hard.

"He wants to hang my Melissa." The words stuck half way up his throat.

"Jesus, Mary, and Joseph! How could you let this happen?" Tears streamed down Bonita's face.

"I had to leave Roswell. I owed Jesse."

"Jesse! For the love of God! Jesse?"

"I had to, Bonita. That's all there is."

Bonita stood, sneered like an animal, and stormed out of the house leaving the brothers to an uneasy silence.

"Why did you take Melissa to Roswell, Sean?"

Sean looked down into the black grounds of his coffee.

"There was something there I needed to do."

"What could be so important that you had to take the woman?"

Sean did not look up. "It don't much matter now."

Before Patrick could speak, a horse snorted and the brothers looked toward the door Bonita had left open.

Liam stepped into the shade of the doorway. Sean squinted up at his youngest brother. Liam nodded and focused his blank eyes on Sean. Then he stepped inside and removed his hat.

"God Almighty," Sean gasped.

SEAN REACHED LINCOLN well after dark. He left his horse in the Wortley's paddock and went directly to the cantina to wash the trail from his throat. Jesse Evans and half a dozen of the Boys filled a table. Some smoked; some chewed. Two men scooted sideways so Sean could sit next to Jesse Evans.

"Did you see your brother today?"

"Yes. The little girl misses her mother."

Jesse nodded. A flicker of compassion crossed his wild face.

"Did you see Sheriff Copeland?"

"I did." Jesse missed a brass spittoon for the second time. "He's still set on wanting to hang her when Judge Bristol comes up. Seems to think it'll give them Regulators something to think about if they come back into town."

"But she ain't no Regulator. She's with the House." Sean sounded hollowed out. "Ain't Jimmy Dolan still keeping her, even with the House closed for good?"

"It don't make no sense to me either." Jesse scored a hit and the brass rang dully.

"She ain't too heavy, Captain," one of the Boys laughed loudly. "He better put sand bags on her so we don't get no Bill Wilson again."

The bearded rustler tossed his head back to suck his
greasy glass dry. He felt Sean Rourke's rough fingers grab
his throat. The man tumbled out of his chair backwards with
Sean gripping so hard that he felt his eyeballs getting tight.
Jesse and two others jumped Sean and pulled him off before
he strangled the drunk like Sheriff Copeland hoped to do
with Melissa.

The man stood up, choking. The commotion stopped the
chatter at nearby tables and everyone turned to the distur-
bance in the smoky saloon at midnight.

"Ain't nothing," Jesse called across the cantina. "Just
funning."

Jesse had to push Sean down into his seat. The others
stepped back to their places. The stunned shootist rubbed
his neck and looked toward Sean. Sean's eyes were still
white, but the man with finger-shaped welts on his throat
did not look hostile.

"I didn't mean no harm, Sean. You know we'll help you
bust her out. Right this minute, if you're willing. Ain't that
right, Captain?"

The tone in his voice forced Sean to sit back and stop
twitching. He looked across the room at the fire in the
hearth.

"I'm sorry," Sean said softly toward the fireplace. "It's
just . . ."

"We know, Sean," Jesse said. "Jake's right: We need to
talk about getting Melissa out of Lincoln before the judge
comes up. Next week, maybe."

Sean nodded without looking up. He had heard the
William Wilson story told merrily over drinks at the Wortley cantina. In December of 1875, while Sean was
panning for California gold, Wilson became Lincoln
County's first judicial hanging. He was convicted of
shooting Robert Casey, a House man, in August. When
the sheriff dropped the trap door for the public execution,
Wilson dangled for ten minutes. After the deputies cut

him down and laid him out, he started breathing again. So they hoisted his semi-conscious body back up for another 20 minutes to get it right. The "double hanging" became saloon legend immediately.

"A breakout?" Sean asked as Jesse spit again.

Jesse Evans looked into Sean's tortured eyes. He spoke proudly.

"Ain't that what the Boys is for?"

The murders of Deputy Morton and Frank McNab flashed into Sean's mind and felt as hot as the red embers in the fire. He thought of his brother Liam who had lost his soul or his mind, according to Patrick. He thought of an unclean little man calling him self a doctor who now lay under the soil of his own paddock. And he thought of the look in Melissa's eyes when she saw Sean with Deputy Mathews and put her hand on her empty belly. Sean had last seen that expression at Shiloh, on men who were dying and knew it. He looked closely at Jesse Evans, murderer and cattle rustler.

"But I ain't one of your boys, Jesse."

"Sheriff Brady paid you three dollars a week to be his deputy. Them dollars come from the House. That makes you one of us."

The logic made Sean's skin crawl.

THE RAIN STAYED long and spring came slowly to Lincoln County. By the end of May, the mile-high air was warm in daylight but cold at night. Drifts of old snow remained in the craggy shadows and on the north side of tree stands were the sun never penetrated. Cyrus taught Abigail how to cover their garden at night with old bed linen to keep frost from killing the fragile green shoots emerging from the moist earth. Born on an Arkansas plantation to slave parents, he knew planting.

Monday morning, May 27, Sean and Jesse Evans rode up

the lane to the Rourke ranch. Bonita saw them coming and
called the rest of the household.

Sean and Jesse dismounted and tied their horses. The
fences were finished and John Chisum's steers were kept
well away from the new garden and the house. Jesse suppressed a smile when he walked past the beef with the
jingle-bobbed ears. He thought of piles of those ears buried
down at Bob Beckwith's spread at Seven Rivers.

"You done good," Sean said to Patrick as they walked
toward the house.

"Cyrus is like hiring three good men," the middle brother
said warmly beside Sergeant Buchanan.

"Strong body; weak mind," Cyrus grinned. Family life
clearly agreed with him. The little girl still stayed close. She
loved him and he had no rules but one: Abigail was never
allowed to call him Uncle. His grandfather had been called
that by two generations of white children whose parents
owned him and had owned Cyrus as a child. So Abigail
called him Cyrus as if he were another of her little friends in
Lincoln.

Liam's hair was finally thick enough to cover his scalp
scars. He had put on weight but still looked troubled. All
trace of his youth was gone from his twenty-one-year-old
face.

The five men sat at the table. Abigail sat on her big
friend's lap. Bonita moved between the tiny kitchen and the
table to set out midday supper. Patrick had been to town
after Sean's last visit. But the brothers did not meet when
Patrick shopped for pantry fare at Sue McSween's store.
Patrick noticed that the rains had finally flattened the
ground above John Tunstall behind the store. Only a plain
wooden marker in the soft soil marked his place.

Sean wanted the child to be elsewhere. But she looked
determined to remain perched on Cyrus' knee.

"Jesse and I are going to fetch Melissa tomorrow morning early."

Abigail smiled and pulled on Cyrus' Army-blue shirt. He patted her head.

"How early?" Patrick asked. His eyes narrowed and he looked hard at Jesse.

"Before daybreak."

"I see."

"We thought you three might want to ride with us. There ain't but a handful of cavalry left in town." Sean looked first at Patrick then Cyrus. It was too hard for him to look into Liam's empty eyes.

Cyrus glanced over the child toward Patrick, then at Bonita. The woman's eyes were worried eyes.

"When?" Patrick asked.

"After we finish." Sean avoided Bonita's face when he looked at Patrick. "You rode with them Regulators. There are warrants out for all the Regulators, you know. It could be ugly if you're seen in Lincoln right now."

"Don't matter."

"Then let's eat," Cyrus said.

Within half an hour, all of the plates were empty except Liam's. Abigail ate from Cyrus' plate.

When the table was cleared, Cyrus and Patrick put on their heavy gunbelts. Liam watched, said nothing, and walked slowly into the sunshine in the direction of the garden. Cyrus watched him leave before going into Bonita's bedroom. Jesse, Patrick, and Sean lingered at the table. Abigail sat smiling in Sergeant Buchanan's chair.

Bonita sat on the edge of the bed. Her hands were folded tightly in her lap.

"There'll be trouble," she said softly so the child would not hear.

"Jesse's men will be there. I don't expect no trouble." He stopped directly in front of her. "You keep an eye on Liam."

Bonita looked up with moist eyes.

"He should go with you. His brother got Melissa into this."

"It ain't his fight."

"It ain't *your* fight." A tear rolled down her left cheek.

"Liam can't fight no more."

"But you're not a soldier anymore, Cyrus. You done your share. Liam should go instead of you. Abbey and I need you." She wept freely.

"He can't. That's all there is to it."

"Then tell me why. You said he went back for you in the battle last year. Why can't he go without you?"

Cyrus sighed. He owed her the story. He stepped to the door, closed it softly, and returned to sit beside Bonita. The tall man put a large hand on each of his knees and he spoke to the floor.

"Liam ran that last time. He couldn't fight no more. He seen too much killing. When we was attacked, he ran. He cut himself with a saber half a mile from the real fight and said he were wounded. It happened twice before, but that was the first time he had to hurt himself to stay out of it. When the others found him, they told him I was dead. That's why he went back. He didn't want them devils to cut me open like they done sometimes. The Sioux cut the *cahones* off our dead at Bighorn. That's why our boys in the Fourth under Mackensie went crazy at Red Fork in '76 against the Cheyenne. Liam just seen too much, Bonita."

Bonita sniffed hard. Cyrus patted her knee and stood up.

"What I told you, no one knows but me and the boy."

The woman nodded. Tears ran off her chin. Cyrus had to look away and walk quickly toward the door.

"Let's go," Cyrus said to Jesse and the brothers.

"You'll bring Mama back, Cyrus." Abigail spoke with certainty absolute.

"What about Liam?" Jesse asked. He looked through the open door to the garden where the youngest brother stood against the purple sky. His outline looked dark and sharp and as desolate as an old, bare tree standing alone under a gray, winter sky.

"He'll stay with the womenfolk."

Cyrus touched Abigail's face as he walked into the May sunshine.

Chapter Seventeen

IF A WOMAN COULD WALK, THE GUNFIGHTERS PRETENDING TO be Texas Rangers ran her down like an animal and raped her face-down in the streets of El Paso. If a Mexican woman could not run, the posse took her where she dropped.

When the El Paso Salt War erupted in west Texas in the fall of 1877, a race war gripped the town. For eight generations, local Hispanics harvested and sold salt from El Paso's salt beds. The mineral was community property available for everyone. White businessmen then claimed the salt as private property. After El Paso's sheriff and two *Anglos* were killed, the new sheriff deputized John Kinney, a Mesilla Valley gunman. He hired thirty of his own kind to put down the protest by Hispanic citizens. The sheriff swore the gang in as Texas Rangers.

Ranger Kinney unleashed his Rangers on El Paso. In October, they gunned down nine Hispanic men and began a rape rampage of Hispanic women. Any woman captured was stripped in broad daylight and violated. The proud Rangers called their mob of animals in rut, the Rio Grande Posse. Five thousand citizens fled to Mexico in terror.

During the last week of May 1878, John Kinney shined his tin star and ordered the Rio Grande Posse to take horse.

"One riot; one Ranger," John Kinney shouted as his men mounted in column of twos and rode north toward Lincoln County.

*   *   *

SHERIFF COPELAND'S OIL lamp burned dimly in the court-house window two hours into Tuesday, May 28th. A faintly yellow glow fell gently on water-filled hoof prints in the dirt street.

Sean, Cyrus, Jesse, and his Boys had been drinking lightly at the Wortley since an hour before midnight. On the same side of the street and five doors closer to the court-house, Patrick looked out the window of the darkened Tunstall store. Patrick had gotten word to Billy Bonney at San Patricio to get word to Sue McSween to leave the back door open. She did, and Patrick stood inside a coal mine that smelled strongly of clove, turpentine, and molasses. He did not pace during his three-hour imprisonment to avoid knocking something over and calling attention to himself. The daytime cavalry sentries left behind by Colonel Dudley to keep the peace had retired to their tents erected behind the jail.

The cantina crowd had thinned out since midnight. But two dozen men still played cards and drank bad liquor. No one paid any attention to Jesse's company at their usual table at their usual hour.

By one o'clock in the morning, the men around the largest table at the Wortley's saloon stopped tipping whiskey and began to sip black coffee. Manuel, from the front desk, was doing the night-shift duties since both Bonita and Melissa were gone. The first round of bitter coffee did not impress him. But with the second, he looked into Jesse's eyes and out the dark window and back at Jesse. The out-of-work rustler looked away.

"Ain't no charge for the coffee," the Mexican said softly, pouring the third round of coffee. "*Via con Dios, Capitan.*"

Jesse Evans only nodded. He pulled a pocket watch from his vest, flicked the case open, and studied the face.

"Two-thirty," Jesse said to Sean.

Sean turned to the only black man at the table who sat at his side.

"You still don't have to do this, Sergeant."

The big man smiled and touched his handiron on his hip.

"All right then," Jesse said. He pushed back from the table and the men around him stood up. When all ten walked into the smoky hallway, only Manuel watched them until the last one disappeared. Then he pulled back the curtain on the adobe wall and peeked into the pitch darkness.

Like one great shadow, the men kept close to the buildings on the north side of the street and walked toward the courthouse. They passed Sue McSween's home where oil lamps still burned. Jimmy Dolan's home across the street was dark. One door past McSween's, they paused in front of Tunstall's store and waited for Patrick who came out quickly. Sean took position at Patrick's side without a word. Cyrus walked on Patrick's other side. The three men led the way with Jesse behind Sean. The Boys walked behind Jesse in two ranks of three gunmen.

At the east end of Lincoln, the silent group paused in the darkness just outside the light cast by the courthouse window's lamp. An overcast sky kept the night close to the ground and the air was still, humid, and utterly silent.

Sean was surprised at how the moist air made cocking his Peacemaker sound like a dry twig snapping. Jesse gestured and Sean took five steps toward the courthouse door. His handiron hung at the end of his arm. Patrick and Cyrus pulled their weapons in one motion when the door opened and bathed everyone in ghostly light.

"Come on in, boys," Sheriff Copeland said with stunning civility. He folded his arms so the party outside could see that his did not wear his gunbelt.

"Well, come on. The coffee's hot, but I ain't got enough cups, it looks like."

Copeland stood out of way so Sean could enter behind

his raised revolver. He looked behind the open door and surveyed the single-room structure. No other deputies hid in
the shadows. Sean lowered his weapon but did not return it
to leather. Jesse put his piece in his holster but he left it
cocked.

Melissa sat on the side of a cot. The other cot in her cell
was empty. Two other cells were also empty. The woman
wore baggy trousers and a heavy cotton shirt. Her boots
looked five sizes too big. The cell door was wide open and
Melissa looked through the cage toward Sean.

The last man inside closed the door and Sheriff Copeland
took his chair—William Brady's chair—behind the desk.
Jesse looked puzzled.

"It's a small town, Captain," Copeland smiled. He was
completely calm and looked up at Sean who still had his
handiron drawn. "You hardly need that, Deputy Rourke."

Slowly, Sean put his iron into its holster. The sheriff eyed
the bothers.

"This must be Patrick? You have your ma's eyes, boy.
Ain't there a third one?"

"At the ranch," Cyrus said for the brothers.

"Sergeant Buchanan." The sheriff nodded respectfully. "I
rode with Custer, you know, in '68 when we killed Black
Kettle on the Washita River. Guess you and I have a lot in
common—killing heathens and such as that."

"I suppose," Cyrus said with a low voice that carried no
pride.

The lawman reached into his pocket and pulled out his
watch. Deep lines around his eyes creased when he studied it.

"Damn near three." Copeland put the watch away, looked
up at Jesse and shrugged toward Melissa. "I fed her good
and kept her blankets clean, boys. She's all yours. Now go
on." He put both hands palms-down on his desk. His gunbelt and sidearm hung conspicuously from a peg on the wall
near the open cell.

"Just like that?" Sean was still surprised.

Sheriff Copeland reached for a crumbled piece of paper on his desk. He handed it up to Sean who immediately handed it to Jesse who looked at it for a long moment.

"Peppin?" Jesse laid the telegram back on the desk.

"Effective tomorrow," Copeland smiled weakly. "Governor Axtell is putting me out to pasture. I should be grateful. What with the House armed to the teeth and them Regulators cooling their heels down San Patricio way. Yes, sir, I should be damned grateful." Copeland's tranquil gaze stopped at Patrick and then returned to Jesse.

"Well, all right, Sheriff. Come on, Melissa." Jesse moved sideways so Sean could approach the cell.

Melissa hesitated and looked down at an empty tin plate on the coarse wood floor.

"Let's go, Melissa," Sean said gently. "Abbey is waiting for you at the ranch."

Without looking into Sean's face, the woman stood and walked head-bowed into the front office. Her too-big boots flopped against the floor boards.

"Oh, boys," Copeland said when Jesse opened the front door. The sudden coldness in the cordial man's voice made the hair on Sean's neck bristle. "George Peppin becomes sheriff again, tomorrow morning. But there's more." The retiring officer stood up with his long arms at his sides. His three-day beard opened into a chilling grin. He faced Patrick squarely and he waited for Patrick to focus on his eyes. "Tell Billy and McSween and them others that Peppin sent for help." Copeland savored a pause. "John Kinney and his posse is coming to town. Let them Regulators chew on that stew."

Jesse said nothing. After all, he and Sean still rode with the House and, now, with Sheriff Peppin. But the wind left Patrick's heart in one long breath. Copeland kept grinning.

"Night, boys."

*   *   *

AFTER DELIVERING MELISSA into Abigail's arms before daylight, Sean rode back to Lincoln. Drinking Bonita's coffee and eating her biscuits, he never even wondered if Melissa would have asked him to leave or begged him to stay, if she could speak. Sean knew only that he could not bear to look at her face. Rocking the child on her lap beside the hearth, the firelight played brightly on the woman's face. From across the room, Sean could clearly see new lines around her shining eyes. He had put them there and he could not stay. By full daylight on Tuesday, he was in his lonesome bed at the Wortley Hotel.

Twenty-five hard men rode easily into town from the west on the weekend. Each wore a star pinned to the breast of his trail duster caked with Texas mud. John Kinney led his regiment of rapists directly to George Peppin's office as if he knew the way. Sean watched them pass from his hotel window. He let the curtain fall back against the whitewashed adobe. For two weeks he only left the smoky sanctuary of loud men and cheap whiskey to brush his horse and pick out its feet to prevent a thrush infection from rotting out the hooves of the only real friend he had.

PATRICK TOOK TO Melissa's silent ways. The feelings the blue-eyed woman fired in him made him uncomfortable. If she and Sean were finished, she could not tell him. And without knowing, touching her would be a bitter trespass. When she moved into Abigail's bed, Bonita Ramos moved into Cyrus Buchanan's bed in the greatroom. Patrick bedded down in the barn with Liam rather than trying to sleep in the loft and laying awake all night thinking of Melissa sleeping in the room beneath his floor.

By the time Melissa joined the widening family circle, Liam's hair had grown down to his ears. With his scars cov-

ered, he no longer frightened the child who still kept close
to Cyrus. Liam spent his time riding the fences or weeding
the garden that flourished from what John Chisum's steers
left behind. Melissa liked Liam's quiet ways. The pain in his
eyes matched her own and a peculiar kinship of silence
warmed between them. When Melissa lingered in the
garden with Liam, Abigail would help, too. Liam learned to
enjoy the child's cheerful company although her heart
clearly belonged to Cyrus.

For two weeks, when bedtime came, Abigail would put
her head in Melissa's lap by the hearth, which was still
needed during the chilly, high-country nights even into the
first two weeks of June. Long after Abigail closed her eyes
for the last time, Melissa would sit and listen to the night's
tall tale, riding blue pipe smoke over Cyrus' head. The
mother would watch her daughter sleep and gently stroke
her brow. Bonita would rock in the corner in Grady
Rourke's chair and watch Cyrus tell his stories.

Patrick welcomed the diversion from thinking about
Melissa when Billy Bonney rode casually up the lane on
Saturday, June 15th.

"Mr. McSween and Mr. Chisum sent me." Billy and
Patrick walked through the handsome garden to keep distance between them and the women. Bonita welcomed Billy
like she would greet a toothache. "Sheriff Peppin is supposed to be rounding up a posse to come down on the
Regulators hard. Those Rio Grande boys is riding with him.
We need your three guns."

Patrick knelt and examined the lush green leaves growing
near his parents' grave.

"We're like a family out here, Billy. With the House
closed up for good, Melissa and Bonita have made a home
for themselves here."

Cyrus and Bonita stood at the front of the house two hundred yards away. Bonita kept looking toward the garden and
Cyrus appeared to be comforting her.

"Sort of salt and pepper," Billy smiled, nodding toward the man and woman.

"It don't matter out here." Patrick stood up, several inches taller than the scrawny boy. "The Regulators hardly need us. They got plenty of men."

"Them Rio Grande Posse men ain't like normal shooters. They're stone cold killers, Patrick. You know that. The Regulators is farmers. You know that, too." Billy sounded anxious. Chisum had sent him to do a job.

"I'm a farmer, too," Patrick smiled. He liked the idea.

Billy looked down and poked the rich earth with his boot between a row of vegetables. When he looked up, his eyes were narrowed against the brilliant June sunshine.

"You saw what they did to Mr. Tunstall. You remember that? And you was there when we done Morton. You're part of us, Patrick."

"I never killed no one."

Billy stifled a smile. He had just won.

"You think John Kinney knows that? You're a Regulator to him and his man-killers. Where you think his posse is going to ride if they make it past us?" Billy looked down the hill toward Bonita who now had Abigail under her arm. Melissa stood behind the child. "You know what the Rio Grande Posse does to womenfolk?"

When Billy turned to face Patrick, the eyes which met his were hard and cold. They were the eyes Billy had been sent to find.

"When?"

"Now."

Patrick shook his head slowly as his mind rejected every argument shouting between his ears.

"I'll talk to Cyrus."

"And Liam."

"Liam's fighting days is over. He can guard the women."

Billy shrugged. "It won't make no difference where he gets skinned alive if we can't hold them."

Patrick led Billy back to the house. Bonita glared coldly at him and he never allowed their eyes to meet. When Bonita made supper, she dropped a plate in front of Billy so hard that gravy splashed onto the table.

After they had eaten, all four men adjourned to the barn on the pretext of checking the animals.

"Your woman don't much take to me," Billy said to Cyrus in the privacy of the barn.

"She don't mean no harm."

Billy repeated his story for Liam and Cyrus. His description of the El Paso rapes was so vivid that Billy licked his lips when he was done. Patrick wondered if Billy missed being there to help the Rio Grande Posse.

"I'll go," Liam said suddenly.

"You ain't fighting no posse," Cyrus protested.

"I'll go," the young ex-soldier repeated. "I seen what men like that do to women and children." Liam looked at Cyrus whose mind flooded quickly with red memories. "You seen it, Cyrus."

"What about the women here?" Patrick could not force from his brain the picture of Melissa under John Kinney—Patrick had slept in the barn for two weeks to stop thinking about Melissa under him. It did not work. "Someone has to stay here."

"I'm going," Liam said dryly. Patrick almost shuddered at the wild look in his brother's haunted eyes. "Sergeant, you stay here."

"No, sir. That ain't right. I ain't hiding behind no women's skirts. No, sir."

Cyrus drew himself up and squared his shoulders. He was broader than any two of the three men in front of him.

"Which of us can hold off an army by hisself?" Billy asked, grinning broadly. He was amazed at his own mental powers.

Patrick, Billy, and Liam watched Cyrus wrestle with the question.

"Well?" Patrick smiled, not quite as brightly as Billy.

Cyrus looked at the ground. "All right."

Billy nodded. "Maybe now Bonita won't throw food in my lap."

ON TUESDAY, JUNE 18th, Patrick and Liam had been at San Patricio for two full days. Patrick mingled freely with the Regulators while Liam kept either to Patrick or to himself. He brought his own demons with him and they were all the company he required.

That same day, George Peppin collected twenty men from town to join the Rio Grande Posse. Twenty-nine black troopers from Fort Stanton still patrolled Lincoln's single street. Susan McSween welcomed their protection as she struggled to manage the Tunstall store on her own without help from her husband, or David Shield, or Billy.

Sheriff Peppin kept his private army camped near the courthouse so they would not trigger any hard words with the soldiers.

Cyrus Buchanan tolerated the company of two women and the little girl for a full week. By the 28th, he had gone as long as he could without hearing from Patrick or Liam.

"I'll come back, woman, if I have to crawl."

Bonita said nothing. Tears ran down her cheeks and splashed on the front porch. Abigail stood under Melissa's arm which held her close.

Cyrus handed two loaded, lever-action rifles to Bonita who took one in each hand.

"You know how to use these. There be more cartridges in the box on the mantle."

Bonita sniffed hard. Cyrus looked at her contorted face and then at Melissa and Abigail. He looked over his shoulder and pointed at the lane running past the barn and on into Lincoln.

"You just keep an eye on that road. I'll be coming down it real soon."

Cyrus touched Bonita's wet face and turned quickly toward his saddled horse tied to the fence surrounding the house. Chisum cattle grazed contentedly behind his mount.

Halfway to his restless animal, Cyrus felt a thump against his back. He turned to find Abigail with her arms wide and her face as wet as Bonita's. The child disappeared for a full minute inside his smothering hug.

Cyrus thought about the home he was leaving for the whole ride to Lincoln. Half a mile from town, the road was blocked by two mounted columns of cavalry. A corporal led the black troopers. The soldiers riding slowly west headed toward Cyrus.

The two-striper raised his gloved hand and the troopers halted in the sun.

"Sergeant Buchanan."

"Corporal."

"We've been recalled to the fort, Sergeant. New regulations have come out from the War Department. We can't take no part in civilian peace-keeping no more without there's an armed rebellion. No more *posse comitatus* for the Army. So Colonel Dudley's called us back."

"What about them Rio Grande boys?"

"They're still in town, Sergeant. Riding for Sheriff Peppin. Damned dangerous, if you want my opinion."

Cyrus reined his horse back. The animal was nervous around so many cavalry mounts.

The proud soldier lifted his hat to Cyrus who wore his faded blue blouse with the gold stripes on the sleeve.

"With my respects, Sergeant."

"With my compliments," the ex-soldier smiled, lifting his hat to return the military courtesy. The troopers pressed forward and rode westward.

Cyrus spurred his horse into a slow walk toward Lincoln which was now protected by an army of Texas rapists and a posse owned by Jimmy Dolan.

Chapter Eighteen

"MAYBE THERE'LL BE FIREWORKS FOR THE FOURTH."

Sean lifted his glass, drained it, and waited for another. Manuel exchanged it for a full one. Cyrus nursed the same drink for half an hour.

"Might be," the soldier said. He looked up when Jesse Evans entered the cantina at midday, July 3rd. Cyrus lifted his half-full shot glass and held it in front of his face.

"To General Hancock."

"To General Pickett," Sean smiled, lifting his new glass to return the toast. Both men threw their heads back and drank to the fifteenth anniversary of Pickett's Charge at the Battle of Gettysburg. They put their glasses down when Jesse pulled a chair to their table. Two of his Boys lingered at the smoky hallway.

"Sheriff Peppin is sending some men down to San Patricio. Wants to remind McSween and Chisum that we're still here, I guess." Jesse took a glass out of Manuel's hand. "Since you still ain't seen your brothers, I thought you would want to ride down with us. Ain't going to be no trouble. Make a little noise, is all."

Sean looked at Cyrus. This Wednesday marked the sergeant's fifth day away from the ranch and he was itching to do something other than sit around the Boys' table at the Wortley.

"John Kinney going?" Cyrus looked closely at Jesse's

eyes. The captain might be a rustler and gunfighter, but he
was not a liar.

"No. Peppin is keeping the Rio Grande bunch here. The
sheriff don't want things to get out of hand. That's why he's
only sending a dozen deputies south. John Long will be in
charge. It's really just to feel them out; see how many Regulators is there."

"All right," Sean said. "Cyrus?"

"Me, too."

Jesse Evans stood and raised his glass. Then he led Sean,
Cyrus and two of the Boys into the tranquil sunshine.

DEPUTY LONG AND twelve men rode slowly south for two
hours toward the blemish on the stage road called San Patricio. Late June had been dry and a little cloud of dust
followed them.

"There's some dust," a farmboy called over his shoulder.

"Dust devil?"

"Don't think so. Sky ain't right for it. Best tell Chisum."

The second gritty man on the hilltop stumbled at a full
run toward the Regulators' headquarters. Alex McSween
stood outside the hovel.

"Dust on the road, Mr. McSween."

"From what direction?"

"Coming south. Could be trouble."

The lawyer's face had taken on a tan after nearly three
months on the lam. His hair had grown over his ears and his
mustache drooped toward his chin. Lawyers are pink and
soft, with hands like women. McSween's time at San Patricio in the loud company of hard men had toughened him, at
least the parts which showed. Sweat had nearly dissolved
his black waistcoat so he wore only his dusty, black vest
over the whitest shirt he owned. Every two weeks, Susan
brought him clean shirts and fresh woollies. Although John
Chisum never packed a handiron in his life—"A six-shooter

will get you into more trouble than it'll get you out of" was his creed—McSween had taken to wearing an old Remington low on his hip like a real man. On days when Susan was not expected, he put a plug of chew in his cheek.

"Best round up the boys." Alexander McSween, Attorney at Law, spit manfully. A ribbon of brown juice trickled onto his yellowed shirt.

"Sure enough, Mr. McSween."

McSween wiped his chin on his cuff and went inside to get Chisum who refused to strap on a pistol.

The dust cloud against blue sky continued to grow from the north. A dozen Regulators crouched atop squat hills on both sides of the main road which ran east and west on the north bank of the Rio Hondo. The Regulators waded across from San Patricio on the south bank. A month without rain had reduced the Hondo to a knee-deep creek. Patrick and Liam Rourke took up picket positions between the road and their camp behind the hills.

John Long rode beside Jesse who could suffer no one to ride ahead of him. Sean and Cyrus rode side-by-side behind them. Half a dozen townsmen followed in a bunch. Less than a mile from San Patricio, the stage road south from Lincoln meets the main road heading east to Roswell and west down to Blazer's Mill. The posse turned right toward the Regulators' camp.

Half a mile from San Patricio, the Regulators on the hills waited nervously. All had laid their handirons on the crest of a hill where their bodies lay flat on the rocky ground. Two or three on each hill looked over the sights of rifles. The long steel barrels had long since been blackened over campfires to keep them from glinting in the sun.

As the posse became larger in the Regulators' gunsights, Cyrus Buchanan's black face in the center of eleven white men made a fine target as they approached from the east and the fork in the dirt road.

A Regulator on the southern ridge with the Rio Hondo at

his back wiped sweat from his squinting eyes. He earred back the hammer on his lever-action Winchester 1873 rifle. He had already chambered a .44 caliber cartridge before he crossed the river. But he had lowered the hammer to keep from blowing his face off if he slipped in the fast-moving water. He drew a bead on the large black face down the slope and three hundred yards up the trail. He held his breath and raised the barrel a full foot. He aimed at nothing but purple mountain sky. Then, waiting carefully for the instant between heart beats, he gently squeezed the trigger at the sky.

Forty grains of black powder exploded in the Winchester's breech.

In the thin, mile-high air, only horse ears flicked forward.

Sean heard a wet thud beside him, the sound made by a dropped melon. He turned to his left where Cyrus sat bolt-upright in his saddle. His arms went rigid and the sudden tension on his reins made his mount jerk his head. Cyrus turned toward Sean.

Sean's eyes widened when he looked at Cyrus. His rumpled yellow cavalry hat was gone. And his forehead was gone.

Still holding his reins in a death grip, the big man rolled backwards out of his saddle. He pulled his screaming horse down on top of him. When Sean's horse side-stepped to keep from being bowled over by the rolling mount, Sean clearly heard Sergeant Buchanan's pelvis snap and pulverize when eight hundred pounds of horseflesh slammed down on his chest. The horse struggled to its feet but could not pull away from the dead man's iron grip on his leathers. The animal lowered his haunches and pulled back with a wild-horse screech. The reins and three brown fingers came loose. He burst into a full gallop. But by the end of the column of possemen, he stepped into the dangling reins, tripped himself, and went limp with a broken neck.

Two seconds after the soldier's head exploded, the posse

scattered into scrub brush along the trail. Men dove from their horses and began firing blindly up the hill. Sean jumped from his saddle and knelt behind a large rock. He blasted upward at an unseen enemy lost in a haze of dust, gunsmoke, and tears.

A rattle of gunfire drifted back toward San Patricio. The mountain air dissipated the gunfire and made it sound miles away instead of eight hundred yards. A few possemen drove the hilltop Regulators from their position and gained a clear shot across the creek toward the encampment and the picket position of Patrick and Liam. The two brothers kept up a slow volley toward the far side of the Rio Hondo.

Lethargic gunfire continued for two hours. A stray round thumped into the top rail of the paddock beside John Chisum's shack. Splinters of dry wood blew into the eyes of one of the skittish horses. In a panic, it jumped the fence and drove headlong toward the creek. The lazy gunplay stopped as hungry men on both sides paused to laugh. The animal ran toward the sheltered hillside where the posse had tied several of their mounts.

When the slackening fire did not stop by evening twilight, Chisum and McSween agreed to make an escape eastward to South Spring River. They left with Billy Bonney and half a dozen Regulators. The rest held their positions since they had no place better to be.

The Regulators stopped firing first. Their ammunition supply had to be conserved. Deputy Long and Jesse Evans waited through half an hour of silence. As the smoke cleared and the guns from the hills stopped, Evans stood on the trail. No fire greeted him and other possemen stood. Behind the hills, the Regulators pulled back across the river.

The road was pock-marked for two hundred yards in both directions. Long shadows of dusk made the trail look like a Moonscape of bullet craters and hoofprints. Sean walked to Cyrus and knelt beside him. He grimaced. The dead man had been riddled by gunfire all afternoon. His cavalry

blouse and trousers with the gold stripe were covered with
small red punctures. Since his blood stopped flowing and
leaking before he hit the ground, only watery juices dribbled
from dozens of wounds.

"Hoist him up and tie him down."

Sean stood when he heard Jesse's voice. Evans stood
holding an unfamiliar horse. The runaway from San Patricio
wore the bridle and leathers from the sergeant's dead mount.
Jesse handed the reins to one of the possemen.

"Give us a hand," Jesse said wearily.

Three men helped Sean and Jesse heave Cyrus across the
bare-back animal. They tied the dead man's hands to his
own feet.

"That'll hold him till we get home." Jesse looked up.
Stars were already erupting in the purple sky. "May have to
camp up the road anyway."

The posse gathered their animals and mounted. There
were no serious casualties other than Cyrus Buchanan who
had never gotten a round off. A few men suffered scrapes
and bruises from hitting the ground when the attack began.

Across the Rio Hondo, casualties were also light. The
executive leadership of the Regulators made good their
flight and were well down the road toward Roswell and
South Spring just across the river.

AT FIRST LIGHT on the Fourth of July, John Long led his
posse back into Lincoln. Saddlesore and hungry, they rode
single-file at a slow walk with horses and riders, heads-
bowed.

Susan McSween was already in the store. With the cavalry troopers gone, she opened Tunstall's mercantile at
dawn so she could stand in the doorway in case House men
came in to make trouble.

The posse walked the length of town toward the courthouse. Sheriff Peppin heard the jingling of spurs and

nickering of horses. He opened the jailhouse door as the posse passed Tunstall's store midway up the street.

Susan McSween watched them pass. Her mouth dropped open when she saw Cyrus Buchanan's stiffening corpse flung across the one saddleless mount. The woman screamed and ran into the street. The caravan stopped beside the crazed woman.

She grabbed the cadaver by the scruff of the neck and tried to lift its head. But fifteen hours of death and bloating had turned the neck bones into stone. She had to kneel in the muddy road to get a good look at the dead face. The eyes were swollen shut and the mouth was locked wide open. The whole top of his skull was missing. Flies feasted on the exposed, gray brain tissue. She shuddered at the ghastly remains.

The lawyer's wife dragged her mud-soaked skirt to the head of the posse.

"What have you vile pigs done to my husband?" She was screaming like a wild woman.

"We ain't seen your husband," Deputy Long said weakly. "Never seen him once."

"But that's Mac's horse! What have you done with my husband?"

Susan began pummelling Long's leg with her clenched fists. She was shouting in blind fury at six-thirty in the quiet morning.

Sheriff Peppin and four men stepped behind the woman and jerked her back from John Long. They bodily wrestled her to the mud from an all-night drizzle. Black ooze laced with rotted manure quickly wadded into her hair. Her face turned bright red.

"Be quiet woman! Now listen to me. You get hold of yourself."

George Peppin was on his knees with muck and mud up to his elbows. As the woman stopped struggling to catch her breath, two dirty boots stopped near Peppin's shoulder. The lawman looked up into John Kinney's glazed eyes.

"I can fix that for you, Sheriff."

Just the sound of his voice made Susan McSween stop squirming. Her eyes became wide, white holes on her mud-caked face.

"None of that talk, Kinney! You go on to Manuel's now and leave us be."

The Ranger laughed loudly and looked down at the filthy, stinking woman.

"Just trying to be a good citizen, Sheriff." He touched the corner of his floppy hat. "Ma'am."

Peppin hauled Susan McSween out of the mud. Her weight doubled with the street she brought up with her.

"John?"

"Sheriff, Mrs. McSween, this here horse ran out of the Regulators' camp. We kept it. That's all there is. The soldier here is the only dead body we seen in two days. I'm sure your worm-stinking husband is all right." Deputy Long smiled as he kicked his animal's flanks and continued up the street. Susan McSween stood with her fists clenched as the lawmen continued on. The look she flashed up at Sean made him flinch and turn away.

Sean led the pack horse carrying Cyrus. The body was rigid when it went past Susan McSween. She stepped forward and spit square into cavity of the dead man's head.

JUST AS SHE had promised, Bonita Ramos watched the lane every day for eight days. She watched the approaching rider grow larger Saturday morning. The new sun was low enough to shine brightly even under the single horseman's broad-brimmed hat. When she could see that half of the distant, bearded face was white and the other half red as raw meat, she lowered her face and went inside.

One day later, Patrick and Liam rode down the same lane. When the braggart who killed Cyrus boasted about it over a

San Patricio campfire, Liam heard the story for the first time. The blood left his face and he lit out hard for the ranch. Patrick could not catch him for half an hour.

JOHN CHISUM, CATTLE baron, had seen enough of San Patricio's privy. One day after reaching South Spring River, he packed his carpetbag, hitched his best team to his best buckboard, and rode east as far as the first rail spur for the train to St. Louis.

Wearing the same shirt he had worn for a week in the saddle, Alexander McSween mounted his horse and rode west with Billy Bonney at his side. The last of Chisum's hired hands followed them back to San Patricio.

Ten miles up the trail to the north, Sean Rourke got drunk in Manuel's cantina and stayed drunk for ten days. At first light every day before the town awoke, he staggered to Tunstall's store and stumbled behind the empty corral. With the sun barely creeping over the eastern mountains, he stood each morning in silence and burped through tears at the fresh mound of soggy earth next to John Tunstall's grave.

Chapter Nineteen

THE LAWYER LOVED IT. RIDING IN THE DARK WITH SIXTY gunmen behind him like an army, Alexander McSween rode with his right hand resting on the handle of his revolver. With Chisum gone, command of the Regulators had fallen upon him. Billy Bonney rode at his side like a loyal lap dog. McSween spit a ribbon of chaw over his knee into the darkness. Leaving behind the squinty-eyed drudgery of his law books, he felt like a gunfighter and it seemed to make his very bones harder.

The night breeze of Sunday, July 14, blew through the corners of McSween's drooping, black mustache. The whiskers tickled the corners of his mouth like invisible fairy fingers. A bright crescent Moon reflected from McSween's grin and happy eyes.

"You all right, Mr. McSween?"

The leader of the Regulators tightened his hand on his holster and turned to the rider at his side.

"Just fine, Billy. Never fitter."

The army of Chisum men rode beside a dozen local Hispanics who felt abused for years by the usurious interest rates charged by the House during its administrations of Lawrence Murphy and then Jimmy Dolan. Near midnight Sunday, they rode into Lincoln from the west in column of threes. Sheriff Peppin and most of his forty deputies were gone from town, out in the wilderness searching for the

Regulators. Only Jack Long and five House men held the
town from their makeshift fortress inside the old Indian,
stone tower, the *torréon,* which Alex McSween owned.
Twenty feet tall and twenty feet wide, it commanded a view
of the entire village.

The Regulators tied up at the Ellis store on Lincoln's far
east end, adjacent to the home of José Montaño and his
store. Across the street and two hundred yards to the south,
the House eyeballs in the stone tower watched nervously as
the Regulators deployed.

During the first minutes of Monday, the Regulators split
into three squadrons of armed men: twenty Mexicans stayed
at Montaño's under the command of Martín Chavez;
another two dozen boarded in the Isaac Ellis home to cover
the eastern end of the street; and fourteen men followed
Billy Bonney and McSween to the lawyer's home.

There was hardly room to move in the McSween house.
Though spacious, the single-story adobe structure was not
designed to accommodate sixteen men. Sue McSween, and
David Shield and his wife made eighteen adults in the light
of oil lamps. The five Shield children slept on the floor with
babies bundled in bureau drawers.

"We got lucky tonight, Mr. McSween."

"How's that, Billy?"

"The sheriff and them Rio Grande Posse boys being out
looking for us."

"Let's hope they think we've all gone to Texas."

LINCOLN WAS QUIET Monday morning. Sixty horses in paddocks and at hitching posts represented an army of
occupation. John Long's men in the stone tower slept on
their weapons. Unless the Regulators chose to starve them
to death, they were safe inside.

Sean Rourke stepped into the overcast day. He looked
up the street toward the end controlled by Regulators.

Beyond the Wortley's paddock, Deputy Long's position
stood against the gray sky. Sean rubbed his forehead. He
had stopped drinking yesterday and awoke with the worst
headache since a Confederate artillery shell had detonated
prematurely on a caisson in front of his face sixteen years
earlier. His eyes could not tolerate even the misty daylight
so he went back into the boarding house for coffee and
biscuits.

"Whiskey, Señor Rourke?" Manuel asked. He knew
Sean's breakfast choice since the San Patricio ambush.

Sean looked at the pleasant Mexican. He thought of the
Regulators camped in and around McSween's house.

"I think coffee today."

Every hour, Sean walked outside to survey the uneasy
quiet. Not a single citizen walked the dirt street. Tunstall's
store was closed tightly, but it was not empty. Taylor Ealy,
the physician, his wife, and their two tiny daughters had
moved into the backroom quarters where Mr. and Mrs.
Shield had boarded.

When Sean went out at one o'clock, the thin air carried a
certain buzz of voices from the concealed Regulators. He
looked to his right just as George Peppin and his posse rode
slowly into town. Sean estimated that Peppin's brigade had
grown to at least sixty men, including Jesse Evans and all of
the Boys, John Kinney's red-eyed Rangers, and a dozen
Seven Rivers Warriors. Sean had to smile as he watched the
group dismount and unsaddle in the Wortley's paddock. The
force of Law in Lincoln looked more like a hall of fame for
cattle rustlers, bushwhackers, and rapists.

Manuel kept the hot coffee coming for an hour until
everyone was wetted.

"They're coming!" one of the Seven Rivers rustlers
shouted from the cantina window.

Sixty men ran over each other to take positions at the
Wortley's outside corners, behind the paddock water
troughs, and around the base of the Indian tower. Up the

road, a dozen Mexicans were jogging in single file from the Montaño store on the south side of the street toward McSween's headquarters on the north side.

The Rio Grande Posse opened fire, throwing large clods of mud into the air around the running Mexicans. The Regulators slunk back toward the store and barricaded themselves inside. They fired from the windows at the stone tower. The boarding house was too far away. No one in McSween's house could fire west toward the hotel since the Watson house was in the way, and they could not fire east at the stone *torréon* since Tunstall's store blocked that field of fire. So everyone just popped in the general direction of the enemy without doing serious damage to anyone. Gunfire rattled for half an hour—the first thirty minutes of the Lincoln County War.

When darkness settled over a brittle stillness, Billy Bonney slipped out of McSween's home and took horse along the Rio Bonito riverbank. He walked his horse by hand until he was beyond the back side of the Wortley. Then he rode hell-bent toward the Rourke ranch. He arrived at nine o'clock to find Liam sitting on the front porch beside Melissa Bryant who held her daughter asleep in her lap. Patrick sat opposite them and did not get up to fetch his iron at the sound of hoofbeats approaching at the gallop.

"Evening, Billy."

The boy dismounted out-of-breath.

"Patrick; Liam. Ma'am. It's started, Patrick. We're all down in town now: all us Regulators and all of the sheriff's boys. You have to come. We need your guns: you and Liam."

"You ain't got no shortage of killers, William Bonney." Bonita answered on words like ice from the doorway. "Now you just git. We're done with all that. You took my Cyrus already. Ain't that enough?"

Bonita was not weeping. Her voice trembled with rage.

Had she come out with one of the sergeant's Winchesters, Billy would have been dead by now.

"I have a ranch to run, Billy. Liam and I ain't leaving. You're welcome to sit and rest for a while. You're welcome to the jug, too. Then you go on."

"Now you know I promised my Ma before she died that I wouldn't do no hard liquor."

Billy sat down on the porch floor. He kept a careful watch on Bonita's white eye.

"Where's Sean?" Patrick looked down at the teenager. His light hair was flecked with mud in the lamp light.

"Holed up with Peppin's bunch at the Wortley."

Patrick nodded.

"I ain't drawing down on my brother no more. I'm staying here."

Billy finally caught his breath as he played with his sweat-stained hat. He spoke to the ground.

"Sean's took up with Jesse and Kinney's Rangers. You know what them Rio Grande Posse boys is after, don't you, Patrick? Sean owes Jesse. I ain't certain for what. But he can't give up if Jesse's there."

Before Billy drew another breath, Melissa stood and shifted Abigail's sleeping weight in her arms. She pushed past Bonita and entered the house. When Bonita followed her, she slammed the door.

"Womenfolk," Patrick smiled until he glanced over at his brother's vacuous eyes. "This ain't our fight no more, Billy."

The boy stood and put on his crumbling hat.

"Then I ain't responsible if Kinney's posse comes after them women and the little girl."

"No, you ain't," Patrick said. His eyes narrowed. "Be careful in the dark."

With a wave of his hand, Billy mounted and spurred his horse toward town.

Patrick looked at Liam. Moonlight glistened in Liam's eyes which seemed momentarily alive again. When Liam's lips moved, Patrick leaned forward. Liam could not make his words come at first. His brother waited until he was ready.

"You done right. It ain't our fight."

"That's right, Liam. But it ain't right for Sean to ride with them kind."

The light behind Liam's eyes went out again and he looked down at the floor for several minutes.

"Yes it is," Liam mumbled.

"What?"

"It's right for Sean to ride with them kind."

"I don't understand."

Liam spoke softly toward his dirty boots.

"Melissa had a field colt."

"What?" Patrick worked to keep his voice low.

"Melissa had a field colt. That doc she done at Roswell got rid of it."

"How do you know that."

Liam looked up with tormented eyes.

"I know."

"This ain't more of your spirit-keeper gibberish, is it?"

Liam lowered his face while Patrick watched him closely.

"It's true then?"

Liam nodded, stood up, and shuffled inside. He closed the door and left his brother sitting alone in the half darkness of a moonlit night. Patrick sat and listened to the braying of Chisum's cattle all around the house. After fifteen minutes, he went inside.

Only a single oil lamp illuminated the greatroom. Melissa and Abigail were asleep in the bedroom. Bonita puttered in the kitchen. When Cyrus did not come home, Bonita claimed the cot in the loft. Sometimes Patrick slept by the hearth and sometimes he joined Liam in the barn. He felt that Melissa joined Liam out there from time to time. But he could not be certain. Patrick knew only that her silence was a gulf between them and that he would never swim in it.

"Liam, I have to go to Sean."

"Why?"

The youngest brother's voice was cool.

"I have to. You can stay here and guard the house."

Bonita came out from the kitchen and stood close to Patrick.

"Ain't Cyrus enough, Patrick Rourke?"

"Liam will stay here. You take good care of Melissa and Abbey. For me."

Bonita read the sadness in his eyes. She knew the way he watched Melissa move. The woman sighed and faced Liam.

"Then you go with him. You watch out for each other."

Liam shrugged and walked outside.

"He still ain't up to it, Bonita. Leave him be."

Without another word, Patrick put on his gunbelt and long duster. He carried his hat and one of the Winchesters when he went through the doorway.

"I'll be back as soon as I can."

Liam nodded and put an arm around one of the timbers holding up the porch roof as if to anchor himself forever to the ranch of his father.

Bonita filled the dimly lighted doorway. The fireplace turned Patrick's back into a shimmering red shadow until the darkness swallowed him as he walked to the barn.

"You go with him, Liam."

Liam held the timber and did not turn around.

"So help me, boy, you go with your brother or I'll go to Lincoln and tell the whole world what you done in the Army." Her words were seething through clenched teeth. Liam turned a questioning face toward her.

"Cyrus told me how you cut and run. You got a spine of jelly."

"I went back for Cyrus at the end."

"Because he protected you. You went back for Liam Rourke." She spoke his name as if it tasted bitter on her tongue. When she went inside, Liam walked head-bowed toward his dark garden.

PATRICK WAITED FOR daylight Tuesday before he rode into town. It was safer that way. Once he was on the trail, he wondered where to go. Because he had ridden with the Regulators, he knew that Sheriff Peppin probably had a warrant for his arrest, too. By the time first light caught the top of the *torréon*, he knew that he should start where he was welcome. He rode along the riverbank until he came to the back of McSween's house. Turning his horse out into the paddock, he looked east to the next building: Tunstall's store. He paused to gaze on the mound of earth where Cyrus Buchanan lay beside John Tunstall.

Billy Bonney waited for him at the doorway. Before they could exchange greetings, the morning crackled with gunfire. Patrick sprinted toward the house where he found shoulder-to-shoulder gunfighters, two women, and five little children.

Men at McSween's windows tried to locate the firing.

"From them hills, looks like," someone called. Alex McSween put hardly more face than an eyeball around the sill of the hole in the adobe wall. Tiny puffs of smoke appeared atop a hill south of town behind Jimmy Dolan's deserted house. The Regulators could see muzzle flashes almost two seconds before each rifle report. Looking eastward up the street, they saw white flecks of adobe dust bursting along the upper edge of the south wall on José Montaño's house where half a dozen sharpshooters lay on the roof. Before anyone could get hurt, the men on the roof inched on their bellies to the front and shimmied down to the ground. Then they ran inside to safety.

"Welcome to Lincoln," the lawyer said, offering his hand to Patrick.

"I come to fetch my brother."

"Not much of a day to walk down the main street," McSween chuckled over the sound of sniper fire outside. "Besides, you're a wanted man down at the Wortley just like the rest of us." The house filled with mean-spirited laughter. "At least until we take our town back."

Patrick stood not quite at ease. He studied McSween's face. He remembered it as flaccid and rather youthful. Now it was wind-burned and tanned with white lines creasing at the corners of the eyes. Gunplay and life on the run seemed to agree with the lawyer.

"Guess so," Patrick said softly.

"Good. Billy, pour the man a drink to wash the trail down."

"Soldiers coming!" a lookout called down from the roof before Billy could answer.

"How many?" McSween shouted.

"Just one. One of them darkies from the fort."

A private approached on horseback from the west, past George Peppin's house on the north side of the street, and on toward the Wortley a few hundred yards further east.

"Put one at his feet," McSween called to the ceiling.

The soldier was bringing a written dispatch to Sheriff Peppin from Lt. Colonel Dudley. The colonel was serving notice that he had declined to grant Peppin's request for troops to quell the running battle on the streets of Lincoln.

When a fist-size clod of earth jumped out of the ground five feet in front of the cavalry horse, the soldier skidded his mount to a halt. The single report of a rifle followed half a second later. While the anxious animal spun under his blue-shirted rider, a second round thudded into the earth. The black trooper right-wheeled and galloped out of town.

"He's riding out," the voice on McSween's roof called down.

"Not hurt, was he?"

"No, Mr. McSween. You said not to."

"Good man." The lawyer turned to Patrick and Billy. "Good day so far, boys."

Desultory gunfire rattled windows for the rest of the day. Only nerves were stung by the sporadic and aimless missiles.

PRIVATE BERRY ROBINSON rode hard back to Fort Stanton. Colonel Dudley was outraged that the anarchists in Lincoln would fire on a blue uniform from the 9th United States Cavalry. Slightly slurring his speech, Dudley ordered three white officers to ride to Lincoln on Wednesday to meet with Sheriff Peppin and to confirm which side popped off at Private Robinson.

The reluctant officers rode slowly toward Lincoln from the west at ten o'clock in the morning. They ordered Liam Rourke to dismount with his hands raised when they approached him suddenly from the rear.

"I rode with Nelson Miles after the Nez Perces," Liam said so softly that the officers demanded him to repeat himself.

"You're one of the brothers? The one who rode with the nigger sergeant?"

Liam nodded.

The officers returned their sidearms to leather.

"We heard he was a hero up north in the Nez Perce war."

Liam thought for several seconds.

"And before that, Lieutenant. Long before."

"Too bad about the sergeant getting killed two weeks ago. Imagine making it through the Cheyenne and Sioux wars just to get bushwhacked out here." The young soldier seemed truly saddened by the loss of one of his own kind.

"Too bad," Liam said listlessly.

"You going into Lincoln?"

"Yes, sir."

"For what, for God's sake?"

"My brothers is there, both of 'em."

"Very well, then. You can ride in with us. We have orders to shoot to kill if anyone looks crosswise at us. You'll be safer riding with us." The regimental guidon snapped at the perfect moment in a sudden breeze.

"I ain't rode under that flag in almost nine months." Liam blinked hard.

"Do you good . . . soldier. Mount up."

"Yes, sir," Liam said from a habit imprinted on his heart.

Lincoln's only street was quiet Wednesday morning as the four men rode up to the Wortley and tied their animals to the outside of the paddock fence. Sheriff Peppin met them at the door. It was pock-marked with bullet holes.

The three soldiers retired with Peppin and Liam found Sean. They retreated to a corner of the cantina. With so many men sitting and drinking, two per chair at some tables, they stood in a smoky corner. Oil lamps burned on the tables, since the adobe windows were shuttered tightly against the daily hail of lead.

"Where's your brother?" Sean asked.

"Come in Monday night. You seen him?"

Sean looked troubled when he answered.

"No. Must be up the road at McSween's with the rest of that rabble."

"You ain't exactly keeping church company yourself." Liam's blank face did not smile. Sean looked around at Seven Rivers Warriors and Texans with tin stars on their shirts.

"Suppose not, Liam."

"We can leave when them soldiers leave."

Sean thought of home.

"How's Melissa?"

"All right. She's back on her feed and putting on a little weight. She looks good. Abbey, too."

A quick smile lighted Sean's face when he thought of the child. Two hard thumps like hammer blows struck the wooden shutter. No one looked up from their drinks.

"Is it like that all day?"

"Pretty much. No real harm done."

The three soldiers appeared at the hallway and gestured toward Liam. Sean followed him.

"We're done here, Mr. Rourke. This your brother?" Sean nodded for Liam. "Captain Purington said you were at Shiloh." Sean nodded again. On the day his face was destroyed, the lieutenant was probably still wetting his pants, Sean thought. "We're going back to the fort now. The sheriff said McSween's people fired on our man yesterday." He looked at Liam. "You can ride with us as far as your spread, if you want."

"Sean?" Liam looked at his brother.

"I can't. It ain't mine." He looked down at the sawdust-covered floor. "And Melissa ain't mine no more. You go on."

Liam sighed so hard his shoulders seemed to collapse around his chest.

"Thank you, Lieutenant. I'll stay with my brother."

"Suit yourself." The soldiers carried their hats toward the front door.

Ten minutes later, a flurry of tiny hammerblows blew dust from the shutters. The throng in the cantina adjourned loudly toward the front room. The door was open and men kept a safe distance from the sunshine outside.

Through the doorway they watched half a dozen deputies run crouching across the street. They were the men who had manned the hilltop south of town. Regulators at the far end of the street were on the Ellis store roof at Montaño's. Their broadside into the running deputies caught Charlie Crawford in the hip. He crawled like a wounded animal toward the door. Two of John Kinney's drunken Rangers walked calmly into the sun and dragged Crawford inside.

John Kinney patted one of the winded men on the shoulder before he knelt to examine the wound. There was no exit wound from the deputy's bowels.

"Be dead in three weeks," Kinney said dryly as he stood up. Crawford held his bleeding side and whimpered softly. He would last five weeks.

NATHAN AUGUSTUS DUDLEY would have been pleased and relieved if the Regulators and the House men managed to kill off each other to the last man-killer in town. But pot shots at his troopers crossed the line.

On Thursday the 18th, he ordered three dozen cavalrymen to prepare for taking back Lincoln on Friday.

Thursday was quiet by Lincoln standards during daylight. After nightfall, a single round from one of Peppin's men thudded in to the neck of Ben Ellis at the Regulator-held store which bore his family name.

Friday morning, the wounded Ellis was in desperate need of medical attention. Billy Bonney crept down the street into Tunstall's store and begged Dr. Taylor Ealy to come up to Montaño's to treat the dying patient.

At nine-thirty, sharpshooters on the Wortley roof blinked in disbelief. Then laughter overcame them. They lowered their weapons and cheered. Taylor Ealy walked into the sunshine. He carried his infant daughter in his arms and his toddler daughter struggled to grip his other hand. The House men held their fire as the physician hid behind his perfect shield all the way to the bedside of Ben Ellis.

Sporadic gunfire erupted when the surgeon was safely beyond harm's way. The gunfire trailed off to silence an hour before noon. Colonel Dudley and three white cavalry officers appeared at the western end of the street. They paused until all fire ceased. Then they led thirty-five mounted troopers in two columns into town. Behind them came one menacing Gatling gun and a nine-pound How-itzer. Their limber chest carried three thousand rounds of small arms' ammunition.

House men cheered as the troopers rode east. The

columns continued past McSween's fortress and past the
stone tower still held by Peppin's weary men. They stopped
directly in front of Montaño's store where Doc Ealy bent
over Ben Ellis. Then the soldiers broke formation in a clearing on McSween's north side of the street and opposite
Montaño's. As they pitched camp, they trained their deadly
Gatling gun on the Ellis store. Within minutes, all of
McSween's Hispanic troops in Montaño's ran into the sun,
mounted their horses, and careened out of town. Mexicans
in the Ellis store joined them. Without the Army firing a
shot, the Regulators lost half of their guns when thirty men
splashed across the Rio Bonito.

As Colonel Dudley's men unpacked the stores of war,
Sheriff Peppin sent Deputy Marion Turner up the street. The
Gatling gun kept the peace as the lawman approached
Alexander McSween's home. Patrick Rourke opened the
door. The deputy handed him a warrant for the arrest of
McSween.

McSween answered by spitting a man-size wad of chaw
into the cold hearth. Turner walked back to Peppin to report.

Outraged, the sheriff sent a dozen deputies outside. The
sun and the bristling weaponry around them brought perspiration quickly to their faces. They kept close to the
buildings on the edge of the street as they made their way
closer to McSween's. They crawled the last ten yards to the
northwest corner of the adobe compound, near the stable.

The men, women, and children inside McSween's home
soon smelled oily smoke. Peppin's men had set fire to the
west wall. But the rock-hard adobe would not catch and the
July wind suffocated the tiny flames. As her home filled
with smoke, Susan McSween opened the door and marched
into the sun. The House men held their fire.

The woman marched up the street, straight to Lt. Colonel
Dudley. She demanded that he put an end to Peppin's incen-
diary plans. On whiskey breath, the officer declined unless
her husband surrendered his garrison. Furious, she walked

back toward her home where she saw deputies piling more kindling next to the wall.

This fire had more spirit and the straw within the adobe began to smoulder. After taking a swig from his bottle, Colonel Dudley sent a small squad to Tunstall's house to escort Mrs. Ealy out of danger.

Black smoke began to rise in earnest from the west side of McSween's home. At four in the afternoon, the Hispanic Regulators who had fled regrouped on the north bank of the river. They crouched and fired several volleys into the Wortley Hotel, eight hundred yards away. When their rounds did no more than plow the ground behind the boarding house well out of range, the men mounted, rode north, and never once looked back as flames engulfed one whole side of McSween's home.

At five-thirty, the eastern sky was darkening. Sparks and flames lapped at McSween's. Colonel Dudley sent another squad into the billowing smoke while Peppin's men held their fire. Under protest, the black troopers escorted Susan McSween, Mrs. Shield, and five children out of the house. They marched the prisoners across the street to Juan Patron's house.

Night comes quickly one mile above sea level and the sun went down hard over the Sacramento Mountains. Lincoln's main street was bathed in the orange glow surrounding the McSween home.

"It's time, boys," George Peppin said with exhaustion in his voice.

Sean felt a firm hand on his shoulder. He looked into Jesse's tired eyes.

"All my Boys will be on the lookout for Patrick. We'll pull him out as soon as we can find him. He must be at McSween's. You coming?"

Sean looked at Liam whose face remained blank.

"All right."

"Good. We'll stick together outside."

George Peppin's troops deployed the width of the street. They advanced on McSween's burning home. A volley from the adobe windows broke the formation quickly. Sean, Liam, and Jesse tumbled together behind a water trough fifty yards west of the flaming structure. Gunfire erupted from McSween's windows.

At the far end of the street to the east, Susan McSween heard the volley and walked into the darkness. The orange flames from her home reflected in her perspiration and tears.

The sheriff's posse and John Kinney's Rangers returned fire. The cavalry across from Sue McSween did nothing.

Inside the burning house, Patrick stayed close to Billy who huddled with McSween as half of his compound burned. Smoke and heat swirled through the room where ten stalwarts coughed and cursed. Several men escaped out the back, toward the river.

"Patrick and I can break for the river like them other cowards just done. But we'll go out the east side, open on Peppin's men and draw their fire. When they come after us down by the water, you and the rest can break out of the north side and make for San Patricio in the dark."

"Patrick?" McSween looked carefully into his eyes.

"I agree with Billy. We'll draw them off you. It'll work." McSween nodded.

Outside, Sean looked at the burning home.

"You stay here, Liam. I'm going in for Patrick."

"Not yet," Jesse protested. "Wait for them to come out. Their Mexicans might be holed up on the river waiting for us to make a move in the firelight."

"Take care of my brother." Sean smiled for an instant, drew his handiron, and rushed across the orange street. He could smell the stench of burning mud when the wind blew into his face.

A kitchen door on the east side of McSween's house opened. Two blazing Peacemakers filled the doorway as

Patrick and Billy ran into the brightly illuminated corral. The fence ran around all four sides of the building. When the fence splintered all around them, they dropped to the ground and rolled among the horse pies.

Sean crept toward the burning, western side of McSween's. As he inched closer, he crawled on his hands and knees. On the far side of the building, Billy and Patrick opened fire through the shattered fence rails. A fusillade from the Rio Grande Posse responded in kind. Patrick bit his lip until it bled.

Two thousand rounds criss-crossed the street inside the brilliant orange cloud of smoke and fury. Alexander McSween and two men ran from the house moments before the roof burst into flames.

Harvey Morris, McSween's law clerk, dropped mortally wounded.

Five bullets thumped into McSween's body. He fell into a bleeding heap. Sparks rained down on the dead lawyer's muddy face.

Sean Rourke crawled toward a corner of what was left of an adobe wall. Moving on his elbows, his revolver led him toward the corner. At the instant he hesitated, a muzzle eased around the corner from the other side. Sean backed away as the Remington at his face extended further. Gunfire rang so loudly in Sean's ears that in a moment he could hear nothing.

As Sean continued to crawl backward, an arm followed the Remington around the corner. Sean rested the grip of his pistol on a hard pile of horse droppings. A sweating face bathed in orange light poked around the corner. The Regulator's wide eyes met Sean's face.

The Regulator earred back the hammer on his revolver. When he looked up, he saw Sean's face illuminated by the burning house. The Regulator blinked when firelight swirled around the folds of wrinkled, purple skin on Sean's right cheek. In the instant the Regulator's face filled with terror at the sight of Sean's grotesque wound, Sean squeezed the trigger that rested just under the stranger's chin. Sean blinked when the blast exploded the top of the Regulator's head in a red and gray slurry.

The crackling of gunfire trailed off at midnight.

The shooting from the Regulators trickled to nothing. Only the roar of the fire filled the night and Susan McSween's face.

George Peppin and John Kinney walked up the street. Approaching the house, they found Alex McSween's body beside two dead Regulators. One of Peppin's deputies lay dead nearby.

Sean holstered his handiron and rubbed the manure from his knees and elbows. Jesse came up to his side.

"Did you find Patrick?" Jesse asked. Although the fire was waning and the shooting had stopped completely, Sean could hardly hear the question.

"Patrick?"

"Yes, did you find him."

"No. Where's Liam?" Sean squinted into the darkness which quickly rolled over the glowing embers of the destroyed house.

"He was just with me." Jesse Evans looked around. Deputies and Rangers walked through the ruins.

"Over here." The voice was Liam's.

Sean and Jesse found him kneeling by the collapsed fence. He was tossing broken rails into the street. Beneath the pile of wood was Patrick's limp body. Sean rolled him over onto his back.

The last of the flames illuminated a ragged and purple, thumb-size hole in Patrick's forehead.

Chapter Twenty

As THE RUBBLE OF THE MCSWEEN HOME SIMMERED ALL Friday night, the looting started. The Rio Grande Posse cleaned out Tunstall's store by dawn, Saturday. When the shelves were bare, they broke into Tunstall's bank and emptied its coffers. When the looting ended because there was nothing left to steal, Colonel Dudley marched his cavalry out of Lincoln at four o'clock in the afternoon. He left a sergeant and two privates behind to patrol the streets.

As the Army rode slowly out of town, they passed Susan McSween standing beside another hole in the ground between Tunstall's store and the muddy Rio Bonito. Scowling at Colonel Dudley as he passed, she threw a clod of earth into her husband's grave next to Cyrus Buchanan and John Tunstall.

SEAN AND LIAM rode up the lane of Grady's Rourke's ranch on Sunday afternoon, July 21st, 1878. The two women and the child met them at the doorway. Liam dismounted. Sean did not.

Under a dazzling mountain sky, Sean Rourke removed his hat and set it on his saddle horn. Beneath him, Liam stepped onto the porch.

Bonita spoke first.

"Patrick's dead, ain't he?"

"Yes." Sean looked uphill toward Liam's garden. "Doc Ealy will bring him home tomorrow. Put him, gentle, up there, next to Ma and Pa." He looked back at the wet-eyed women. Liam unbuttoned his muddy shirt and pulled out a folded piece of paper. He handed it to Melissa Bryant. Tears ran from her eyes, the color of the Sunday sky.

"That's why we didn't come up yesterday." Sean spoke slowly and looked down lovingly at Melissa. "McSween's partner, Mr. Shield, drawed that up for me last night. It's what he called an election against Patrick's estate. Pa ain't left me nothing here. But when Patrick died"—Sean blinked hard and looked back toward the garden—"his half of the ranch under Pa's will went half to me and half to Liam." He looked back at his family. "That there paper is my quarter of the ranch. I'm giving it to you, Melissa. You and Abbey have a home now. Liam will take care of all of you. That goes for you, too, Bonita. Cyrus would have wanted you to stay here. None of you needs to be kept by no Jimmy Dolan no more."

"But Sean," Bonita stepped forward and raised her hand to the mounted man's leg.

"No." Sean squinted in the sunshine at John Chisum's steers and Liam's full garden. "This is good land. You can all grow old here. The war in Lincoln is over."

"What about you?" Bonita's face softened and her eyes glowed. It was the face Cyrus had loved.

"There's still gold in California. I'm going to find it."

Melissa and Abigail stepped to Bonita's side. Liam stayed in the porch shadows.

Sean looked at Melissa.

"Give my brother his soul back, Melissa. Make up for the one in you that I killed."

Melissa held her daughter's shoulder tightly.

"Maybe one day, I'll come home." Sean gathered his reins. "God bless you all."

The women and Liam watched the lane until the hot earth

sucked up the last of the cloud of dust that followed the first son of Grady Rourke.

SUNDAY NIGHT WAS closing in on Sean after riding easily for thirty-five miles. On the stage road into the Sacramento Mountains, he reined up beside the Rio Tularosa and Blazer's Mill. He could still see the bullet holes in the old sawmill under the quarter moon in a perfectly clear sky. He groaned when he climbed down and tied his weary horse to the front porch.

"Ain't your ranch the other way?"

William Henry Bonney stepped out of the shadow.

Sean looked hard at the boy who was not yet twenty. When Sean saw that he was not wearing his gunbelt, he lifted his hand from his handiron inside his duster.

"I made some coffee inside," Billy said with his front teeth shining in the moonlight.

"Thanks."

Sean uncinched his saddle and laid it on the porch.

"Where's Doc Blazer?"

"Gone to Santa Fe. Too hot for him lately." Billy smiled.

"Yes."

"You can bed down here, if you want. It's just me."

"Where you going, Billy?"

"Sheriff Peppin still wants my hide. Thought I'd hide out in Silver City for a piece. My ma is buried down there. She died of the consumption when I were just fifteen."

"It's hard, ain't it, Billy?" Sean's face sagged in the moonlight.

"Sometimes." Billy smiled easily. "And sometimes, it ain't."

Sean nodded.

"What about you, Sean? Where you headed?"

"California."

"Ain't been there. Maybe one day."

"Look me up." Sean stepped onto the porch. He inhaled the delicious smelling coffee through the broken window.

"You can tell folks out there you know'd me when."

"I'll do that, Billy."

William Bonney's clean-shaven, boyish face became serious.

"When you do, I'm thinking of changing my name."

"Oh?"

"Yes, sir. I'm going to call myself Kid."

"Kid Bonney?" Sean tried not to smile as he walked inside. His spurs made music on the wooden floor.

"No. Billy the Kid."

Introduction and Acknowledgments

An historical novel should be slightly less than a post-graduate dissertation and must be slightly more than a pack of lies. Nearly all of the principal players in this story are real, historical figures from the 1878 anarchy in New Mexico now known as the Lincoln County War. Actual names are used for such persons. The author assumes responsibility for offense taken by their living heirs and descendants. Of the primary characters in this story, only Grady Rourke and his sons, and Cyrus, Melissa, and Bonita are fictional.

The author acknowledges his debt and abiding gratitude to the scholars of the Lincoln County War whose texts are the sources for the historical accuracy of this story:

Maurice G. Fulton, *History of the Lincoln County War,* University of Arizona Press, Tucson, 1968 (Robert N. Mullin, editor). Susan McSween's frontispiece quotation is from page 270.

Joel Jacobsen, *Such Men as Billy the Kid: The Lincoln County War Reconsidered,* University of Nebraska Press, Lincoln, 1994. John Tunstall's frontispiece quotation is from page 20.

Donald R. Lavash, *Sheriff William Brady: Tragic Hero of the Lincoln County War,* Sunstone Press, Santa Fe, 1986.

John P. Wilson, *Merchants, Guns and Money: The Story of Lincoln County and Its Wars,* Museum of New Mexico Press, Santa Fe, 1987.

THE BEAR PAW HORSES

THE BLAZING SAGA OF ONE MAN'S BATTLE TO SAVE THE SIOUX NATION—AND TO WIN A FIERY REBEL!

Con Jenkins is a horse-thieving murderer who can charm a whiskey drummer out of his sample case or a schoolmarm out of her virtue. With his razor-sharp mind and lightning quick draw, he has carved a reputation for himself from Hole-in-the-Wall to Robber's Roost. So why is Jenkins helping an ancient Indian and his white-hating granddaughter carry out the last orders of Crazy Horse, the most-feared war chief of all the Oglala Sioux? And why is he so determined to save the old medicine man from harm?

Before he can answer those questions, Con Jenkins is thrown headfirst into the deadliest struggle of his life—a battle for the very horses that will bring the Sioux—or the white settlers—their greatest victory.

_4055-7 $4.99 US/$5.99 CAN

SAN JUAN HILL

Bestselling Author of *Death of a Legend*

The year is 1898 and Fate Baylen of Arizona's Bell Rock Ranch joins the cavalry to fight the Spanish. But it looks as if the conflict is turning into a haven for graft grabbers, a heyday for incompetent officers, and a holiday for Fates and other boys from the West. Then the fighting starts, and men sweat, curse, turn cowardly, become heroes—and even die. Under the command of the valiant Teddy Roosevelt, Fate musters all the courage he can. Yet as he and the Rough Riders head into battle after battle, Fate can only wonder how many of them will survive to share in the victorious drive to the top of San Juan Hill.

_4045-X $4.99 US/$6.99 CAN

WILL HENRY

JESSE JAMES
DEATH OF A LEGEND

Beneath the bandanna, underneath the legend, Jesse James was a wild and wicked man: a sinister and brutal outlaw who blazed a trail of crime and violence through the lawless West. Ripping the mask off the mysterious Jesse James, Will Henry's *Death Of A Legend* is a novel as tough and savage as the man himself. Only a great Western writer like Henry could tell the real story of the infamous bandit Jesse James.
__3990-7 $4.99 US/$6.99 CAN

RIP-ROARIN' ACTION AND ADVENTURE BY THE WORLD'S MOST CELEBRATED WESTERN WRITER!

GUN GENTLEMEN

MAX BRAND

Renowned throughout the Old West, Lucky Bill has the reputation of a natural battler. Yet he is no remorseless killer. He only outdraws any gunslinger crazy enough to pull a six-shooter first. Then Bill finds himself on the wrong side of the law, and plenty of greenhorns and gringos set their sights on collecting the price on his head. But Bill refuses to turn tail and run. He swears he'll clear his name and live a free man before he'll be hunted down and trapped like an animal.

_3937-0 $4.50 US/$5.50 CAN

MARBLEFACE

MAX BRAND

"Packed with reckless deeds and hairbreadth escapes...no fan will be disappointed!"
—New York Times

He'd almost been a middleweight champion of the world, but then his heart went bad. If he doesn't want to get dumped in a pine box, he has to take it slow and easy for the rest of his life.

But a man can't live in the Old West without putting up a fight. So he learns to use a gun and make money at poker. It isn't long before every desperado and lawman knows he packs a Colt and a deck of cards—and the man hasn't been born who can beat him at either.

_3799-8 $3.99 US/$4.99 CAN

RIP ROARIN' ACTION AND ADVENTURE BY THE WORLD'S MOST CELEBRATED WESTERN WRITER!

MAX BRAND
THE OUTLAW TAMER

Sandy is a gentle giant with the mind of a child but the brute strength of any ten cowhands on the ranch—and the ability to tame the meanest outlaw horseflesh alive. He is a miracle worker with animals and he wouldn't hurt a fly—unless he's crossed. Then he can outwrassle a grizzly or outshoot the quickest gunman.

When his boss tricks Sandy and goes back on his word, he knows he will have a deadly enemy when the giant finds out. So he makes a devil's bargain with the lowest outlaws in the county to get rid of Sandy first. But even with an army of hardcases on his trail, the smart money is still on the outlaw tamer.

_4076-X $4.50 US/$5.50 CAN

Dorchester Publishing Co., Inc.
65 Commerce Road
Stamford, CT 06902

Please add $1.75 for shipping and handling for the first book and $.50 for each book thereafter. NY, NYC, PA and CT residents, please add appropriate sales tax. No cash, stamps, or C.O.D.s. All orders shipped within 6 weeks via postal service book rate. Canadian orders require $2.00 extra postage and must be paid in U.S. dollars through a U.S. banking facility.

Name _____

Address _____

City _____ State _____ Zip _____

I have enclosed $_____in payment for the checked book(s).
Payment <u>must</u> accompany all orders.☐ Please send a free catalog.

MAX BRAND

RONICKY DOONE

First Time In Paperback!

"Brand is a topnotcher!"
—New York Times

Doone's name is famous throughout the Old West. From Tombstone to Sonora he's won the respect of every law-abiding citizen—and the hatred of every bushwhacking bandit. But Bill Gregg isn't one to let a living legend get in his way, and he'll shoot Doone dead as soon as look at him. What nobody tells Gregg is that Doone doesn't enjoy living his hard-riding, rip-roaring life unless he takes a chance on losing it once in a while.

_3738-6 $3.99 US/$4.99 CAN

Dorchester Publishing Co., Inc.
65 Commerce Road
Stamford, CT 06902

Please add $1.75 for shipping and handling for the first book and $.50 for each book thereafter. NY, NYC, PA and CT residents, please add appropriate sales tax. No cash, stamps, or C.O.D.s. All orders shipped within 6 weeks via postal service book rate. Canadian orders require $2.00 extra postage and must be paid in U.S. dollars through a U.S. banking facility.

Name _____

Address _____

City _____ State _____ Zip _____

I have enclosed $_____ in payment for the checked book(s). Payment <u>must</u> accompany all orders.☐ Please send a free catalog.